Recipe for Life

Nicky Pellegrino

First published in Great Britain in 2010 by Orion Books,
an imprint of The Orion Publishing Group Ltd
Orion House, 5 Upper Saint Martin's Lane
London WC2H 9EA

An Hachette UK Company

1 3 5 7 9 10 8 6 4 2

A CIP catalogue record for this book is
available from the British Library.

ISBN (Hardback) 978 1 4091 0091 1
ISBN (Trade Paperback) 978 1 4091 0090 4

Typeset by Deltatype Ltd, Birkenhead, Merseyside

Printed and bound in the UK by CPI Mackays, Chatham ME5 8TD

The Orion Publishing Group's policy is to use papers that are
natural, renewable and recyclable products and made from wood
grown in sustainable forests. The logging and manufacturing
processes are expected to conform to the environmental
regulations of the country of origin.

www.orionbooks.co.uk

For Hatty who is right at the beginning ...

Prologue

At Villa Rosa there was an old dog barking in the garden, running between the straggle of artichokes, chasing a bird as though he was still a puppy. He ran across the terrace where the bougainvillea had taken over, through the dappled lemon grove and across the sun-bleached lawns. When at last the dog stopped barking the only sound was the breeze rushing through the pomegranate trees and the pounding of the sea on the rocks below.

The house was empty and locked against intruders, its high gates tightly closed. Only the little dog and the green-backed lizards knew how to squeeze their way through the hole in the wall that was almost entirely overgrown with weeds.

It seemed like a lost, forgotten place. The flowerbeds had long since surrendered and the wisteria grown wild. But someone had been there. The trees had been stripped of fruit at the end of last summer and the pathways swept clean of autumn leaves.

The weather always hit this house hard. The salty wind and the harsh sun had blistered the varnished shutters and faded the wash of pink on the walls. If the roof hadn't been weighed down with stones then the tiles might have lifted in the wilder storms and the heavy winter rains soaked through. Inside the house dust lay undisturbed, coffee cups sat upside down on a draining board where someone had left them, a bed was still unmade. Pictures had been taken down from walls and only their shadows remained.

Cobwebs decorated the ceiling.

It might have been months since anyone had lived here. Or it might have been years.

PART I

'Your time is limited so don't waste it
leading someone else's life,'

Steve Jobs, CEO, Apple Inc.

Alice

It was his weight I felt first, unfamiliar and wrong, pressing down along the full length of my body. I opened my eyes but all I could see in the darkness was the shape of his hair, curly and long. I suppose I must have screamed and he'd have told me to shut up but I don't remember that bit clearly. My memory is of the sharpness of whatever he was pushing into the side of my face, a kitchen knife or scissors perhaps, and the thoughts that ran through my mind ... not that he was going to kill me but that I would be left with a scar. A cheek ruined by a knife cut. It seems like such a stupid thing to worry about the moment you are raped.

It was a fumbling, messy business that didn't last long. Afterwards I lay still and listened to him running down four flights of stairs. Only when I was sure he was gone did I get out of bed and go downstairs to Charlie's room.

'I've been raped.' I opened my mouth so wide to scream out the words that my jaw hurt.

I'm not sure anyone but Charlie believed me at first, not until they found the stolen money he had dropped as he ran away down the front path. The police even suggested I'd dreamed the whole thing. But that was in the days before they'd had all that special training. I'm sure they wouldn't do that now.

I heard them on their walkie-talkies describing me as 'the victim'. I hated that. And I hated being made to stand on a sheet of brown paper while I undressed in front of a doctor who put my clothes in clear plastic bags and took them away somewhere. I hated being poked and prodded by him and then left to sit for hours with a weak cup of tea in a brightly lit room. I hated seeing the headlines – 'Student Raped' – on the front page of the next day's newspaper and knowing it was about me. And all my friends, everyone who'd ever been in my little room, being fingerprinted so there was no chance of me keeping it quiet, of not being pointed at whenever I was on campus. 'That's the girl who was raped look.'

It changed everything. If I went out to a pub I'd always be thinking, 'He could be here'. The others would be chatting, listening to the band or playing darts, I'd be looking for the man with the long curly hair.

The nights I was at home alone I'd listen for him coming up the stairs. Sleep was impossible. I barely even tried.

Charlie stayed with me a lot more than I expected. I suppose he felt guilty. If he'd still been my boyfriend he'd have been sleeping in that bed beside me when the stranger came into the room.

It had been such a nice house to live in: high ceilings, thick carpets, central heating. No wonder neither of us had wanted to move out when we broke up. A place like that was hard to come by. So we hung on, Charlie in one room, me in another, both convinced the other should go and too stubborn to see how ridiculous we were being.

In the end it was the bed linen that helped me leave. They'd taken it away to do forensic testing but now, I told the police, I needed it back because I was broke and couldn't afford to buy more. They looked surprised but fetched it anyway. Once it was spread out on my bed I realised my sheet was still covered in stains. They'd circled some in blue chalk and cut out swatches of the fabric here and there. I balled it back up and threw it in the bin.

That's when I knew it wasn't right for me to stay there,

hanging on to the torn edges of my life. I had to be some-where else. Anywhere else.

I packed up the things I cared about into a couple of bags and caught a train south, not letting anyone except Charlie know I was going. As the train rocked me, I made plans for my new start. I began thinking of this as extra time ... life after 18 November 1985, the date a stranger held a knife to my face. I stared out of the window at England blurring past and decided to treat every day from now on as a bonus. I would use time properly. I was going to squeeze life dry.

Babetta

Babetta looked towards the sea trying to work out what her husband had been staring at for so long. He was sitting in an old cane chair he'd pulled out onto the terrace and, even though it was chilly, he showed no signs of moving. It was as though he was waiting for someone. But no one was expected today. It was rare that anyone came.

This morning there was work to be done. Babetta wanted to plant out a crop of onions – the crisp red ones that tasted so good in summer salads. Usually Nunzio would be out there by now, his back a little hunched but his arms strong as he wielded his bent old spade and made the ground ready. But this morning the cane chair had claimed him and he was busy squinting at the horizon.

He stared, hardly blinking and not bothering to look at her although she was scratching her broom over the terracotta tiles to attract his attention. His dirty brown hat was pulled down hard on his head and he gripped the chair's arms as though he was worried she might try to tug him out of it.

She stopped sweeping. '*Buongiorno*, Nunzio,' she said loudly – he was becoming a little deaf.

He turned to look at her at last, his eyes cold and his face expressionless. '*Buongiorno* is dead, Babetta,' he said, his voice low. '*Buongiorno* is dead.' And then he turned back towards the horizon and it was as though he hadn't spoken.

They were the strangest words he'd said in their many

long years of marriage, mused Babetta as she found the spade and began turning the earth for the onion bed. Now and then she glanced up and saw he was still there, staring into space wordlessly, unconcerned that she was doing all the heavy work.

At lunchtime Nunzio came inside and took his usual place at the kitchen table, waiting for her to bring his food. He soaked his bread in the steaming thick soup of beans and pasta until it was soft enough for him to chew and spooned up the food quickly and noisily. With the last mouthful swallowed, he pushed the empty bowl away and left it there for her to clear while he returned to his post in the cane chair.

By nightfall he had come inside but still he hadn't spoken. Babetta wrapped a woollen shawl around her head and went out to fetch more wood for the fire. It was a windless night, the moon the tiniest sliver. As she picked up her basket of logs, Babetta looked up towards the mountain where the tall white statue of Christ was illuminated as always.

She and Nunzio had lived here for many years, ever since old Umberto Santoro – the previous caretaker – had died, and every night it gave her a feeling of peace knowing Christ was hovering above them in the blackness.

This was a lonely spot. They had no neighbours to talk to and no car to take them up the hill into town. When she was a girl Babetta had lived not far from here and once a week she and her sisters had walked into Triento to sell the baskets her father made. But now the ribbon of road that wound round the coast was so busy with fast cars she wouldn't have dared to walk it even if she'd thought her legs could carry her that far. So she stayed here with only Nunzio and the distant statue of Christ the Redeemer for company.

There were some visitors, of course. On Tuesdays the vegetable man came in his open-sided flatbed truck and

Babetta would sell him the surplus of whatever crop she had harvested from her garden. On Wednesdays it was the butcher in his refrigerated van and, if they needed more money, Babetta would sell him a chicken or a side of prosciutto that had been hanging to age in their cellar since she'd last killed a pig. Every other Thursday the fishmonger would call to offer her some baby squid or a bag of clams. She never bought much, just enough to mix with a little pasta and serve for dinner that night.

Living like this meant Babetta rarely had to touch the money she and Nunzio were paid for tending the gardens of the empty house next door. Villa Rosa was a lonely place, hidden behind high walls. When they'd first come here the family that owned it had travelled south every summer to swim in the sea and sail their boats, and Babetta remembered how it had come alive. But it had been many years now since anyone had bothered to come and the house looked neglected; paint peeled from its pink walls and, Babetta suspected, its roof was beginning to leak.

Still, the house wasn't her responsibility. She and Nunzio were paid only to care for the terraced gardens that stepped down to the sea, covered with lemon trees and pomegranates and, threaded between them, the crops of artichokes and fava beans they'd planted in the cinnamon-coloured earth once they'd realised the place had been abandoned.

Babetta was surprised the money kept appearing in their bank account every month. Why would anyone care if the gardens of Villa Rosa became wild and overgrown? For years her fund had been accumulating until now there was a respectable amount. Whenever her daughter Sofia came down from Salerno, Babetta always insisted they went to the bank to make certain it was all still there as it should be.

Her daughter couldn't understand why she refused to spend it. 'Buy yourself some new clothes, Mamma, or some bright curtains to cheer up the house. Treat yourself to something.'

Babetta always shook her head stubbornly. She already had everything she needed. And it was comforting to know the money was there, growing steadily month by month.

Chilled by the wind that was whipping up from the sea, Babetta hauled the wood inside and found Nunzio sitting in his armchair, staring into the flames of the fire. She wondered what was wrong with him now. For as long as they'd been married he'd been buffeted by bad moods. Her sisters had always told her she should never have married a man from Calabria – their blood was heated by too much chilli and there was a skein of blackness twisting through them. 'You should have chosen a local boy,' they would say whenever she complained about Nunzio's temper.

Even as they stood in front of the priest, she'd wondered if she was making the right choice. He was ten years older than her and not the husband she'd imagined taking. But by then it was too late. She'd chosen the direction her life would travel in. She had to follow it.

As the decades passed she and Nunzio had grown used to one another. When he flew into one of his rages, she would lock herself in the cellar until he came to the door crying and promising he'd calmed down. Sometimes his bleakest moods could stretch from weeks to months and Babetta knew all she could do was live in his silence until something inside him changed and he came back to her.

But this new mood of Nunzio's seemed very different. She had never known him shirk a day's work before. No matter how forlorn or angry, he would always manage to pick up his spade and go out into the garden. His jobs were the routine ones: trimming back the grape vines in winter or breaking up the ground before she planted out seedlings in spring. He worked hard until the day grew too hot or the light faded.

Never before had she known him to sit in a chair and stare at nothing from morning till night. Nor had she seen that look on his face, blank and still as though he was slowly shutting down.

Babetta began to worry that her husband might be losing his mind.

Alice

Leila was the person I fled towards after I'd been raped. The one I trusted to help me fix up my life again. We'd been in the same halls of residence the first year of university, and I'd been dazzled by her. I remember her giving me red wine and talking about things I'd barely ever thought about: hunger striker Bobby Sands, or the situation in Iran.

There was no way I could help being drawn to Leila's vivid colours. She was like a dress I knew didn't suit me much but wanted all the same. In all my dull, plain suburban life I'd never met anyone like her

Leila drank Guinness in pubs and claimed she was a vegetarian, although once I found her half-hidden behind a pillar near the bakery, scarfing down a steak and kidney pie. She wore second-hand clothes; beaded silk dresses with a woollen greatcoat over the top or stiff men's dinner jackets that still smelt of cigars.

I barely saw her the second year. She moved into a house in town with some people who wore only orange and were obsessed with an Indian guru called Bhagwan. Once I called in to visit her and she served me some smoky-tasting tea and then sat on the sofa repeatedly drawing the same picture on sheet after sheet of paper.

When Leila dropped out of university I'd been disapproving but not surprised. Now I was doing the same, following in her footsteps all the way south to London.

She was living in an apartment her mother owned in a Maida Vale mansion block. It was so clean and white it looked like an operating theatre. 'Don't touch the walls, don't touch the walls,' was Leila's constant refrain. Apparently they'd been painted with some stuff that marked really badly if you fingered it.

'Why didn't your mother use a paint that could be wiped clean?' I asked.

'You don't get the same effect,' said Leila, sounding as if she was repeating something she'd been told. So I took to walking round the apartment with my arms crossed over my chest. After all, I was staying there for free and didn't want to do anything to upset Leila's mother on one of her rare trips back to London from her house in the south of France.

Every afternoon I bought the Evening Standard and trawled through the job section while Leila sat and smoked French cigarettes. I went for a few interviews at recruitment agencies and one at a restaurant in Covent Garden but it proved more difficult to find work than I'd imagined. Either I didn't have enough experience or they were worried that, since I'd managed only half of an English degree, I would quickly grow bored.

My mother might have sent some money but she was furious with me for not graduating and I hadn't been able to explain why. All alone, my father long gone, she thrived on worry and regret. Usually she wanted to talk for hours, shed feelings and tears, fret away at the things I didn't want to think about. Somehow I knew telling her what had happened would only make me feel like I was being raped all over again.

'If I don't get a job soon I don't know what I'm going to do,' I said to Leila one morning as I sat drinking smoky tea and opening rejection letters while she filled up an ashtray with cigarette butts.

'Why don't you take my job?' Leila offered. She'd been waitressing at a little place down the road called the Maida Vale Brasserie.

'What are you going to do instead?'

Leila pulled a strand of hair into her mouth and started sucking it. She shrugged one shoulder at me. 'I don't know,' she said through the hair. 'Maybe I'll live like Holly Golightly in *Breakfast at Tiffany's*.'

She was the only person I knew who would decide to say something so ridiculous.

I laughed. 'And how would that work?'

'Well I'll eat when men buy me dinner and I'll drink when men buy champagne.' She lit another cigarette and smiled. She really was gloriously beautiful with raven's-wing hair, black kohl-ringed eyes and generous lips she liked to stain red. I could see how she might be able to live on the things men bought for her.

'But won't they mind at the brasserie?'

She shrugged again. 'Who cares if they do?'

So that night I turned up for her shift and, although the maître d', Robbie, didn't seem too pleased, he gave me Leila's apron and let me do her work. That first night I was busy trying to keep up with everyone and my shift passed in a blur of cassoulet and goat's cheese salads. I couldn't balance plates up my arms like the other waitress and struggled to remember more than two orders. By midnight my feet hurt and my knees felt creaky.

'You're young and strong,' the chef boomed at me when I admitted I was knackered. 'How do you think I feel eh?'

He poured me a glass of red wine but I noticed he didn't take one himself. 'I'm Guyon by the way,' he said. 'Bit rude of Robbie not to introduce us.'

'I'm Alice,' I told him. 'I'm a friend of Leila's and she's sort of given me her job.'

'Ah, that explains it then. Robbie's mad about lovely Leila. He reckons she brings in extra business and he may be right. Not that you're not lovely too,' he added hurriedly.

I laughed to show I wasn't offended. It was hardly news

to me that I wasn't in Leila's league. I've always been this little brown person: quite small and sort of one-tone. Not awful looking but nothing special either.

'Will Robbie let me stay on do you think?'

'Don't see why not. After all, it's easier to keep you than to look for someone else. Just try not to drop anything,' he advised. 'Oh and come in earlier tomorrow. I do a staff meal at four thirty. I like everyone to taste the specials so you can describe them properly to the customers.'

'Leila didn't tell me that.'

'Yes, well, Leila didn't seem to do much eating,' Guyon said drily.

The brasserie was quite a simple place with white wrought iron tables and chairs that could be pulled out onto the pavement on sunny days. The walls were pale and covered with bright paintings by some local artist and there was always one really extravagant floral display in a big vase up on the bar. It was one of those neighbourhood cafés that people would go to on nights they couldn't be bothered to cook, but Guyon liked to run it as though it was a high-end restaurant.

He was especially fussy about how food was arranged and often made us wait while he wiped the rim of a plate clean of a few spots of creamy sauce or drizzled a dessert with a perfect swirl of raspberry coulis. It caused a lot of fights because speed was Robbie's thing. 'Get them in, get them fed, get them out,' he liked to say. Guyon would shake his head and insist on re-plating a dish that looked perfectly fine, just to annoy him.

'Bloody washed up old alky,' Robbie raged whenever he was out of earshot. 'He's lucky to have a job after what happened.'

You could tell Guyon had been a drinker. He had cheeks reddened by burst capillaries and his nose was a bit lumpy looking. Robbie whispered to me that one time Guyon drank so much he lost control at the smart Mayfair restaurant where he used to be head chef. The fridges ended up full of rotten food and the kitchens dirty and infested. Eventually he managed to poison some customers and the place never recovered from the scandal. No one would touch him after that, no matter how good a chef he'd been. For a while he could only find work as the cook in an old people's home. And now he was here – a recovering alcoholic – serving up steak and *pommes frites* at the brasserie.

'Pretentious old bugger,' Robbie complained as he chalked up the day's special menu. '*Poulet aux olives vertes* indeed. Why doesn't he just call it chicken and olive stew?'

I'd been wondering the same thing so I asked Guyon about it one evening when things were quiet and Robbie wasn't around.

'The thing is, Alice,' he explained, 'people don't come to restaurants just to eat. It's about an experience. Even a place like this, they come because they want to feel special for a few hours before they return to their lives.' He was wiping clean his skillets and hanging them in order of size along the kitchen wall. I wondered if he found it difficult not drinking when he worked only a few steps away from boxes and boxes of wine but didn't dare ask him that.

Then one busy Sunday lunchtime Robbie threw a tantrum and walked out and the next week the owners offered me his job. 'You haven't got much experience,' they said. 'But Guyon tells us you're smart and you've got a nice way with the customers so I think we should give you a go.'

When I went to thank Guyon, he laughed. 'Bear in mind that they're paying you about a third of what Robbie got. They can get away with it because you're so inexperienced. And they'll be planning on working you hard.'

I didn't mind the extra work or spending longer hours at the brasserie. In some ways it was a relief because Leila's plans to live like Holly Golightly weren't quite working out. Yes, she had lots of men but they were all musicians, artists or sculptors and none of them seemed to have any money.

When I got home from work I never knew which one she'd have in her bed but I'd hear them because the apartment had wafer-thin walls. One night Leila shrieked so loud I got worried and burst into her room. I found one of the men – the artist, I think – perched on top of the wardrobe naked. It completely freaked me out.

'Sorry, darling,' Leila said the next morning after he'd gone. 'We were both a little drunk.'

'You seem to have a different man in there every night. Don't you ever get sick of it?'

'No.' She smiled at me. 'I'm good at sex, Alice. Really, really good at it. Wouldn't it be a shame not to make the most of that?'

Mostly I didn't mind the greedy pleasure Leila took in sex. It was a reminder that what had happened to me was something else: violence and hate, not passion. And Leila's men were non-threatening, so physically caught up with her they barely noticed me. In the morning I'd find them drinking tea in the kitchen, and they were kind to me but disinterested.

Often I got lonely and thought of Charlie. I still missed being physically close to him. He hadn't written to me in a while and as far as I knew he was still with Sarah White, the girl who'd stolen him from me.

The funny thing was I'd always imagined I'd be able to keep Charlie for ever. He was far from handsome, with pale skin, gingery hair and barely any eyelashes. The first time I found him lying in bed beside me after a drunken first-year party, I couldn't wait to get rid of him. Even his body wasn't that good – it was slim but soft from lack of exercise.

What Charlie had going for him was he was clever and

very funny. He made me laugh and moved into my life, scattering his shoes, clothes and records all over my tiny student room. Gradually he imprinted himself on me. I started listening to the northern bands he liked, The Smiths and Big Country. I spent hours flicking through albums with him in record shops and watching movies with foreign subtitles. I moved out of my halls of residence and into his house-share and every night he slept with me in my room.

Perhaps, if I'd any proper friends, they'd have told me to stop being such a sap. But this was a new life and everything about it was half-formed, especially the friendships. Charlie was a second year. He pulled me into his circle of friends and, aside from Leila, they became my whole social life. I couldn't imagine existing without him.

And then Sarah White appeared on the scene. The first time we bumped into her was at the campus Worship Centre. We used to go there because they gave out plates of baked beans or spaghetti on toast. They only did it to trap you so they could talk about God but Charlie enjoyed a good argument and I liked filling up on free food.

I noticed Sarah seemed to pay him a lot of attention but it didn't bother me. It never occurred to me she was any sort of threat. Now I realise it must have been flattering for Charlie. Just because he wasn't good-looking didn't mean he wasn't vain. And Sarah appealed to his vanity.

She moved in on him one weekend when I'd gone home to see my mother. The moment I got back I sensed a change in Charlie. He seemed withdrawn and grumpy. Once or twice he reached out to me in bed, pulling me to him then pushing me away just as fiercely. And then there was the night he just didn't come home. I woke up alone the next morning and knew he must be with her.

Devastated and humiliated, for a while I think I may have lost my mind. I certainly behaved like it. Leila took a childish pleasure in hearing me repeat the mad things I'd done. How I'd stormed over to Sarah's house when Charlie was there, and started sobbing and wailing. How I'd kept turning up night after night, creating scenes, making it impossible for them to spend time together.

'Tell me again how you found them having a pub lunch and threw your beer over her,' Leila would encourage me.

She said she'd have gone further, rubbed the food in Sarah's face or stabbed her with a fork. She made me laugh as she described all the things I could have done to get revenge. But really I was ashamed. I'd pestered Charlie and Sarah White. I'd made a fool of myself.

And then, just when I'd thought life really couldn't get any worse, some stranger with long curly hair had gone for a night out stealing, found me alone in my bed and taken his opportunity. So that was me, dumped and raped within a few short weeks. If it hadn't been for Leila, writing to me and coaxing me to London, offering me her mother's spare room, I don't know how things would have turned out.

As the months rolled by my life began to revolve around the brasserie and the people who worked there. I loved the routine of staff meals every afternoon, talking nonsense as we gathered around a table in the cramped kitchen to taste that day's specials. The extra responsibility of organising rosters and cashing up at the end of the night kept my mind busy and my days full. Only Mondays were difficult because the place was closed. The thought of all that empty time scared me so I took to hanging out with Guyon. On sunny days we'd walk through London for miles and when it was wet we'd go to the movies or a museum. He seemed as desperate as I was to stay occupied and exhausted.

'You're no fun,' Leila complained early one morning as she threw herself onto my bed. 'Wake up and talk to me. What's the point of you if you never talk to me?'

'Please go away,' I begged. 'I didn't get to sleep till past two a.m. I need another hour at least.'

She lay across me and pushed her face into mine, so close I could smell the coffee on her breath. 'You're always either at work or with that great ugly poof Guyon,' she complained. 'Why won't you ever come out to play with me?'

I opened my eyes and stared into her face. 'I will,' I promised, 'but not right now.'

She jiggled a bit on top of me. 'I love you, Alice,' she said.

'I know, I know.'

'I'm bored, Alice.' She jiggled some more. 'And you're getting boring.'

There was no hoping she'd go away. 'All right, what do you want me to do?'

'Get dressed quickly.' She sprang off the bed. 'I want to show you the most beautiful view in London.'

Leila put on a yellow silk dress and a pair of Doc Martens, stuffed some French cigarettes into a little beaded bag and made me walk all the way to St James's Park. We stood on a bridge in the middle of the lake. 'There, not like London at all, is it? More like a fairytale,' she said triumphantly.

Once she was satisfied I'd fully appreciated the best view the city had to offer, we walked up to Chinatown and ate some dim sum in a restaurant on Wardour Street. Then we went to a pub round the back of a theatre in Soho where we spent the afternoon drinking. We must have been starting to look a bit messy because an older man, who'd been buying us wine, insisted on taking us to the restaurant next door. Actually, he claimed he owned the place. Perhaps he was telling the truth because, even though we were very drunk and much too loud, they brought us champagne and let us order pizza.

Living in Leila's slipstream turned out to be dangerous

and decadent. As we caught the last tube home, flushed and reeking of wine, Leila laughing about what that rich man had thought he was going to get from her, I realised I'd managed to forget myself for nearly a whole day.

I spent a year like that, living in the flat in Maida Vale and being careful not to touch the walls. Some days I'd work too hard, others I'd drink too much. And then one afternoon I was helping set up tables in the brasserie when I happened to glance through the window and I saw him: a gingery man smoking a roll-up cigarette as he strolled across the road. It was Charlie, of course, heading towards me, heading back into my life.

Babetta

For a long time no one but Babetta noticed what had happened to Nunzio. It had been months since he'd spoken or worked in the garden. She had lined his cane chair with cushions and given him a rug to make him more comfortable. As she struggled to manage the work alone, she watched him carefully for signs of more change.

Eventually Sofia, their daughter, realised something was wrong. 'Every time I come here Papa is sitting in that chair as still as a statue. What's the matter with him?'

Babetta wasn't certain how to explain it.

'Is he depressed, do you think?' Sofia pressed her. 'We should take him to the doctor, get him some pills.'

'No need for that. He's fine. I can look after him.' Babetta was afraid they might lose their job caring for the gardens of Villa Rosa.

Sofia sighed and launched into her usual tirade. 'But you're so isolated here. No phone, no car. I suppose I can come down from Salerno more often to check on you but still ...' She stared at her father. 'It would be better if you moved up the hill to Triento. Maybe if there were more life around him Papa would cheer up. And you wouldn't have to work so hard. You could buy your vegetables at the market instead of growing them.'

Babetta imagined some gloomy apartment in one of Triento's narrow alleyways. 'We're fine here,' she repeated. 'Nunzio doesn't want to live in town. He likes to look out at

23

the sea and have the land around him. That's what he's used to.'

Her daughter shook her head. 'You'll have to move at some point. This place is too big, too much for you. What if you had a fall? Think about the future, Mamma.'

Babetta didn't like to look too far ahead. It seemed as if there were only bad things in store: weakness, illness, loss. Easier to work hard and not think too much about any of it.

'We're not ready yet,' she insisted. 'We don't want to move. We can manage.'

She didn't tell Sofia that already the vegetable plots they'd planted on the terraces of Villa Rosa had run to seed. Or that there were weeds straggling through the flowerbeds near the house and there hadn't been time to trim back the bougainvillea that spread over the terrace.

'No need to worry about us,' she said instead. 'Our lives are good.'

Three months later Babetta noticed the money had stopped appearing in her bank account. She kept tending the gardens of Villa Rosa as best she could and waited to see what would happen. But there was no explanation, no word from the family in the north. Babetta wished she could discuss the situation with Nunzio but he remained locked in his silence, staring unseeing into the distance and only moving at mealtimes or once it grew dark.

'*Buongiorno* is dead,' Babetta muttered to herself bitterly as she stared up at the statue of Christ on the mountain top.

It was only when the strange car appeared that Nunzio showed a small flicker of interest. He walked all the way to the end of the path to get a better look at the shiny black Fiat, parked outside the gates of Villa Rosa.

Earlier Babetta had seen a young woman get out of the car, well dressed in a red woollen suit and high heels. She'd held a key to the gates and let herself in. By now she must be looking at the flowerbeds, tangled like unbrushed hair, and the fallen bougainvillea blossoms that needed sweeping from the path. Officially none of that was Babetta's responsibility. No one had paid her for the work so why should she do it? Still, she was sorry someone had come to inspect the place when it wasn't looking its best.

She watched the open gates for half an hour, staring just like Nunzio, but the woman in the suit didn't reappear. Curious, Babetta moved closer, peering into the courtyard to see if she could catch a glimpse of anything, and was rewarded by the sight of the stranger, standing beside the pomegranate tree, making notes in a big leather folder.

The woman looked up and saw her. '*Buongiorno*,' she called out in a friendly voice.

Babetta took a few steps through the open gates. '*Buongiorno*,' she responded uncertainly. 'I'm the gardener here. Can I help you with anything, signora?'

'I don't think so.' The woman gestured at the unkempt grounds. 'It doesn't look like anyone has done any gardening here for a while.'

'The money stopped coming,' Babetta said awkwardly. 'I still tried to do a little but my husband has been ill recently and it all—'

'Don't worry.' The woman interrupted her. 'We'll need to have a gardening crew come in anyway. The place needs repainting too. There's quite a lot to be done.'

'Are the Barbieri family coming back?' Babetta asked her.

'No, they're selling the place. Well the wife is. Her husband died a few months ago. He used to be someone quite famous round here, I believe.'

'That's right.' Babetta nodded, keen to share what she knew. 'He was an American. He built that big statue of Christ up on the mountain. So he's gone now, eh? Well at least his statue remains for people to remember him by.'

'I suppose.' The woman shrugged. 'His wife doesn't care to come and see it though. My instructions are to sell the place as fast as I can.'

Babetta turned to look at the old villa with its pink-washed walls, varnished shutters and its wide terrace of brightly painted ceramic tiles. 'It's sad to see the house lying empty like this,' she said.

'Should be worth a bit once it's spruced up. There's access to the sea, isn't there?'

'Yes but the steps down aren't safe any more. They're crumbling away.'

The woman frowned and made another note in her leather folder.

'This gardening crew you spoke about,' Babetta said hesitantly. 'They'll want lots of money for the work. My husband will be better soon. He and I can go back to caring for the garden again. We'll do it for a much better price.'

The woman looked doubtful. 'We'll see,' she said.

'Well, at least let me offer you something to drink. What can I get you? Some coffee? A juice made from our own oranges?'

'Espresso, please. That would be wonderful.'

As she made the coffee, Babetta talked to Nunzio even though he showed no signs of listening. 'Can you believe they're selling Villa Rosa? It must be more than fifty years that the Barbieri family has owned it. Now someone will come and fix the place up at long last. I expect there'll be all sorts of people coming and going. It'll make the view from that chair of yours a bit more interesting, eh?'

She put the coffee pot on a tray with some tiny cups and a bowl of sugar. 'Hurry up and get better,' she hissed at him as she carried the tray towards Villa Rosa. 'We need to sort out that garden or we're going to lose the work.'

She and the signora sipped their coffee beside the

pomegranate tree in the centre of the courtyard. It was a spot Babetta often stopped at, sitting on the low wall to rest her legs and enjoy the warmth of the afternoon sun.

'I wonder who will buy all this,' she mused, looking down at the rows of fruit trees and the blue slice of sea on the horizon.

'Foreigners, maybe,' the signora replied. 'Or a business that will rent it out as a holiday home.'

Babetta had been hoping for an Italian family with children she'd be able to hear playing in the courtyard.

'It's such a beautiful place.' She knew she sounded wistful. 'Someone will fall in love with it I'm sure.'

Alice

Charlie looked out of place standing beside the bar of the brasserie. He was clutching a brown canvas satchel stuffed with the day's *Guardian*, some copies of the *NME*, and one of those old Penguin Classic novels with the orange covers. Everything about him was so familiar and yet he seemed all wrong.

'I've missed your face,' he told me.

Those weren't the words I'd expected to hear and for a moment I was disarmed. Then I found my anger again. 'What about Sarah White?' I asked.

'It was a mistake. It's over.'

'A mistake?' The brasserie was no place for a fight so I kept my voice soft.

'We're still friends, aren't we? You're pleased to see me.'

'Yes ... no. I don't know. Why did you come?'

'I just wanted to see you again. It's been almost a year.' He looked as though he wanted to touch me. 'Your hair is longer and you seem thinner.'

I pushed my fingers through my hair. 'Running around here six nights a week keeps me thin,' I told him, and then was annoyed at myself for being too friendly, too soon. 'Look, Charlie, I can't really talk. This place will be busy soon and there's a lot to do.'

'What about later?'

'I'll be tired.'

'Coffee in the morning then?'

'OK. I'll meet you at the café near the tube station if you like. But not too early.'

I watched as he walked away. His stride was less confident, his head carried low. A year ago I'd never have imagined being anything but pleased to see him.

'Was that an old boyfriend?' Guyon had been nosing at us through the kitchen hatch.

'What makes you think that?'

'The look on your face, Alice,' he said. 'You look stricken, you do.'

I smiled a bit. 'Stricken? That's dramatic. But the thing is I was sort of getting used to life without him.'

'Send him away then. Tell him you're not interested in seeing him.'

'It's not that simple.'

All evening, as I greeted regulars by name, took their coats and showed them to their tables, I kept thinking how Charlie must be somewhere close by. He'd missed my face; Sarah had been a mistake. For so long I'd wanted to hear words like those from him.

Once we'd said goodnight to the last customer I let Guyon pour me a glass of wine and bother me with questions.

'Why did you split up with him then?'

'He ran off with one of my friends.'

'Nice guy.' Guyon put the wine bottle away.

'I think they're finished now though. At least that's what he said.'

'So she's dumped him and he's come looking for you.' Guyon sounded indignant. 'I hope you're going to tell him where to go.'

'I don't know.' I sipped my wine. As always, I felt awkward about drinking in front of Guyon. 'I fell apart when he left me, I thought I'd kill to get him back ...'

'Tell him he's too late, say you've got someone else.' Guyon suggested.

29

'But I haven't.'

'This is no time to worry about telling the truth.' Guyon pulled out the wine bottle again and topped up my glass. 'Think Gloria Gaynor, darling.'

As he went off to finish clearing up the kitchen, he was singing 'I Will Survive' and camping it up more than usual. I laughed because that's what he wanted but when I went over to the till to start cashing up, I felt more like crying.

If Charlie wanted me again would I give myself to him? For two years we'd been so close. We'd slept together in a single bed and, except when we were in lectures and tutorials, done everything together. It seemed like a part of me was almost always touching a part of him.

I knew he didn't get on with my mum but I thought that was her fault. She lived in such a narrow world, obsessed with her shopping lists and her new front-load washing machine. She'd never come across people like Charlie and his family. She didn't know what to make of them.

To begin with I was intimidated by Charlie's family too. His dad was a doctor and Charlie's two older brothers had followed their father into the profession. They lived in quite a big house, full of books and old things, and were always talking about the qualifications people had. 'Have you met Jane, she's got a degree in biochemistry' was how a conversation with one of them would usually start. They were the kind of people who could make any social occasion feel like a prayer meeting. They liked to pull their chairs round in a tight circle and have proper discussions. It made me want to giggle.

None of them thought much of me. I could tell because they were always bringing up Charlie's ex-girlfriend and updating him on what she was up to. Once they actually invited her round for tea while I was there. She sat on one of the wooden chairs, pulled into the circle, while I stayed

30

on the sofa flicking through some magazines I'd bought. Charlie's mother told me I'd wasted my money on them; I could have bought a book for the same amount.

After a while they seemed to accept my part in Charlie's life. They must have seen how he was always holding my hand or playing with my hair, and realised he was serious about me. Or perhaps they'd added me to the list of his other failures and obstinacies. An art history degree instead of medicine, a little brown-haired thing with a northern accent instead of the hometown girl. Something else they had to grin and bear.

It's funny how the power shifts in a relationship. At first it was all about Charlie pleasing me. He used to plan little day trips for us. We'd go up the coast and sit in deckchairs on the seafront, or he'd learn all about some historic place and take me round it, exploring the church and the grave-yard, wandering down old walking tracks and having chips and beer in a pub for lunch.

We were in Scotland when the balance changed. We'd taken the train up and then hitched our way around the lowlands, sleeping rough because we didn't have the money for a B&B. We weren't very well equipped. We hadn't even brought a torch and only had the flame of Charlie's cigarette lighter to see by once the sun went down. The first night we lay in our sleeping bags in a bus shelter and I tried not to think about rats. The second night it was dark by the time we found a church with its door unlocked. We slept on the floor near some pews and it was hard and cold.

'Just think of all the people in the cottages nearby,' I said longingly. 'They'll be lying in their comfortable beds, covered in eiderdowns with their radiators on.'

'Boring people,' Charlie said. 'Not having an adventure like us. We can go anywhere, do anything.'

When we woke we left some coins in the collection plate and then stepped out into a spring morning. The church turned out to be in the middle of nowhere, on the edge of a lake and surrounded by rolling fields and tall leafy trees.

'It's gorgeous isn't it,' I marvelled. 'Last night in the dark I had no idea that all this was out here.'

Charlie hugged me to him. 'That's the thing with adventures,' he said. 'Unexpected things happen.'

Suddenly I had this moment of pure happiness when everything, including us, seemed completely perfect. It felt like bacon smells when you're really hungry, or the first bite of chocolate.

Charlie seemed to sense my surrender and, over the following weeks, he pulled away. It was a subtle thing. He didn't touch me quite so much; he teased me a little more; he didn't always tell me where he was going. That was how he held me to him. And now he had followed me to London and I wondered what he wanted.

Distractedly, I helped Guyon lock up the brasserie and walked back to the apartment, longing to sleep and forget about everything till morning. I found Leila still awake and all alone. She was sitting at the kitchen table scribbling something on a thick pad of lined paper.

'Hi,' she said without looking up.

'Night,' I replied, slinking past, grateful not to have been caught in conversation.

Sleep didn't come easily. My mind was flickering and I couldn't seem to shut it down. Every now and then I'd hear Leila moving about in the kitchen, making tea or lighting a cigarette from the gas hob. Perhaps sleep was eluding her too.

I must have dozed off because reality got all mixed up with dreams and Charlie was in most of them. He was carrying his brown satchel and taking me on an adventure but we never seemed to get anywhere.

In the morning I felt terrible, worse than hungover, my

eyes looked piggy and my skin yellow. Leila was where I'd seen her last, still filling pages of the notebook with her mad spidery handwriting, a full ashtray at her elbow.

'What are you doing?'

'Um ... writing a book,' she said, her voice all rattly from smoking too much.

'Really? What's it about? Can I read it?'

She put down her pen and groped round for another cigarette. 'Yeah, maybe when it's finished. It's about dogs.'

I was confused. 'Like how to train them or ...?'

'No, no, it's a novel. English people are obsessed with dogs, aren't they? So how could a story about them not be a best-seller?'

'You'd have to get it published first. I don't think that's easy.'

Leila wasn't one for worrying about the obstacles in life. 'There's a guy I sometimes drink with at the Coach & Horses who's a literary agent. He'll help me get it published, I expect.'

I tried to read some of what she'd written but she laughed and covered it with her arm. 'No you don't.'

'Oh, go on.'

'No, I've got a long way to go before I'll be ready for anyone to see it. You can do me a favour though?'

'Oh, OK, what?'

'Get me a few waitressing shifts at the brasserie. I need some cash.'

It had taken ages for Leila to run through the allowance her mother had left her. She didn't have many expenses. I filled the fridge with food, mostly taramasalata and sesame seed bread from the local Greek shop, and she didn't have to pay rent so really the only thing she ever bought was cigarettes, and she scammed them when she could.

'I don't want to work more than two or three nights a week because I need to focus on my writing,' she added.

33

'OK, I'll have a look at the roster tonight and see if I can squeeze you in somewhere,' I promised. 'But you have to get in at four thirty for staff dinner, remember. Guyon goes nuts if everyone hasn't tasted the specials.'

She frowned. 'I just want to work, not eat there. Robbie never minded if I skipped staff meals.'

'Yeah well Robbie's not there any more. I'm the maître d' now, remember?'

She just laughed at me. 'What's up with you anyway? Why are you out of bed so early and so grumpy?'

I knew she wouldn't be impressed if I told her I was meeting Charlie.

'I'm going out, catching up with a friend for breakfast,' was all I said.

'Oh yes? Who?'

'I'll tell you about it later. I need to jump in the shower now.'

I was late and Charlie was there waiting for me, his brown satchel on the chair beside him and the café table spread with pages of his newspaper. He pushed them to one side when he saw me and stood up.

'Alice.' He leaned in and held me, smelling of tobacco and wet wool which I found oddly comforting.

'Charlie.' I made myself pull away.

'It's so good to see you.' He smiled as we sat down opposite each other. 'You look fantastic, you know?'

I pushed my hair about a bit. 'Do I? Thanks.'

'Here, have a look at the menu. Let's have a big blow-out breakfast like we always used to on Sunday mornings. They've got that egg thing you like with the gooey yellow sauce on it.'

'Hollandaise.' I glanced at the menu. 'I'm not really hungry, to be honest.'

'Have something,' he insisted. 'It's my treat.'

He was being so formal and mannered, as if we were

on a first date. 'Charlie, I just don't know why you're here or what you want from me and I can't eat because I'm freaking out,' I blurted.

'Actually I'm freaking out a bit too,' he admitted.

'Are you? Why?'

He pulled something out of his satchel and put it on the table between us. It was a small square box covered in green velvet. I stared at it, hoping it wasn't what I thought.

'What's that ...?'

'It's a ring.'

The waitress came over at that moment and seemed to take for ever scratching down my simple request for coffee and a croissant on her notepad.

'Charlie, why have you brought me a ring?' I asked once she'd moved away.

'I think you know why.' He reached out across the table and gripped my fingers tightly. 'Because I've missed you and I've realised I screwed up. And I wanted to show you we have a future together.'

'Please don't ...' I said, but I didn't try to pull my hand away.

'Alice, will you marry me?' He didn't get down on one knee but he sort of performed the words.

'Not now. It wouldn't be right.'

'But you still love me, don't you?'

'To be honest I don't know.'

'At least look at the ring. It's an emerald. It'll suit you.' I thought I could see tears forming in his eyes.

'Put it away please. I don't want to see it.'

'Are you absolutely sure? It's beautiful. It took me ages to pick it out.' There really were tears. Some of them were starting to trickle down his cheeks.

'You dumped me, Charlie,' I said softly. 'And I don't think I've forgiven you for that yet. And also what about all that awful stuff I did to you and Sarah? All that madness?

Stealing your drinks in bars and turning up at her house in the middle of the night crying.'

He managed a smile. 'You had Sarah worried. She wanted to call the police at one point. But you know, looking back I think it was kind of funny.'

'Really?'

'We never knew when you'd turn up. You were this tiny furious thing and I thought she was pathetic to be afraid of you. She's about twice your size. Anyway, she probably deserved it. She ruined you and me, didn't she?'

'She only gets half the blame,' I reminded him.

The waitress brought our order and then lingered, wiping up spilt sugar from the table. I wondered if she'd noticed Charlie had been crying.

'Yes, I know it's my fault too.' He stared at the ring box still lying there between us. 'But it was a mistake, a huge one. And even if you don't want to marry me, I think we should be together.'

'I don't see how it's possible.'

'Of course it is. I'll come to London if you like. We could get a place. Please, Alice.'

'I'm not sure ...' I said indecisively. 'I need time to think.'

'But you're not seeing someone else?'

'No.'

'Has there been anyone since ... you know, since that night?' Charlie sounded awkward.

'Do you mean have I slept with anyone? No.'

He shook his head. 'Psychologically this can't be good for you, Alice. You have to get past it, begin to heal.'

'I'm fine actually,' I insisted.

'Have you even talked to anyone?'

'No, I haven't.' I didn't want counselling or, even worse, to share my story with other women who'd been raped. It seemed better to ignore the whole thing, store it away in the back of my mind until I knew what to do with it.

Still, Charlie was probably right. It had been over a year now and perhaps I did need to see how it felt to be with someone.

'I'm staying at my brother's place in Camden.' He let go of my hand and slipped the ring box into the front pocket of his satchel. 'You could come back with me, if you like. Just for a cuddle.'

I folded my arms across my chest. 'That doesn't sound like a great idea.'

'Just this one time, Alice.' Charlie smiled at me as though he knew how comforting it would be to crush myself against him, to curl up in a tent of sheets and blankets, warm and safely wound up in his arms.

He folded his newspaper and put away his book. 'It's up to you, Alice.'

'Perhaps just a cuddle then.' I yielded. 'But only for half an hour.'

He grinned as though he had won. 'Yeah, absolutely, if that's what you want.'

Charlie took my hand again as we left the café, his other arm already in the air to hail a black cab. Once we were sitting in the back of it, he pushed his leg against mine and a part of me touched a part of him all the way to his brother's flat in Camden.

Babetta

Even on days when the sky was bruised and full of rain and the cold wind ripped up off the sea, Babetta wrapped her head in an old shawl and went to work in the gardens of Villa Rosa. She collected fallen fruit from the lemon grove beside the house, pulled weeds from the flowerbeds and arranged pots filled with red geraniums along the rough stone walls. She didn't care if her own garden lay neglected or if the fire burned down in her hearth and her husband was left to look after himself. He could sit at the kitchen table all afternoon if he liked, there would be no bowl of soup placed before him, no rough-cut bread or shards of grainy Parmesan. For now Babetta wasn't concerned about him, only Villa Rosa.

Despite the ache in her left hip and the stiffness in her knees, she felt excited. Nothing had happened here for so long and now so much was changing. As she worked through the day without taking a break, she imagined the family that might come to live in the old house; the wife so glamorous in all the latest designer clothes, the children who would play in the courtyard beside the pomegranate tree, the husband who would drive down from the city at weekends in a fast car. They would appreciate someone like her who could keep an eye on the place when they were busy with the rest of their lives. Perhaps there would be parties in the summer, with strings of lights twisted through the trees and music playing all night. Then she would find a second cane chair and sit with Nunzio for hours on end watching people come and go.

Babetta was beginning to feel as though she had control over the garden at last when the three men turned up. They backed their white flatbed truck right through the gates of Villa Rosa.

'Be careful, be careful,' Babetta fussed, eyeing the equipment strapped down in the back. She saw a bundle of rakes and spades, something that looked like it might be a chainsaw, and other tools it would take a strong man to handle.

'What are you doing here?' she demanded to know. 'Who are you?'

'We're the gardeners,' the older one said. 'We've come to tidy the place up.'

'There's no need. I'm taking care of it.'

He looked confused. 'This is the right place, isn't it? Villa Rosa?'

'Yes, yes but perhaps there's been a misunderstanding,' she told him. 'You're not wanted here any more.'

'Signora, we have our orders.' He pulled a creased sheet of paper from his pocket and his eyes flicked over it. 'Trim back the climbing plants. Pull out the vegetable beds and sow grass seed. Spray weeds, water-blast paths, mow lawns. There's a lot to be done, you see? Best let us get on with it.'

All morning Babetta was pained by the sound of them working, the clatter and throb of their machines, the crashing of branches falling to the ground. She tried to distract herself with all she'd been neglecting in her own garden but kept being drawn back to the terrace where she stood by Nunzio's chair and wondered exactly what was happening behind the high wall that blocked her view of Villa Rosa.

By lunchtime she could stand it no longer. She squeezed some lemons into a big glass jug, added a few sprigs of mint and lots of ice and carried it, carefully balanced against her chest, over to Villa Rosa.

'*Ragazzi*,' she called out to the men. 'You must be ready to eat by now. I've brought something to refresh you first.'

They were grateful for the cool, bitter drink. As they finished it Babetta looked about her. Everything had been hacked back, even the tangle of flowering wisteria on the upstairs terrace, and the garden looked bald and embarrassed. Here and there she saw weeds they'd left to grow and seedlings they'd ripped out instead. Babetta shook her head and clicked her tongue against her teeth but managed to hold her silence.

Alice

Charlie had only been staying in his brother's flat for a couple of days but already he'd filled the spare room with pools of loose coins, eddies of discarded shoes and dropped things. I lay on the old double bed and remembered how irritating it had been trying to live with someone so untidy. A few minutes earlier, despite all our talk of only wanting cuddles, he and I had been busy setting the bedsprings creaking. It had been exactly the way I remembered it. Both of us knew the order of things, how they were supposed to fit together for a pleasant, safe sort of passion. And now it was over what I felt mostly was relief. It was as though we had pushed the night of my rape just that little bit further into the past.

Two things struck me as I lay there, examining the mess Charlie had spread around the room. One was that I could so easily sink back into a life with him, rent a little flat, spend our weekends taking long walks and watching foreign movies. It seemed a lot more appealing than the alternative – living alone – even if I did end up having to constantly pick up after him. The other thing I realised was that I'd preferred myself when I was with Charlie. Somehow I'd felt smarter and more interesting back then.

I could tell he was feeling happy. His body was curled around mine and he was drifting in and out of sleep. One moment he was making little snuffly snoring noises, the next his eyes were open and he was smiling at me. It was comfortable. I could have stayed there with him all afternoon and perhaps even have made the bedsprings creak once or twice more.

But then I remembered Leila. I'd left her to go out for breakfast and now it was past lunchtime. Shifting the weight of Charlie's arm from my shoulder, I slid out of bed. He grunted a bit and rolled over, falling further into sleep. It seemed a bit mean to wake him so I found a pen amidst all his rubble and wrote a note along the white margins of his newspaper. 'Come and see me in the brasserie soon.' The words curled down the side of the page. 'I'll buy you some dinner and a bottle of wine.'

I left the newspaper next to his tobacco, got dressed quickly and slipped out of the flat. All the way back to Maida Vale I felt weirdly exhilarated. I wasn't ready to look at his emerald yet but I was beginning to think we should be together. Surely the little bits of love I'd shed when he left me would soon return. It would be as easy as gaining back a couple of kilos. And if I were with Charlie then the future wouldn't seem so muzzy and unknown. I could keep working in the brasserie, he would find a job somewhere and things between us would be like they used to. Safe, comfortable. The thought of it pleased me.

But I'd reckoned without Leila. When I told her what I was planning she grew quite stormy.

'So you've wasted this entire time you've been rebuilding your life.' She stubbed out a cigarette viciously. 'You're just going to do a complete U-turn. Get sucked back into being Charlie's little sidekick?'

'I don't know why you object to him so much,' I complained.

'Because he's bad for you. He eats up all your personality.'

'That's ridiculous,' I told her.

'No, but I mean it. You've been more yourself without him.'

'Have I?' The idea struck me as odd. After all, I'd been living in Leila's house, doing her job, going to her favourite pubs. How was that being myself? Perhaps the truth of it was that I was really quite bland, like human tofu, taking on the stronger flavours of everyone around me. The thought was depressing.

'Don't go back with him,' Leila said. 'Promise me you won't.'

'But I can't stay here for ever,' I pointed out. 'And I don't want to live alone or with strangers.'

'You can stay here for as long as you want.'

'Won't your mother mind? What if she comes back and needs her room?'

'My mother?' Leila laughed. 'She's far too caught up in her own dramas to care whether you're here or not. The last I heard she was leaving the south of France and planning to move to Italy. She says she feels more inspired there but I suspect she's had a love affair with some French man that's gone wrong and needs to get away.'

Leila's mother was a painter. Some of her earlier work was hanging in the flat. They were large canvases, with big blocks of varying shades of blue arranged next to each other. I didn't know much about art but it seemed to me she just churned out variations of the same picture. It was working for her though, they sold for a small fortune and she was always getting written about in the Sunday papers.

'Sooner or later I'll have to move on,' I pointed out. 'Your mother will come back to live in London eventually.'

'Probably, but there's no point in worrying about that right now.' Leila let out a hiss of breath. 'Look, Alice, I think you should see him if you really want to but don't move in with him. Stay here with me, stay working in the brasserie, stay in the life that you created after he ruined the last one.'

'If you're sure you don't mind me being here ...'

She came and wrapped her arms around me, her long hair falling over my face. 'I love you being here, Alice. I'd be lonely without you.'

I felt as seduced as any man she'd brought home. 'Then I'll stay,' I promised. 'But Charlie might come over from time to time. Will you be OK with that?'

'I suppose so.'

'So that's settled then. Everything's settled.' I felt soothed, happy that some decisions had been made.

Only it turned out everything wasn't so settled after all. Because when I got to the brasserie later that afternoon Guyon dropped a bombshell. The moment he saw me arrive he beckoned me over to a corner of the kitchen.

'I'm leaving,' he hissed at me. 'I've got a new job. A really fabulous one.'

'What?' I was shocked.

'It's a new place called Teatro being opened by a hot young chef.' His face was flushed with excitement. 'I'll be running the morning kitchen, in charge of all the prep: the stocks, the soups, boning and jointing the meat, filleting fish, that sort of thing.'

'But why do you want to do that?' I was confused. 'Isn't it a step backwards? Here you're in charge of your own kitchen.'

'It's all about the food, Alice. This menu will be exciting, the sort of stuff I ought to be cooking and the place will have a buzz about it. It's a step towards where I was before everything went wrong.' Guyon had never talked to me about his fall from grace and he hesitated for a moment before adding, 'It's where I want to be.'

'It'll be awful here without you,' I couldn't help saying. 'What am I going to do?'

He grinned. 'Come with me. I can recommend you for a job. Not as maître d' though, obviously. You'd have to take a few steps back too.'

'I don't know. Let me think about it.'

All through that night's shift I wondered about Guyon. How could he be so passionate about working in a kitchen? It seemed like hard slog to me with suffocating heat and too much stress. And then there were the customers who pushed their meals around their plates or looked for things to complain about. What was so important about food that he put up with all that?

As I trotted back and forth to the kitchen I watched him cook. He moved fast and with a sort of rhythm. Meat sizzled in oil, long flames flared out of pans and Guyon sweated over them, his expression slightly distracted.

To my surprise I felt envious. I wanted to know what that passion felt like, to be driven and consumed by what I did as Guyon seemed to be. But I was certain it was never going to happen while I was waiting on tables.

'I'll do it, I'll come with you to this new place, Teatro,' I said impulsively at the end of the night.

'That's great – I'll talk to the boss.' Guyon sounded really pleased.

'There's just one thing. I don't want to waitress. If I come it has to be to work in the kitchen with you.'

'But Alice, you're not trained.'

'Does that matter? I'll start at the lowest level, do all the chopping and the grunt work. I'll be the kitchen slave.'

'It'll mean an early start every morning, long hours, hard work and not much money,' he warned me. 'Why would you want to do that?'

'For the same reason you want to. It's a step towards something. I just want to try it out, OK?'

He took my hand and held it in front of my face. 'See how your skin is all perfect and unmarked?'

I nodded and then watched as he put his own hand next to mine. It was covered in scars from knife cuts and burns. 'I get your point Guyon. I know it's going to be tough,' I said. 'But still I think it's worth giving it a go. I can't be a waitress for ever, can I? It's time I got on with life.'

'All right, Alice, I'll see if I can get you in,' he promised. 'But don't ever tell me I didn't warn you.'

Walking back to the flat that night I felt more excited than I had in ages. A year ago I'd promised myself I was going to use my time wisely, squeeze life dry. So far I hadn't managed it at all. Maybe this was my chance at last.

Babetta

More and more often Babetta found herself staring through the open gates of Villa Rosa. It seemed as though the house was waking up at last. The shutters had been flung open and the courtyard was filled with ladders and paint pots. All day long people came and went. Many of them hardly noticed Babetta, and even those who did offer her a bare *buongiorno* quickly went on their way. They had work to do, walls to wash a rosy pink, tiles to fix, steps to cut into the rocks that led down to the sea. Babetta wasn't part of any of it. But still she was drawn back to the open gates where she could stand and watch.

Even Nunzio had come and paused by her side once or twice. He had held up a hand and nodded at the workmen. But when she tried to speak to him he turned and shuffled back to his cane chair.

The person Babetta most hoped to see was the signora with the clipboard. She wanted to remind her of the offer to take back the responsibility of caring for the grounds. Surely it was obvious what a mess those idiots from the gardening crew had made. Far better to put her in charge even if they had to bring in a man every now and then to help her with the heavy work. But when the signora did drive up in her smart Fiat she seemed harassed. She nodded brusquely in response to Babetta's greeting and hurried through the gates without stopping. She seemed to be angry about something, barking orders at the workmen, telling them they had to work faster. Babetta could have told her it wasn't the right way to go about things but instead she just stood and looked on.

'Signora, can I have a word with you?' she asked when the woman returned to her car. 'It's about the gardens.'

'I don't have time to talk about that now.' She was already climbing into her Fiat and Babetta's chance was slipping away. Then the signora paused and looked back at her. 'Actually, you might be able to help me. Would you mind doing a small favour?'

'Of course not.' Babetta was eager. 'What is it you need?'

'Well, the house isn't officially on the market yet but I have a client who wants to view it anyway. She's coming later this afternoon and the trouble is I can't be here. If I leave the key with you, could you let her in and show her round a bit? I know it's a lot to ask but ...'

'It's no problem at all. I'd be happy to do it.' Babetta held out her hand and took the key, slipping it quickly into her pocket before the signora could change her mind. 'What is this client's name?'

'It's Aurora Gray. She's an Englishwoman but she speaks some Italian and understands quite a lot so long as you talk slowly. Show her the house and the gardens. I wish I could be here but ...'

She tore off up the hill in her Fiat, raising dust as she went. Babetta put her hand over the pocket where the key to Villa Rosa lay, feeling like she'd been given a prize. She hadn't seen inside the house before. She'd never imagined she would.

All day long she was bursting to tell someone her news but there was no one there who'd care, certainly not Nunzio who'd abandoned his cane chair and gone upstairs to lie down in bed. So instead Babetta got on with her chores and kept an eye out for the Englishwoman. She wondered what she'd look like, if she were rich and why she was interested in buying Villa Rosa.

It was getting late and Babetta was beginning to worry no one would come when she saw the car sweeping down the hill. She ran to the gate, the key in her hand so she would be ready.

'*Buonasera*,' she called out as the Englishwoman slammed the car door behind her.

The woman smiled at Babetta. She was tall with long coppery hair and a face that was still lovely.

'*Buonasera*,' she replied. 'Isn't it a beautiful evening? I was so afraid it would rain and I wouldn't see the place looking its best.'

'You are Aurora Gray? My name is Babetta. The signora asked if I would show you round Villa Rosa as she has some other commitments this evening. If you come with me I'll take you into the house right away.'

'No, no, if you don't mind I'd like to walk through the gardens first and down to the sea. The house can wait.'

Babetta was disappointed but she led the English woman through the gardens, pointing out the different fruit trees and being careful to mention several times that until recently she had been the one who had helped them flourish.

They followed the path to the sea and Babetta saw that the steps that led down onto the rocks still hadn't been repaired properly. 'It's too dangerous to go further, signora. But in the summer it's very beautiful. There's a metal ladder you fix to the rocks and then you can climb down and swim in the sea on days when it's calm enough.'

'That sounds nice.' The woman was eyeing the steps. 'I'm sure I could get down onto the rocks, you know. I just need to take it carefully.'

Before Babetta could stop her she began to clamber over the crumbling steps. She may not have been a particularly young woman but she was agile and soon she was standing at the very edge of the rocks looking out over the layers of blue the sky made as it fell towards the sea.

'Perhaps this is it,' the woman murmured.

The house itself didn't seem to interest her much. Babetta took her through every room, frowning at the dust that lay over the white ceramic tiles and noticing how the tasselled curtains were beginning to rot, taking it all in because who knew if she'd ever be allowed inside again. But Aurora Gray seemed more fascinated by the views from every window. She stood and watched while the sun began to set and the layers of blue turned pink, and then turned to Babetta and said. 'I think I've seen enough.'

As the Englishwoman drove away, Babetta's eyes lifted to the statue of Christ high above her. She stared at him for a while and then shrugged and went inside to find something to cook for poor Nunzio's dinner.

Alice

It was as if I'd entered some sort of hell, a seething pit walled with stainless steel and crammed with bodies. All I could do was work harder and faster because if I stopped, even for a moment, I'd fall behind and that wasn't an option.

The kitchen at Teatro was at the front of the restaurant with windows onto the street so anyone passing by could see us in our chef's whites, bending over a chopping board or struggling to strain a vat of chicken stock. To get to the dining room customers had to walk past the kitchen down a narrow corridor, feeling the heat of the ovens and flames, smelling whatever was cooking. Even as they ate they could watch the act of cooking through an entire wall of plate glass.

The other thing that was different about Teatro was there was no wine cellar. Instead, all the bottles were stored on shelves that reached up the full height of the three remaining walls. There were ladders for the sommeliers to climb up and little baskets on pulleys for them to pass the bottles down.

'We're not just feeding our customers,' Guyon told me. 'We're giving them a night out at the theatre.'

Of course, when we were there, the dining room was empty as Teatro only opened for dinner. Our job was to prepare as much as possible in advance for the evening chefs who would finish off the cooking and plate up the food.

The head chef, Tonino Ricci, was famous for his modern Italian cuisine so we were making lots of light sauces and stocks, filleting fish and boning meat. At first I wasn't allowed to try my hand at any of that because it was considered too advanced. For what seemed like weeks all I did was dice vegetables.

The first day Guyon gave me a sack of carrots and told me to cut them into square cubes. It took me over two hours, and every now and then he'd glance over to make sure I was getting it right.

'What will you do if they're not perfect?' I asked him.

He nodded towards the stockpot. 'Toss them in there.'

'You're kidding, right?'

He shook his head grimly. 'So much is at stake here, Alice. So much money has gone into this place. We can't afford for anyone to screw up ... not even the kitchen slave.'

I'd never heard him use that tone of voice, strict like a teacher. Surprised to find myself on the edge of tears, I bent my head and kept chopping.

Once I could dice vegetables perfectly, they let me cube meat for a ragu, or zest the citrus fruit. Only when Guyon declared that I'd learnt to use a knife properly – not lifting it but rocking back and forth – was I allowed to move on to other things: jointing a duck or chicken, preparing herbs for a salad, slicing veal thinly for involtini. Eventually I was shown how to make the pasta dough, roll it out and cut it into whatever shapes were needed for that night's menu.

By mid-afternoon the night chefs had arrived and started setting up their stations. That's when the kitchen became really overcrowded and busy. The smells were of braising meat, bubbling stocks and sauces. The odd thing was there was hardly any noise, just knives knocking against chopping blocks and the occasional clang of pans.

It was brutal work. By the end of the day my arms and

shoulders ached, my hands and hair smelt of food and I was so tired all I could think of was lying down, but still I felt reluctant to walk away from the kitchens of Teatro just when things were getting interesting.

'Do you think one day I'll be good enough to work the evening shift?' I asked Guyon as I diced celery one morning.

He laughed and pointed his knife at me. 'You've caught the bug,' he said. But he didn't answer my question.

At night the restaurant was bustling because this was the hip new place in town and Tonino Ricci was the chef everyone was talking about.

'But those people don't really care about food,' Guyon told me. 'They'll be gone as soon as the next trendy place opens up. To get the right sort of customers in here we need some good solid reviews.'

Even I found myself racing out first thing on a Sunday to buy the papers and see if Teatro had got a mention. I could sense that everyone was on edge waiting to find out how the restaurant would fare. Only Tonino himself seemed disinterested. A quiet man, he looked more like a marathon runner than a chef. He had dark brown eyes and a voice you had to strain to hear. It was Nico, the sous-chef, who made all the noise. Tonino just drifted about, whispering in people's ears or gently moving them aside and show-ing them how things ought to be done. He was still quite young, only in his mid-twenties, but Guyon told me he'd worked in the kitchen of his family's restaurant in southern Italy from the moment he was old enough to hold a knife.

When the reviews came they were good but still we couldn't relax because Tonino wanted to work towards getting his first Michelin star. He added more specials to the menu and that meant Guyon had to get in even earlier to write up his list of the things we had to cook for the day. He was starting work at six a.m. and putting in twelve-hour shifts; I was worried about him.

We were all stressed and exhausted but everything was running OK until a year or so after opening Tonino got that Michelin star he'd wanted so much. That afternoon he poured glasses of champagne for everyone, made a little thank-you speech and proposed a toast to all of us at Teatro. Guyon lifted his glass and sipped along with everyone else. Draining it, he accepted another.

I didn't say a thing because I wasn't supposed to know Guyon had a drinking problem – he never spoke about it to anyone. Anyway, it was nearly the end of his shift, we were celebrating a big success and surely a couple of glasses of bubbly couldn't do any harm?

At first Guyon held it together. No one but me noticed that his breath had a strange new sourness to it, or that he went in and out of the walk-in fridge repeatedly after mid-day. It was me who found the half-drunk bottle of white wine in there, hidden behind some stacked trays of morel mushrooms, but still I didn't say anything. How could I broach the subject? It seemed easier to watch and wait.

Then the mistakes started. Once Guyon left a dish of meat braising in the oven so long all the liquid burnt off and the meat began to catch. There were other things. One of the line cooks borrowed his knife and complained it wasn't sharp, a sign of sloppiness in a kitchen. He forgot to make a sauce and so Tonino had to take a pasta special off the menu. Lots of little things, none of them disastrous. And Guyon didn't seem drunk, not wobbly on his legs or slurring his words. So I left it, hoping he would sort it out.

There wasn't a drama, no customers poisoned, nothing broken even. But Tonino, in his quiet way, watched everything in his kitchen. If I'd noticed that Guyon was off-key, then he had seen it too. One morning I came in and, instead of Guyon, I found a thin girl in chef's whites standing at the counter, writing up the list of what had to be cooked that day.

'Where's Guyon?' I asked.

'Gone,' she replied.

'What, like, gone on holiday?'

'No, just gone,' she replied shortly. 'I'm Chloe. You answer to me now.'

I couldn't wait for my shift to be over so I could go round to Guyon's flat and see if he was all right. I caught a taxi there I was so impatient. But there was no sign of him, even though I knocked and rang on the door for ages. So I went to the brasserie to see if Leila was working.

'I think it was crappy of Tonino to let him go like that,' I said to her, accepting a large glass of wine. 'He's worked so hard. If Teatro's a success then Guyon is a big part of that.'

'They might have him back at this place, I suppose.' She glanced up at the new chef who was busy dropping things in the kitchen. 'Things don't seem to be working out so well. But Guyon will have to prove he can stay away from the bottle. Do you think he can do that?'

'I don't know. Maybe the problem is worse than I thought. Anyway, he's not opening his door to me at the moment.'

'So what about you?' Leila asked. 'Will you leave as well now?'

'No, I think I'll stay there.'

'Why?' She sounded surprised.

I shrugged. 'What else would I do?'

'Well, I don't know. I thought you had some sort of plan.'

I laughed. 'Not really. I'm just working hard and learning as I go. And I'm so knackered at the end of the day I can't think properly, never mind make a plan. I mean who has a plan?'

'I do,' Leila said with complete certainty, and then she moved off to take an order, wipe down a couple of tables and seat some customers so I had to wait ten minutes or so until I could ask what it was.

She wouldn't tell, of course. 'You'll see,' was all she said, twirling a strand of hair round her finger and smiling.

I walked home, pleasantly muzzy with wine, alternately wondering about Leila and worrying about Guyon. When I got in I found a message from him on the answerphone.

'I screwed up, Alice,' he said in a voice as thick as one of his favourite creamy French sauces. 'I really, really screwed up.'

Babetta

The silence was the first thing Babetta noticed. No screaming brakes of concrete trucks trying to negotiate the hill, no men calling to each other, no cleaners arriving with buckets and brooms. The work on Villa Rosa was complete and the house lay behind closed gates, waiting for someone to claim it.

The Englishwoman Aurora Gray hadn't been back but there had been a stream of others. Sometimes the signora showed them round the house but more often, especially if they were locals and only there to ogle at the place, she gave Babetta the key and let her take care of them.

There had been a few faces she recognised amongst those who had come to look. Fabrizio Russo – wealthy from doing things she'd rather not think about – scathing about Villa Rosa, declaring it far too simple for his tastes. His brother Stefano, owner of the linen shop in Triento and pushed around the place by his ambitious, greedy wife. Babetta moved them through as briskly as possible, not stopping to let them admire the views or run their hands down the new butter-soft velvet curtains.

The only one she had time for was beautiful Raffaella Ricci, who admitted she'd come simply because once she'd worked at Villa Rosa and wanted to take the chance to see inside it again.

'This place holds so many memories for me,' Raffaella said as she sipped the espresso Babetta had poured her. 'When I was very young I cooked here for the *Americano* who built the statue of Christ on the mountain. Do you remember him?'

Babetta smiled. She had always liked Raffaella and her second husband Ciro. They were good people, generous and hard-working. 'I remember seeing the *Americano* the day they blessed the statue,' she replied. 'He was a handsome man. Such a shame he and his family never bothered coming back here. The place has been so neglected.'

Raffaella looked out at the terrace with its painted ceramic tiles and generous view of the sea. 'Strange, but it seems that's always been the way. It's so pretty here and yet no one wants to stay for long.'

'Why don't you buy it?' Babetta asked hopefully.

'No, it isn't for me. I'm happy living in my parent's old house down by the port. That has lots of memories too.'

Years ago Raffaella had been the most beautiful girl in Triento. She'd been widowed very young and Babetta remembered how people had hated her for it. There was so much jealousy and gossip up in town, even back then. That was one reason Babetta liked to live hidden away here, where there was no one to care about knowing her business.

She followed Raffaella out of the house and along the path that led to the sea. 'I haven't been down to the port for a long time,' she remarked conversationally. 'Not for years and years.'

'It's changing. Crowds of tourists, lots more cafés and restaurants. My parents wouldn't recognise it now if they were still around.'

'Still, all these new people must be good for business?' Babetta said, negotiating the newly rebuilt steps down onto the rocks.

'Yes, our restaurant is busy all summer. And the pizzeria up the hill does pretty good trade all year round. My son, Lucio runs that now.'

They were standing side by side, looking down at the waves hurling themselves over the rocks. 'Your family has done well,' Babetta remarked. 'You must be very proud. And what about your eldest son? I heard he went to England.'

Raffaella sighed. 'Tonino's opened a big restaurant in London, very expensive, very smart. He works such long hours he has no time to think about a wife or family. All he cares about is cooking. If only he'd come home. But he's still young and ambitious so I suppose the time isn't right.'

They walked back up through the gardens and Raffaella apologised for wasting so much of Babetta's time. Then she climbed on her old Vespa and took off up the hill, her long hair streaming behind her just as it must have when she was a young girl.

Babetta took a last look back at Villa Rosa, freshly washed in pink, its shutters flung open, and then she locked the gates behind her and returned to her own house. Soon her daughter would come to drive her up the hill to Triento so she could fill her basket with the things she and Nunzio needed to keep them going. A wedge of Parmesan, maybe a bag of flour and a little yeast, some vinegar, olive oil, salt and sugar. Her shopping lists were never very long because they lived a simple life here, tucked beneath the hill on the edge of the sea. She'd never seen any reason to change it.

Alice

Without Guyon the prep kitchen of Teatro was a lonely place to work. I diced vegetables, rolled out pasta and filleted fish in silence, wondering what had become of him.

Every day for a week I'd been back to his flat but there was no sign of him. Even knocking on the neighbouring doors hadn't helped much. One woman said she thought he'd gone away but she seemed vague and there were small children screaming in the background, so I wasn't convinced she'd really noticed much.

The more worried I got, the more I blamed Tonino. In all the time I'd worked at Teatro, the head chef had barely spoken to me. His kitchen had a strict hierarchy, with him at the very top and me at the bottom. If he bumped into me while I was working then it was my fault and I apologised. If he wanted me to do something, he'd get Guyon to tell me. So when I walked right up and asked if he could spare a moment, he looked surprised.

We went into the walk-in fridge for privacy and I stood beside a tray of beef cheeks, shivering a little as I told him I was handing in my resignation.

'Can I ask you why?' His voice, as always, was calm and measured.

'It's because of Guyon.' Righteous anger made me brave. 'You fired him, right, chef?'

He nodded. 'Yes, I did.'

'Well, I don't think that was very fair of you. Why couldn't you have given him a bit longer to sort himself out?'

'Because it would only have got worse.' He sounded matter-of-fact. 'I've seen it before. Guyon shouldn't be cooking at this level. He has the talent for it but not the temperament.'

'But now he's disappeared. No one seems to know what's happened.'

'He's in some rehab place in Kent. I drove him there myself.'

'Oh.'

'Happier now?'

'Yes ... sorry ...'

'And I'm not accepting your resignation.' Tonino had a quiet Italian arrogance about him. 'I think it's time you had a change though. I want you to work evenings. You can start on the pasta.'

'Really, chef? Do you think I'm ready?'

He shrugged. 'I don't know. But it's time to see if you've got the talent and the temperament. If it doesn't work out then I'll accept your resignation. OK?'

'Yes ... I—'

Tonino didn't wait to hear me out. Turning away, he strode back to whatever he'd been doing, leaving me standing in the walk-in fridge, chilled and astonished.

The pasta station in a restaurant like Teatro is always busy because almost everyone likes to order a pasta course when they're eating Italian. So although my new job wasn't as tough as working the grill, for instance, it was still difficult. Speed and stamina were needed; pasta, the others kept telling me, was only ever a young person's station.

At night the kitchen changed its mood. Tonino, or Nico the sous-chef, stood at the pass calling out the orders and the rest of us reacted like well-trained hounds, scrambling to obey as fast as we could.

There were lots of things I found tough; the constant heat was one – most nights I sweated over that pasta boiler for at least five hours. Keeping the orders straight in my head, remembering which sauce went with which pasta shape, and plating the whole thing up properly, all of that was difficult.

There was a cheat sheet pinned above my station to remind me how each dish was meant to be composed but the constant steam from the pasta boiler had rendered it soggy and mostly unreadable. Even when I wasn't at work I kept repeating the dishes to myself: the tortelloni filled with goat's cheese is served with a butter emulsion and crispy fried thyme, the pappardelle comes with a rich duck ragu, thinned with a little pasta water, enriched with butter and sprinkled with fresh herbs ... until it got so I could recite the contents of each dish like a favourite poem.

The first few nights I got so many things wrong. I left the chilli pepper out of one dish, the chopped fresh tomato from another. Nico hissed at me, 'Get it right next time, Alice. Get it right.'

I lived on adrenalin, but then we all did. The guy on the grill turning out perfectly cooked meat, the girl on the vegetables, all of us line cooks doing our bit to make sure the diners got their food on time, each dish tasting and looking exactly the same as the last time they'd ordered it.

'It's about consistency as well as flavour,' Nico kept telling me. 'So get it right.'

Within a week I had ugly red scalds up my arm where I'd flicked myself with boiling salty water as I pulled out the pasta with my tongs. I'd found a rag and tied it round my head so I wouldn't sweat into the food and I'd learnt that I still had so much more to learn.

There were nights when I was so clumsy my pans fell crashing to the ground, sauces were spilled and Nico, pulling me out of sight of the diners, yelled at me. Other times I got so much wrong he pushed me aside and made me watch while he worked my station. 'See, this is how it's done, Alice. Now you try it. And get it right.'

I kept expecting Tonino to tell me I didn't have the talent or the temperament and that he'd accept my resignation. But every afternoon I got in, pulled on my chef's whites and started setting up my station. And every night I left well after one a.m. when I'd finally finished cleaning the pasta boiler. Eventually I realised Nico wasn't scolding me any more. The orecchiette was cooked perfectly, the correct amount of softly steamed Italian broccoli had been stirred through and the chilli pepper had been remembered. I was getting it right.

It was around then the crying started. I never cried in the restaurant or in front of anyone from work, only when I was alone. I'd cry when I woke up, while I drank my first strong coffee and took my shower. Once or twice I had to get off the tube a couple of stops early and walk through Green Park, my head down, letting the tears slide out. I cried on my days off and at night before I fell asleep, but quietly, with my face pressed into a pillow, so Leila wouldn't hear. I didn't really understand what was going on. All I knew was I had the strength for just two things: cooking pasta and crying.

Charlie noticed my reddened eyes once or twice. We'd fallen into the habit of seeing each other on Sundays because it was the only day we both had off. Teatro was closed and so was the film production company where he was working as a runner. Usually we met for brunch at the brasserie and then spent the rest of the afternoon in bed. Lying there with Charlie's arms around me was the only time I didn't feel like crying. Still, he knew me well enough to realise there was something wrong.

'What's the matter?' he kept asking. 'Are you all right?'

'Yes, I'm fine,' I always insisted. 'Stop asking me that.'

I couldn't explain because I barely understood it myself. I actually felt sorry for people like Charlie, nine-to-five office workers who lived without the massive buzz I got every night as I hovered over the pasta boiler, turning out dish after dish.

I could feel Teatro was taking a huge toll, both physically and mentally but I was sure anything else would seem dull after it. So I enjoyed that little Sunday afternoon hiatus, knowing I'd be back in my chef's whites the next day, half-sick with anticipation.

Sometimes, when there was a lull in the orders at the pasta station, I'd let my eyes sweep around the kitchen and take in all that I could see. And I'd wonder, how did I end up here? How did this become my life?

Then an order would be called and I'd snap back to work, buzzing with fear and exhilaration.

Babetta

So much about Triento had hardly changed at all. The market traders still set up stalls in the main piazza, festooning them with strings of dried chillies and thick trunks of salami, piling them high with gourds of waxy caciocavallo cheese and the season's fresh produce. The town hall still stood proud and tall and beside it the burnished bronze statue of a naked mermaid spouted water just as it had when Babetta was a girl.

It was true there were more tourists here now. She could hear the babble of foreign voices as she queued in the *salumeria* or walked past the corner bar. There were more cars clotting the streets and more traffic officers equipped with loud whistles to move them on. But Triento hadn't been spoilt like so many other towns. Its old houses and churches were packed in so tightly there was no room to put up modern buildings. No space for supermarkets, petrol stations, no vacant lots for American hamburger joints.

In Triento life went on much as it had for centuries. Women shopped with baskets over their arms, pausing to greet friends or exchange a morsel of gossip. Young Fernando the butcher stood in the doorway of his shop, like his father and his grandfather had before him, waiting for some trade. Fine linen fluttered in the breeze outside the Russo's shop. Above it on a terrace two old women were knitting woollen shawls and keeping an eye on the ebb and flow of locals in the piazza.

Whenever Sofia brought her up to town Babetta followed

the same routine. First they would go to the bank, so she could check her money was still nesting there safely. Then Sofia usually insisted on stopping for coffee and choosing some sweet little treats to go with it.

'If you'd told me you wanted coffee I'd have made you one for free before we left home,' Babetta liked to grizzle as they settled at an outdoor table. In truth she enjoyed sitting there, watching people walk by and greeting old women she had known as girls.

Then they would shop together, Sofia urging her to fill her basket. 'What about this wild asparagus, Mamma? So delicious fried with a little egg. Perhaps I'll buy some to take home for dinner.' Sofia's husband worked on the railways. He didn't earn much money and Babetta worried what little he had was quickly spent on things they might have managed without.

Sometimes they stopped at the bakery for a wheel of freshly-baked bread stuffed with caramelised onion and prosciutto or dusted with rosemary. Old Silvana was there most days, sunning herself on the bench outside the shop, even though she'd long ago sold the place. She was quite deaf and half blind but her mind was still sharp and if anything was happening in town then Silvana was sure to be told about it. Not even that had changed.

Babetta was in no hurry. She moved slowly through the market stalls choosing carefully and haggling over the prices.

'Don't think you can charge me like you do the tourists,' she warned as a slab of pecorino was wrapped up for her. 'What about that little waxy end bit? No one will buy that. You may as well give it to me.'

The market traders muttered in complaint and Sofia looked embarrassed but Babetta didn't care – a few coins saved here and there would soon add up.

It was as they were walking back towards the car that

Babetta saw her, the Englishwoman she'd shown round Villa Rosa weeks ago. She was sitting alone at a café table, sipping a glass of Prosecco and raised her hand to wave as they walked by.

Babetta barely nodded in return but still Sofia had noticed the exchange. Now she would be curious and was bound to bother her with questions.

'Who is that woman who waved? How do you know her?' Sofia was craning her neck to look back.

'Don't stare. Look where you're going,' Babetta scolded, hurrying on.

'She's very glamorous. Why was she waving at you?'

Babetta tutted impatiently. 'She's just someone I showed round Villa Rosa weeks ago. Why do you have to pester me, Sofia? What is it to you if some woman waves?'

Her daughter ignored her. 'If she's come back to Triento a second time that must mean she's interested in buying Villa Rosa. I'm sure she has the money. Did you see her smart clothes and that big leather handbag beside her on the table?'

Inevitably Sofia began her favourite refrain. 'If she buys the house what will you do?' she demanded. 'She might not want to keep you on as caretakers. If you lose your house where will you and Papa go? Have you thought of that?'

Babetta stared towards the mountains and tried to shut the words out of her ears.

'Why wait until you're turfed out,' Sofia went on relentlessly. 'Especially with Papa so sick in his mind, you need to find a little place in Triento sooner rather than later. I don't understand why you won't listen to me. Why must you be so stubborn? If you moved into town then I wouldn't have to worry about you so much.'

Babetta set her face into a frown and refused to discuss it. Wordlessly she kept on towards the car, aware of how annoying it must be for Sofia. But when her daughter grew older she'd understand better. Then she would know how it felt not to want to change anything, to hold what was left of your life curled up in the palm of your hand.

Alice

All of us seemed so busy with our lives. Leila had bought a second-hand typewriter and set it on the kitchen table. When she wasn't waitressing at the brasserie, she was busy hitting the keys with an odd sort of ferocity, pausing only to dab at the page with Tippex every now and then. Charlie was busy too, caught up in his new job and working longer hours in the hope of speeding up the whole process of getting ahead. All of us were trying to jam so much into every day: so many experiences, so much learning. It's no wonder we didn't have much time for each other.

There was only one person I knew whose days were moving slowly, and he was in a rehab centre somewhere in Kent. I wanted to talk to Guyon so much but Tonino had refused to give me his address.

'Guyon is there for a reason,' he had said in his arrogant way. 'He doesn't need interruptions. When it's the right time for him then he'll get in touch.'

He'd made me feel guilty for wanting to talk about my problems with someone who already had enough of his own. So I tried to put Guyon out of my mind and knuckled down to working in Teatro, anchored by the pasta station, barely thinking beyond the next order.

What's amazing is how addictive the rush of cooking can be. It was the single thing that most reminded me I was alive. So when I heard they were short-staffed in the prep kitchen I offered to do double shifts, and took to spending calm, quiet days making light pillows of ravioli and little knots of tortellini, and then frantic, steamy nights cooking them to order. It was oddly satisfying. Instead of just doing my bit in the line, I was making a dish from start to finish, really cooking at last, and I liked that idea.

Work took over almost completely. My mother grew plaintive as the weeks sped by and I never found time to head north to see her. Charlie and I carried on having our Sundays lazing in bed, and I managed the odd late-night glass of wine with Leila. Aside from that my world had shrunk and all I saw was the inside of the restaurant kitchen, the flat in Maida Vale and the tube train as I shuttled from one to the other.

It was Tonino who put a stop to it. One afternoon he called me over and steered me through to the dining room where he sat me down at a table. This was the first time I'd really experienced the restaurant from a customer's point of view and the skew in perspective threw me off balance.

'So, Alice, how's it going?' Tonino took a seat opposite me.

'OK, I think, chef.'

'You seem to be doing fine on the pasta station.'

'Thanks ... yes, chef ... I'm getting the hang of it.'

'And are you enjoying it?'

He was staring at me, making eye contact in a way I found disconcerting. Suddenly I felt the pressure of tears forming and, to my horror, they started spilling down my face.

'It's just a bit stressful ...' I managed.

Tonino acted as if he hadn't noticed I was crying. There was no neatly-pressed handkerchief passed over, not so much as a tissue. Instead he shrugged: 'Of course it's stressful. You have absolutely no training and you're working in the kitchen of one of the city's top restaurants. I'm amazed you've coped as well as you have.'

I rubbed at my face with my sleeve. 'Are you going to fire me?' I asked.

He didn't answer the question. 'The trouble is, Alice, you don't actually know how to cook. You can make the dishes you've been shown but you still don't understand the first thing about food. Do you know, for example, why it is we stuff a goose or duck instead of cooking it with an empty cavity?'

I shook my head. 'No.'

'Do you want to know?'

'Yes, of course.'

'The stuffing slows the cooking of the bird so the fat is rendered properly and the full flavours develop. It's one of the basics of being a chef. Cooked fat is delicious, un-cooked fat is not. But you don't know these things, Alice. You can't know them because you've never been taught.'

'So you think I need to go back to college, get a catering qualification?'

'I think you need to find a way to learn.'

'Are you firing me?' I asked again.

'No.' He smiled at me. 'You work hard and you're not untalented so why would I fire you? But I don't want you pulling double shifts. Prep kitchen or pasta station? Your choice.'

'Pasta,' I said, without needing to think about it.

'Good, so that leaves you with your days free to find out more about food.'

'But chef, how do I know if this is really what I should be doing?' I asked. 'Perhaps, like Guyon, I haven't got the temperament for it?'

Tonino shrugged. 'You've got this far. Only you can decide if you want to keep going.'

I didn't tell him about the tears I dribbled into my morning bath and pressed into my pillow most nights. Nor did I admit how much I hated the idea of spending time in some dreary college kitchen getting a proper qualification. Instead I nodded my head compliantly.

'OK, I'll see about getting some training then, chef.' Just the thought of it exhausted me.

'And one more thing. In your time off I want you to start eating in restaurants. Not expensive ones. Cheap Asian places, Turkish cafés up in north London, little neighbourhood spaghetti joints. Think about what you're eating, what's good about it and what's bad. And get some food books, cook at home. Become passionate, Alice. Fill your life with food.'

He left me sitting in the empty dining room, staring at the towering walls of wine bottles and more than ever wishing Guyon was there to listen to me talk.

Babetta

Her house was as nice as Babetta had been able to make it. Years ago she'd covered the walls with hand-woven baskets, each one a little different in pattern and design. The living room was hardly ever used but still Babetta wiped down the floors nearly every day with a damp rag tied to a brush. She and Nunzio stayed mostly in the kitchen where they had an old television up on the counter and a radio she left on for much of the time. They'd been comfortable in this place. It had been easy to forget it belonged to someone else.

Now Sofia had forced her to think about how things were going to change whether she liked it or not. Babetta woke every morning wondering if this might be the day they came, and she found herself peering out the kitchen window every time she heard a car. For his part Nunzio seemed not to care what happened. He shuttled himself from his bed to his cane chair, turning his face away and infuriating her.

'This is all your fault,' she cried at him more than once. 'If you hadn't given up on life none of this would have happened.'

It was almost a relief when the signora's car pulled up and she saw the Englishwoman, Aurora Gray, climb out of the passenger side. The pair went through the gates of Villa Rosa and it was half an hour or so until they emerged. Babetta felt a little stab of anxiety as they wandered up her front path, the signora stopping every few steps to point out things of interest in her garden.

'You see there is quite a lot of land here. It's all being cultivated at the moment but could easily be put back into garden. This house would be perfect for extra guest accommodation, or you could turn it into two apartments and rent them out.'

Aurora nodded but looked uncomfortable. She must have been aware of Babetta hovering within earshot.

'So this place was built at the same time as Villa Rosa?' she asked.

'Yes, yes.' The signora hugged her leather folder to her chest. 'It's always been used to accommodate servants and gardeners. If you rented it out you could get a nice little income. You might even want to put in a swimming pool.'

Babetta moved out on the terrace and waited in silence while they made their way up her steps.

'Miss Gray would like to see inside the house. Is it convenient now?' The signora smiled brightly.

Babetta nodded but still didn't speak. She led both women into the tiled kitchen and remained there while they moved through her home, into the sunny front room where Sofia once slept, her own space with its neatly-made bed, and the one at the back of the house where Nunzio often went to avoid her. At one point she heard the Englishwoman exclaim at the old baskets on the upstairs landing, the ones made by her sisters all those years ago. Perhaps she thought she could buy those along with everything else.

It was only when they came back downstairs that Babetta found her voice.

'Can I offer you a coffee or a cool drink?' she asked.

'No, no that won't be necessary.' The signora sounded brisk.

'Actually, I'm parched.' Aurora was apologetic. 'I won't hold you up for long but I'd love to have something to drink.'

As she filled two tall tumblers with chilled lemonade,

Babetta took her chance. 'So you will buy Villa Rosa,' she said to the Englishwoman.

'I'm not sure.' Aurora took the drink gratefully. 'When I came the first time I hadn't understood that the property included two houses. It's more than I intended to spend.'

'But I think you'll buy it.' Babetta topped up her glass. 'You would like to live here.'

'Yes I think I would,' she agreed.

'I've lived here for many years. It's a good place, peaceful. Nunzio and I have been happy here.'

Aurora nodded and there was an awkward moment before the signora interrupted, tapping her watch. 'Sorry to rush you but I need to get back to town.'

As they walked out onto the terrace and down the steps, Nunzio barely seemed to notice. His expression hadn't changed at all.

Babetta watched the two women drive away, feeling infuriated with him once more. 'This is your fault, you stupid old man,' she repeated in a hiss. 'If we were still the gardeners over there then we wouldn't have this problem.'

Alice

Leila was always obsessively tidy around the flat just in case her mother sprang a surprise visit, but this morning there were photographs scattered all over the kitchen table. I went over to have a look while I waited for the kettle to boil. Most showed a shuttered house with pale pink walls and little wrought-iron balconies covered with pots of geraniums. There were a couple of views of the sea and then about five just of the sky, stretches of blue broken up by clouds.

'What's this?' I asked Leila.

'It's the place my mother is buying in Italy. It's right down south. She says it has the right kind of sky.'

'But sky is sky, isn't it?' I wondered. 'The same the world over.'

'Apparently not.' Leila lit her first cigarette of the day from the gas ring on the hob. 'Anyway she's keen for me to go and stay for a while. You should come too.'

'Can't,' I said automatically. 'Work.'

'Don't you get holidays like everyone else?'

Hoping to avoid the conversation, I went to make the tea.

'Well, don't you?' Leila wasn't going to drop it.

'Yes, probably.'

'So why don't you take one?'

'I can't right now. Tonino wants me to get some training so I'm looking at catering courses and stuff. Maybe some other time.' Putting the full teapot down next to her,

I glanced at the photos again. 'It does seem lovely though.'

Leila stopped me before I could slip back to my room. 'Don't think I don't know what's going on,' she said.

'What do you mean?'

'All this crying ... the state you're in most of the time. I'm totally pissed off with you, Alice. Why won't you talk to me, tell me what's wrong?' She poured two cups of tea and pushed one over to me. 'Sit down and start talking.'

'The problem is I don't know what's wrong.' I took the tea but stayed on my feet. 'I feel ... overwhelmed, I suppose.'

'With your job?'

'Partly ...'

'So stop doing it. Go back to waitressing for a bit. Be nice to yourself, Alice. You've had a tough time, after all.'

Giving in to her, I took a seat at the table. 'But I don't hate it.' I tried to explain. 'Actually, it's the most amazing thing I do. It's only when I'm not doing it that I seem to fall apart. I don't know what's wrong with me. Maybe I need drugs or something. But I can't take time off to go on holiday. I can't stop, not now.'

'Just for two weeks.'

'No, if I stop then I might not be able to start again.'

'Would that be so bad? I mean, there are a million other things you could do.'

Even I didn't understand what it was that made me want to keep cooking. But the idea of two weeks in Italy, lying on a sun lounger, left me feeling heavy-limbed. I was certain I'd never be able to pick myself back up.

'You know what?' said Leila. 'I'm just going to buy you a plane ticket and you're coming whether you like it or not. I mean, this is Italy, Alice. The Italians are mad about food. If you want to really learn about cooking then better there than catering college, I'd have thought.'

'I can't—'

'Yes you can.' She passed me a photograph of the pale pink house. 'You're coming to Triento and you're going to stay at Villa Rosa for at least two weeks. Come with me, Alice. Come and see the sky.'

'But Leila—'

'Don't bother trying to argue. Just tell Tonino you're taking a holiday.' She grinned at me. 'He can get someone else to boil his pasta for a couple of weeks.'

'Yes, but if I take time off then I ought to go back home to see Mum. I haven't seen her in ages.'

'She'll understand you need a proper holiday. I bet she's worried about you too.'

When Leila became obsessed with an idea it was exhausting trying to stand up to her. She mentioned Italy every chance she got, steamrollering me into the plan, and in the end the easiest thing was to do what she wanted.

'You win,' I told her.

She only laughed. 'I knew I would.'

The funny thing was Tonino seemed overly excited by the plan from the outset. I'd never seen him quite as warm and animated as he was when I broached the idea.

'Italy, yes, yes,' he kept saying. 'You should go for longer than two weeks. This is spring vegetable time, tender beans, wild asparagus, little buds of artichokes. Go and stay for the summer. Cook the whole season.'

Later, as I was cleaning down my equipment at the end of the shift, he came over to talk some more. 'Where in Italy is this house your friend's mother has bought?' he demanded to know.

'I'm not sure,' I admitted. 'It's some place down south, called Triento. But I don't know anything else about it.'

He looked surprised. 'Triento? You're kidding, right?'

'No, I'm sure that's what Leila said, chef.'

'But that's where I'm from! You knew that?'

There had been endless profiles of Tonino in the

newspapers that banged on about his Italian upbringing but I can't have been paying much attention because the name of the town hadn't meant anything to me.

'How weird. What a coincidence,' I said.

'Better than a coincidence. It's the best of luck,' he told me. 'I'll call my mother in the morning. You can spend some time with her and my father in their seafood restaurant. This is your chance to learn about food the way I did, Alice. I'm very excited for you.'

'But what about my job here?'

He laughed. 'I can easily get someone to work the pasta station. And when you come back perhaps there will be new opportunities. You'll have learnt so much.'

And so suddenly I was meant to be spending the summer in Italy. I was going to see the sky Leila's mother had fallen in love with and learn to cook the way Tonino had. Leave Charlie, work and worry behind me for a while. Of course, I was excited, who wouldn't be? But I was scared too, more than a little bit scared.

Babetta

Babetta had hatched the plan one night as she was standing at her front gate staring up at the floodlit statue of Jesus standing high on the mountain. First thing next morning, she took her spade and went over to Villa Rosa. She stood where the gardening crew had dug up the vegetable beds that she and Nunzio had once planted with sweet red onions and vines of cherry tomatoes. Now there was nothing left but flattened, cinnamon-coloured earth. Babetta had expected someone to come back and fill the space with useless flowers that would shrivel and die that summer unless that same someone remembered to give them water. But no one came and the earth stayed bare.

She marked out an area with her spade and planned how she would plant it. Artichokes at the back where they could spread and grow gangly; two rows of wooden stakes for tomatoes; a tangle of wild rocket in a shadier corner, and hardy herbs where the sun beat most fiercely.

She began the work of turning the earth. Later she would dig in the rotted compost made of trimmings from her garden and rich with dirt from her chickens and pigs. Then she would gently put in the plants and seeds and water them well till they were established. This was to be her gift to the Englishwoman, Aurora Gray.

Babetta suspected her life in this place was almost over. Soon she and Nunzio would be asked to pack up their few belongings, say goodbye to the house she'd scrubbed clean every day, and the land that had fed them for all these years. The thought left her numb rather than sad. Perhaps, like Nunzio, she was beginning to collapse inside, to retreat into some empty space deep within her that she would never find a way out of. She had been so angry with her husband but, as she sank her spade into the soil, she began to wonder if his might be the easiest way to live out her final years. Maybe he had made the sanest choice after all.

She was getting old, Babetta realised, even though her body was still strong from the long days of physical work and the things she wanted from her life hadn't changed so much from since she was a girl.

Just like her sisters she had followed the path their father had chosen for them. In the mornings they helped him make baskets, in the afternoons they worked beside their mother growing food, all of them waiting until the right man took them and they could have families of their own.

In many ways Nunzio had been a good prospect. He'd had a regular job on the road crews digging tunnels through the mountains. Every morning she'd sent him off with enough food to keep him going: crusty bread, mortadella sausage, a dish of rigatoni and meatballs baked early that morning and covered in foil. Then she'd spent the days tending the vegetables, pigs and chickens and making baskets until, after such a long, long time, Sofia had finally come.

And now her daughter was grown and gone, trying desperately for babies of her own, and she and Nunzio were coming closer to their ending. Babetta didn't feel sad. She didn't feel anything at all.

She would plant this garden for the Englishwoman and then Sofia would have her way. There would be an apartment for her and Nunzio in Triento, tiny rooms with no view and certainly no earth for her to turn with a spade. Babetta's body would grow buttery and soft with age but that wouldn't matter. No one would notice but her.

She bent her head and dug more fiercely, pausing now and

then to push back the hat she wore to protect her old eyes from the sun. There wasn't much time. The Englishwoman would be here soon and Babetta wanted the garden to be planted and ready for her.

It was the sound of a second spade rattling against the stony earth that startled her. She looked up to find her husband at the other end of the vegetable bed. His back was bent and he was digging with some energy. Beside him lay his hoe and a sack of compost he'd carried over.

Nunzio glanced over and his eyes met hers but he didn't say a word. Babetta held her silence too. Turning back to her work, she carried on as though this day was just the same as the one that had gone before.

Alice

Leila claimed driving a rental car from Naples to Triento was going to be no problem at all. She'd had her licence for years and, even though she hadn't had much practice lately, was sure once she got behind the wheel it would all come back to her.

But even she seemed alarmed as we stalled two or three times and then bunny-hopped out of the car park. Once we hit the *autostrada* things got tense. The road was bristling with traffic, all of it moving too fast. Huge trucks barrelled past inches away from us, drivers leaned on their horns and, if there were any rules, no one seemed to care.

Leila hugged the inside lane and swore a lot while I clutched a map and tried to get us on the right road. There were a few missed turns and some panicked shouting but finally we found the route south.

Near Salerno we stopped at a service station so Leila could drink coffee and settle her nerves. While she smoked a couple of cigarettes, I went and browsed through the shop and was amazed at what I found. Fresh buffalo mozzarella from Avellino and Caserta, sides of prosciutto, bundles of leafy green vegetables I couldn't identify, stuff you'd only find in some pricey deli in London and yet here it was for sale by the side of the road. I filled a big basket with things I couldn't wait to taste.

We set off again, the back seat now covered in bags and the car filled with the enticing smell of cheese and cured meat. At first it was a relief to strike off from the motorway and take the smaller roads that skirted ravines and cut through tunnels. But Leila kept being distracted by the prettiness of a terraced lemon grove or the drama of a town perched on top of a mountain.

'Eyes on the road, Leila … slow down,' I muttered once or twice.

'Oh shut up, Alice,' she replied. 'Shouldn't you be enjoying yourself by now?'

At last we had our first glimpse of the sea, a tablet of blue on the horizon, and then I spotted a tall statue of Christ on a mountain.

'Can't be far now,' said Leila. 'My mother told me she can see that statue from the garden of Villa Rosa.'

When we got to the coast there was a perilously narrow road to negotiate and then finally a steep lane that ended at some high gates.

Leila hooted her horn. 'We're here,' she called out. 'Open up.'

Villa Rosa was so beautiful, I laughed when I saw it. The house was quite simple really but it had gardens that tumbled in terraces all the way down to the sea. Its back was to the mountains and it faced a little courtyard with a pomegranate tree in the middle.

Leila's mother Aurora brought out glasses of iced limoncello and we sat together watching the sun go down.

'I think I might be enjoying myself now,' I told Leila, steeping myself in the drink's lemony sourness.

We topped up our glasses and sat, mostly in silence, staring out at Aurora's piece of sky. For a few moments I thought about all I'd left behind: my nagging guilt at neglecting my mother, my half-life with Charlie, the heat of Tonino's kitchen. This place was so gorgeous that just being here made all of it seem so much less important.

Once the light had faded there was some talk of going up the road for a pizza but instead I made up a platter with things I'd bought from the little motorway shop. I quickly blanched the unidentifiable greens and dressed them with lemon and olive oil, set out cheeses, salami, preserved artichokes, green olives and a piquant paste made of tomatoes, anchovies and chilli. Aurora poured red wine from an unlabelled demijohn and we sat around the kitchen table.

It was fast, easy food and yet it had so much flavour. As I filled my plate a second time I thought about how choosy Tonino had always been about where he sourced his ingredients. If a supplier couldn't deliver something he often dropped a dish from the menu instead of looking elsewhere. It had seemed to me as though he was being picky but now I'd learned my first lesson – raw ingredients are as important as the things you do to them. If they're not good, nothing will be.

We ate and talked for a while about Aurora's art and her plans to paint the sky. But I was tired so, once I'd cleaned up the mess I'd made in the kitchen, I grabbed my suitcase and went upstairs to find my room and get some sleep.

Only once I got up there did I realise there was going to be a problem. Aurora had given me a small bedroom tucked away down a long corridor at the side of the house. It had French doors that opened onto a little terrace covered in flowering wisteria that had steps down to the courtyard below. I suppose she'd thought it would be nice for me, private and pretty. But, as I sat on the bed, I began to panic. There were too many ways for a stranger to come into this room. The locks looked perfunctory and the house was isolated. I didn't think I could sleep here.

It had always been easy for me to feel safe in Maida Vale. The flat was on the top floor and there were at least four deadlocks between my room and the outside world. Leila was right there on the other side of a thin wall. But here all was silent and lonely. I felt afraid. I felt like a rape victim again.

In the end I pushed the bed right up against the French doors and hoped Aurora hadn't heard the scraping sound it made on the ceramic tiled floors. I slept fitfully, waking with every strange sound, wishing the walls of the house weren't made of stone or that Charlie were lying beside me. Probably I should have said something, asked if I might move to another room. But admitting I was frightened would have scared me all the more.

As soon as it grew light I got dressed and let myself out. I thought perhaps it would help if I explored the area, knew what lay around the house.

First I took the path down to the sea where I found some new-looking steps and then a ragged area of wildflowers and gravel that gave onto jagged rocks. Beneath them was a boiling mess of waves and froth.

Reassured, I walked back up through the gardens and out of the gates of Villa Rosa. There was another house here, surrounded by well-tended vegetable beds. I heard chickens clucking in a coop somewhere nearby and wondered if I could sense the sour smell of pigs on the breeze. Whoever lived here could watch Villa Rosa, see who went in and went out. But it was still very early and there was no sign of a soul.

I went back to put on a pot of coffee and, as I pottered round the kitchen, made up my mind to stop being afraid. Already I'd been driven away from university and set on a different path because of what some stranger had done to me. My anger at him still felt fresh, my disappointment with myself hadn't faded. I couldn't bear the idea that now I might be frightened away from this place as well.

I was determined to stay at Villa Rosa the whole summer long just as I'd planned to.

Babetta

Babetta had been watching and waiting. First, she'd seen the removal trucks arrive and strong men unloading Aurora Gray's belongings. Then Aurora herself had disappeared inside the house. Now, just a couple of weeks later, someone new had come. A small brown-haired girl with a pinched, exhausted look to her face was standing at Babetta's gate looking across her garden. Before too long she turned and went back to Villa Rosa, but still Babetta wondered if it was time she offered a proper welcome.

She took a basket and wandered through her garden filling it with fat pods of fava beans, sweet baby peas and young shoots of spring onion. Babetta loved the smell of earth first thing in the morning when there was still dew on the ground, and she spent a moment or two standing between the young climbing vines of tomatoes and beans letting the beginnings of the day's sun touch her face. Then she lifted her loaded basket and took it over to Villa Rosa.

There was a strong smell of coffee coming from the kitchen and Babetta saw the brown-haired girl busy at the stove.

'*Buongiorno*,' she called, offering her basket of vegetables.

The girl looked startled. 'Oh, is that for us? Thank you so much. I mean, *grazie*.'

Babetta gave her the basket and the girl peeked inside. 'Oh how lovely. Freshly-picked and everything.' She looked up and touched her fingers to her chest. 'I'm Alice.

So sorry but I don't speak Italian and you probably don't understand a word I'm saying.'

Babetta smiled and shrugged. She offered her own name and then beckoned the girl outside.

'*Viene, viene qua,*' she urged.

Herding the girl down the path that led to the sea, Babetta took her to the spot where a hole had been made and steps cut through to a natural pool sheltered by towering walls of rock. Babetta made a swimming motion with her hands and the girl nodded.

'Yes, yes I see,' she said smiling.

Next, Babetta urged her to walk back up towards the new vegetable garden where she showed her how the young tomato plants were already tall enough to be tethered to their stakes, and how to sink her fingers into the earth to free a weed or two. The girl seemed perplexed. She smiled at Babetta but didn't bother bending to help tidy the garden.

When a voice called her name from the house, the girl took the excuse to leave but Babetta stayed, crouched over, working in her slow, quiet way. It seemed a waste to let the garden run wild and, since no one at Villa Rosa cared about tending it, then she would carry on, at least for a time.

Once she'd finished she went to find a brush to sweep the pathways clean of fallen pomegranate flowers. She found Nunzio closer to the house busy in the lemon grove, collecting dropped fruit before it spoiled. He stared at her without really seeing anything then went back to gathering windfalls.

Smiling to herself, Babetta picked up a broom and kept on working.

Alice

I hadn't wanted to follow the old lady down to the sea but she was insistent and it was impossible to explain I'd already been once that morning. Still, she showed me a perfect place to swim on calmer days and then took me up to a vegetable garden I hadn't noticed earlier, planted on one of the terraces. I think she expected me to help her with the weeding but thankfully I heard Aurora calling from the house and was able to slip away.

'Is that old woman your gardener?' I asked her. 'She's incredibly fit.'

'Oh, is it her again?' Frowning, Aurora glanced out the window. 'She keeps going down there to water something. And her husband is always pottering about the place. It's a bit awkward really. The pair of them used to do the gardens here.'

'But not any more?'

'Well, no, not officially. But they appear every day and do at least a couple of hours' work then disappear without saying anything.'

'That's odd.'

'Sort of.' Aurora chewed at the ends of her hair in a very Leila-like way. 'Most likely they're worried I'm going to evict them from their house next door. They've lived there rent-free for twenty years but it belongs to me now.'

I hardly knew Aurora but couldn't imagine her doing something so awful to two ageing people. 'Will you let them stay?' I asked.

'I think so. It depends though.' She picked up the strand of hair again and started to worry at it. 'I over-committed myself buying this place. So long as I start painting again it should be OK. But really even if they do stay I can't have them slaving in my garden. I mean, look at them, they're getting old. And I suspect he's lost his marbles.'

I followed her gaze to see the old man shuffling along, balancing a basket of lemons against his ribs. There was a dirty brown cloth hat crushed onto his head and his mouth was hanging half open. Leaving the lemons by the kitchen door, he went on his way without even bothering to nod at us.

'Well at least the pair of them are making sure we don't run short of food,' I told Aurora. 'The old lady brought over that huge basket of home-grown vegetables earlier. Have you got any recipe books? I'm trying to work out what to cook with them.'

I'd been dreaming up a plan to bring the peas, fava beans and spring onions together, turning the ideas over in my mind. A pasta in a light broth perhaps, that would intensify the nutty taste. I saw how there was a lacework of holes through some of the leafy greens, pock marks on the bean pods and insects that needed rinsing out. This was real food, not the bug-sprayed, flabby vegetables piled too high in London supermarkets. I couldn't wait to start cooking with it, playing with the flavours.

While I rifled through a box of old recipe books, Leila helped with the unpacking. There was so much stuff to get through: loads of paintings stacked in the living room, more boxes of books, cartons of things like paintbrushes and photographs. I couldn't see how there would be space to store it all in what was really only a holiday villa.

Just as I'd suspected, it didn't take Leila long to grow tired of trying to order her mother's belongings. After an hour or so she appeared in the kitchen dressed in a black swimming costume and a long cream hooded cardigan.

'Come on let's go to the beach. I want to swim.'

'It feels a bit cold for swimming, doesn't it?' I said. 'It's not proper summer yet after all. And actually I was just about to think about cooking something for lunch.'

Like the Italian woman from next door, Leila wasn't about to take no for an answer. She chivvied me out of the kitchen and together we walked down the narrow lanes Aurora had told us would take us to the public beach. In the summer there was a proper lido here with deckchairs and boats to rent and a bar where you could eat a simple lunch, but it wouldn't open for at least another month and right now the beach was deserted.

We climbed down the steps from the cliff-top and picked our way over the pebbles. 'You're not really going in?' I asked Leila as I saw the way the waves were surging onto the shore.

But she'd thrown off her cardigan and was already ankle-deep in water. Tipping her face towards the sun, she took a deep breath and then she charged right into the sea, screeching as she went.

'Oh my God, it's fantastic!' she yelled. 'Absolutely freezing. Now I know exactly what swimming in a gin and tonic would feel like!'

I stayed on the beach, stacking little piles of pebbles and enjoying the thought that this was the very first day of my break. There were weeks and weeks ahead before I'd have to return to my real life.

Leila didn't stay in the water too long. She was shivering, lips blue, skin goose-pimpled, and I helped dry her off with a towel, tasting the salt water that flicked from her hair. It would have made a nice snapshot: two girls standing on a beach laughing, one much more beautiful than the other but both happy to be right at the beginning of a long, hot summer.

'Let's go back home. I want to make some fresh pasta,' I told Leila.

She laughed. 'Don't you ever relax any more? Still, if you're mad enough to make it then I'll be happy to eat it.'

Swathed in towels and covered in the cardigan, her wet hair falling in black ringlets, she led me back up the steps. We were at the top when we heard a mewling noise coming from a rubbish skip in the corner of the car park.

'There must be an animal trapped in there.' Leila ran over to take a look. She poked her head in the skip and her voice echoed out to me. 'Oh, poor baby. Who put you in there? Are there any more of you? Let's see ... no, good. Now don't bite me if I try to help you out. Here you are. Come on. Good boy ... or girl ... whatever you are.'

In her arms was a dirty ball of white and ginger fluff with frightened eyes. Leila wrapped it in one of her towels and held it close. 'Who'd dump a puppy in a skip and just leave it to die?' she asked, her voice wobbling. 'I bet no one comes down here usually this time of year. He's so lucky we found him.'

I peered at the little dog. 'He might have fleas,' I warned.

'Well we can go up to town later and buy some flea stuff for him. And some puppy food. But let's take him back and give him some milk now.'

Leila held the puppy the whole way home. It seemed to enjoy being nestled against her warm chest. The mewling had stopped and its eyes were drooping closed. 'It would have died in there,' Leila said again. 'God, people can be so cruel.'

We saw the old man from next door when we got down as far as Villa Rosa. He stared at Leila as though he were trying to work out what she was carrying.

'It's a puppy, see.' She pulled back the towel and showed him. 'Abandoned in a bin down by the beach. I'm going to see if I can find something to feed to him.'

He continued to stare, nothing registering on his face, and I was sure he was much too far gone to understand, even if we had been speaking in Italian.

Fortunately there was no chance of Aurora being angry with her daughter for bringing the stray home as she was equally crazy about dogs. The pair of them fussed about, warming a bowl of milk for the puppy as I searched fruitlessly through the kitchen for flour and eggs to make pasta.

'I'm going next door to see if I can borrow some stuff from the old lady. What's her name again? Babetta?'

'Hmmm, yes, that's right.' Aurora was distracted by watching the puppy lap up his milk hungrily.

The windows of the house next door had been flung open and I could hear a radio chattering inside. I found the old man sitting in a cane chair on his terrace, staring out to sea. He seemed a bit creepy but I'd decided his wife Babetta was lovely. She had one of those square old lady's bodies and wore a flower-sprigged scarf on her head like a gypsy.

I mimed to her that I needed eggs and flour to make pasta and she took me to her kitchen, basic but scrupulously clean, and opened up her cupboards. 'Take whatever you need,' she seemed to be saying.

Then she went to her chicken coop and found me six fresh eggs still sticky with feathers and dirt. I felt embarrassed to be taking so much from her and when she pushed a small covered dish into my basket I tried to refuse it.

But the old woman insisted. '*Per il cane.*' She made a funny woofing noise. '*Capisce?*'

'Oh, it's meat for the puppy.' I understood at last. 'Your husband must have told you we'd rescued it.'

I tried to thank her but Babetta seemed happy to see me leaving with her basket stuffed with gifts. '*La mia casa e sempre aperta,*' she said as I walked down her path.

I memorised the words and, when I got back, repeated them to Aurora whose Italian was quite fluent. 'Ah, she was saying her house is always open to you,' she exclaimed. 'What a nice woman.'

'And she gave me this,' I added, taking the dish of left-over meat from the basket. 'Will I boil some rice to put with it and then we can feed it to the puppy?'

The poor thing had curled up to sleep on a blanket that Leila had put down next to the milk bowl.

'Oh how lovely,' Aurora said when she saw the meat. 'Thank goodness there are some good people in the world.'

'Yes, thank goodness.' I took some small comfort in having this woman, old but kind, there like a sentry just beyond the gates of Villa Rosa.

Babetta

Babetta still couldn't quite believe Nunzio had spoken. He had walked into the kitchen and said, in a low, hoarse voice, 'There is a puppy'. And then before she could reply he'd hurried back outside and taken to his chair in silence.

She'd been wondering if she should try to coax another word or two out of him when the little brown-haired girl, Alice, had appeared on the doorstep. She'd wanted to borrow food, just a couple of things, but Babetta had slipped in the meat because she hated to think of anything starving, even a dog. She'd never kept an animal herself unless it was for food but she knew that Nunzio often used to leave out stale things for the feral cats that lived in the bushes nearby.

Lately, Babetta had been looking at the few photographs she owned of her husband as a younger man. There was one showing him with the other workers from the road crew, all of them so young, stripped to the waist, olive-skinned and muscled. Nunzio was easy to pick out amongst them with his round face and slightly gummy smile. He had never been a handsome man but when he was lit up with happiness, the day Sofia was born or on Sunday afternoons when they went to the beach together, his charms lay closer to the surface.

As the years stretched by he had shrunk and his skin collapsed into his face but Babetta thought she could still find that young man in the old man's mask of wrinkles. And now these Englishwomen had come and a little spark inside Nunzio seemed to have caught. First he'd come to work beside her in the gardens of Villa Rosa, now he'd spoken those few simple words.

Babetta tried not to feel too encouraged, but still she was eager for more.

Alice

Leila seemed amazed at how quickly I'd made the pasta, fat little pouches of ravioli filled with a purée of fresh peas and fava beans and some soft white goat's cheese I'd found in the *autostrada* shop. We ate them covered with melted butter and sage leaves that I'd fried quickly until they were crisp.

The three of us pulled the kitchen table out into the sun and Aurora produced a bottle of rose-coloured wine. 'This is heaven,' she said, as she forked open one of the ravioli pouches. 'Leila, how do you stay so slim eating food like this all the time?'

'Actually, this is the first time Alice has ever made pasta for me. The most ambitious we get in the flat is a cheese and onion toastie,' she laughed.

It was true that I tended to save all my energy for work. At home the thought of making a proper meal exhausted me. I only prepared the most hurried snacks: taramasalata from the Greek shop up the road or feta cheese with tomato. Leila had never seen me cook before.

'Later we'll go up to the village to stock up and then I'll make it up to you,' I promised.

'But you don't have to do all the cooking,' Aurora put in hurriedly. 'We can take it in turns.'

Already I felt possessive over the kitchen of Villa Rosa. I'd looked through Aurora's sad little collection of battered pans and splintering wooden spoons and made a note of things we needed to buy. It was all very well using an old rolling pin to make pasta but the right equipment would make everything so much easier.

'I don't mind. It'll be fun to play around with different ingredients,' I told them. 'Anyway, Tonino told me I had to. He said I should spend time learning to make simple, honest food from local produce.'

'You don't get much more local than vegetables grown in the neighbour's garden.' Leila was licking remnants of purée from her knife. 'So when are you going to introduce yourself to Tonino's family? Aren't you supposed to be working with them?'

'I'll go soon, I suppose,' I said without much enthusiasm. What had seemed like a great idea when I was in London now looked like a poor alternative to lazing away the whole summer.

'Well, that pasta was wonderful.' Aurora pushed her empty plate away. 'Alice, I'm more than happy for you to cook if that's what you want.'

While the pair of them cleaned up, tiptoeing around the sleeping puppy, I took the leftover ravioli over to Babetta. I felt a bit cheeky offering my food to an Italian but the pasta wouldn't keep for long and it seemed a pity to waste it.

She seemed amazed when I offered her the tray. Even the old man looked curious, peering over to see what I'd brought although he didn't bother getting out of his chair.

Using my newfound mime skills I tried to explain that we were heading up to Triento and we could give her a lift if she wanted. I hadn't noticed a car anywhere on their property so couldn't imagine how they ever managed to do any shopping.

She grinned when she realised what I was offering and held up a finger to ask me to wait a minute. When she reappeared she'd changed her headscarf for a prettier one in a less faded fabric and produced another hand-woven basket she put over her arm ready to fill with shopping.

'*Pronto?*' she asked, treating me to such a wide smile I could see several of her back teeth were missing.

Babetta was silent on the drive up to Triento, busy looking down at the view she must have seen thousands of times before. It was spectacular, with ruined towers on rocky outcrops, bay after unspoilt bay and the sea, a gleaming jewel blue, stretching out to the huge canvas of sky that Leila's mother had fallen in love with.

The little town was halfway up the hill, a tangle of narrow streets built long before anyone had thought of cars. With a jabbing finger and a lot of, '*Si, si, no, no,*' Babetta showed us where we could park. Then she led the way up steeply stepped lanes until we came out in a pretty piazza bustling with market stalls.

Babetta stayed by my shoulder while I shopped, making sure I only bought the freshest and the best. She shook her head at some tomatoes I was tempted by and instead made me fill my basket with a tangle of wild asparagus and handfuls of tender baby artichokes. Then she took me to her preferred butcher and *salumeria*, pointing out the best quality prosciutto, the tastiest cheeses, the most delicious local sausage. Once or twice voices became a little raised and I think she may have been haggling with the shopkeepers but it almost always ended in laughter. Babetta must have known these people for a long, long time and they were used to her.

Shopping for food bored Leila very quickly so she went in search of supplies for the puppy. She came back a short while later loaded down with flea powder, a collar, a lead and several squeaky toys. 'So you're keeping him then?' I said, and Leila just grinned in reply.

It was pointless trying to explore the town properly while we were weighed down with bags of shopping so we headed back to the car and stowed everything in the boot.

'Let's drive down to the other part of Triento on the way back,' suggested Leila. 'Apparently there's a fishing village and lots of little cafés and boutiques down there. We could maybe have a quick drink in the sunshine.'

So we took another road that curved round the hill then dropped towards the sea. Sure enough, we soon saw the sand-coloured houses stacked above a marina, with green-painted shutters and balconies covered in pots of bright flowers.

Here down by the port it seemed Babetta wasn't so sure of herself. She glanced round as though she too was a stranger, and made no objection when we headed to the nearest waterside café.

'I think Tonino's parents have their place somewhere down here,' I told Leila once we'd sat down and ordered our drinks. 'It's a seafood restaurant called Trattoria Ricci.'

The waiter brought the drinks and we clinked our glasses together. Admittedly it seemed a little odd to be hanging out with an aged Italian woman who couldn't communicate with us properly but she looked happy enough, staring at the people passing by and nodding every now and then if she recognised someone.

'Babetta,' a strong voice called out. Striding towards our table was one of the most attractive older women I've ever seen. Her face was fascinating. She looked a bit like Sophia Loren, all sleek dark hair, olive-toned skin, full lips and perfect bone structure.

'*Raffaella, ciao.*' Seeming delighted, Babetta stood and kissed her on both cheeks. The two chatted for a while in quick-fire Italian and then the beautiful woman turned to me and said, in far more hesitant English, 'You are Alice, yes? I am Tonino's mother, Raffaella Ricci. He said you would be here by now.'

I felt a little embarrassed that she'd found me before I'd had a chance to go to her trattoria and introduce myself properly. 'Oh, so pleased to meet you. I was planning to drop in some time this week,' I said hurriedly. 'I'm very grateful for this opportunity you're giving me.'

Raffaella smiled and shrugged in that very Italian way. 'Don't come too soon. My son Tonino, all he thinks about is work. But there's plenty of time for that. Explore, have fun, relax a little first. We'll be there when you are ready.' She pointed to a small white building right at the end of the marina where there were a few outdoor tables with blue sun umbrellas fluttering in the breeze. There was no sign pointing to it, not even a small one above the door as far as I could see. I might have struggled to find the place alone.

'It looks lovely,' I said politely.

Raffaella laughed. 'You will find it very different to Tonino's restaurant but I think you will enjoy it. No rush. Come when you are ready.'

As she walked away I saw how men's heads turned to watch her. Raffaella held herself as if she knew they were looking but didn't much care, picking her way through the café tables with her head high and her stride long.

'She's a foxy old thing, isn't she?' remarked Leila. 'Is her son Tonino as good-looking? How come you've never introduced me?'

'Not your type,' I told her.

'Oh yes? What is my type then?' she challenged me.

'Impoverished artists, grungy musicians, slightly raffish men with smart clothes and no money ... should I go on?'

Leila's laugh was rueful. 'Well, I want an introduction to Tonino when we get back to London. He might be my new type.'

We ordered more drinks and sat chatting for a while as Babetta closed her eyes and half dozed beside us. It was pleasant here soaking up the empty time and the warmth of the sun, and I realised with some surprise that I hadn't cried for no reason since we'd arrived at Villa Rosa. Almost an entire day with no tears. I wondered how long I could keep it up.

Babetta

Although she knew that the English girls would leave just as suddenly as they had come, Babetta let herself enjoy the way they'd changed things. Each day they offered to take her somewhere different; a drive round the coast perhaps, or a jaunt further south towards Calabria. The serious one, Alice, liked to shop for food wherever they went and Babetta helped her find the best: the freshest mozzarella, the most tender cut of beef. Often, when they got back to Villa Rosa, she'd follow her into the kitchen and show her how to prepare them.

The girl was quick and clever with some things. She had nimble fingers for pasta and could chop an onion faster than Babetta ever had. But there was so much no one had shown her, dishes any Italian mother would teach a girl. Babetta clucked over the pans of bubbling sauces and the trays of meat and somehow the girl seemed to understand, even though she barely spoke a word of Italian.

Each day the sun grew stronger and climbed higher in the sky. Babetta stopped waiting for someone to tell her that she and Nunzio must leave the house. She gave up looking at their possessions and planning which she would take and what she'd leave behind. Worries might have filled her mind if she'd let them but she looked away from them, pretended they weren't there and carried on cooking food, feeling her way through this strange, silent friendship with the English girl and watching the gardens she'd planted grow.

Often, in the cool of the morning, they worked together planting herbs for the kitchen, rows of beans that would climb up bamboo stakes and bushy little chilli pepper plants. There was going to be a lot to harvest later in the season. Babetta hoped the girl would still be here to taste it.

The other one, the dark-haired beauty, never came to join them. She spent her time smoking cigarettes with a book in her hand or sometimes tapping away at a typewriter while that little dog she'd rescued tugged at her skirt and begged her to play with it. Only the mother, Aurora Gray, seemed to have nothing to occupy her. She passed much of each morning sitting down on the rocks, her face shaded by a hat, gazing out at the sky. At lunchtime she'd come up to open a bottle of wine and eat what had been prepared but still it was the sky that commanded her attention. It was a mystery what was so interesting about it but Babetta was reminded of Nunzio in his cane chair, stranded and staring, waiting for something to happen.

Alice

Leila was laughing, covering her mouth with her hand like a mischievous child. 'That old man is trying to steal my dog,' she said. 'Look at him.'

I watched for a while and saw she was right. The puppy was following Nunzio as he moved about the garden pulling weeds and sweeping the pathways. Every now and then he'd slip his hand into a pocket and quietly produce some little treat to feed it with.

'Isn't it strange how the old guy never speaks?' I remarked.

'Maybe he just doesn't have anything left to say.' Leila was still staring at her puppy through the kitchen window. It was running in excited circles around Nunzio and she started laughing again at the sight of it.

'What are you going to call that little dog anyway?' I asked.

'I thought I might name him Sky. If it hadn't been for my mother falling in love with the sky at Villa Rosa then we wouldn't have come and he'd never have been rescued.'

'Good name,' I agreed, and then my mind drifted from the old man and the dog to Leila's mother. For the last few days I'd been wondering about her. I'd noticed she seemed edgy and distracted, always staring out towards the horizon with an expression that looked almost resentful at times.

'She's not painting yet, is she, your mother?'

'No.' Leila frowned. 'She says she can't decide how to begin.'

Personally I'd have thought she could have started by throwing loads of blue paint on a canvas and she'd have ended up with the usual result but, of course, I didn't say that.

'Is it always like this when she's trying to work?' I asked instead.

'Sometimes. I think it's difficult to start because once she does it takes over her whole life. Just wait and see, you'll barely be able to get her to speak, never mind come and eat meals.'

The plan had always been that I would stay on at Villa Rosa for the entire summer while Leila went to spend time with a school friend who lived in Rome, maybe returning later for a few more weeks. I was hoping she'd change her mind about leaving now she had the puppy, especially if her mother was going to be mad and monosyllabic. But Leila needed excitement – men to fall in love with, nights drinking herself dizzy, scrapes and escapades. With each day that passed at Villa Rosa we seemed to slow down more and I was afraid she'd soon get bored.

'Sky, Sky,' she was calling to the dog. He might not have known his new name yet but he recognised the sound of Leila's voice and, tilting his head comically, he came trotting over.

'Isn't he adorable?' She kissed the tip of his nose.

'What will happen to him when we go back to England?'

'My mother can keep him. He'll be company for her. And I'll see him whenever I come.'

We breakfasted late that morning on toast spread thickly with pomegranate jelly that Babetta had made last autumn with fruit from the many trees in the garden. I could see her at work already on the terrace below, hoeing a patch of earth where she was going to plant corn, but I didn't have time to go and help her. The plan was for Leila to drive me down to the port before lunchtime so I could talk to Tonino's parents about what they expected from me. It had been such a casual arrangement to go and help out in their restaurant. I wasn't sure if it was a proper job with set hours or if they needed me at all.

At least I'd had almost three weeks of relaxing and playing with food in the kitchen of Villa Rosa. I'd made little dumplings of gnocchi from ricotta cheese and covered them with a light tomato sauce, I'd pan-fried squid and stuffed it with herbs and rocket leaves from the garden, I'd cooked up lusty stews of fish and fresh garlic. There was far too much food and often we had to share with Babetta and Nunzio or we'd never have got through it. The old lady had been great, showing me how to make all sorts of peasant dishes she'd been taught by her mother. Now the time had come for me to learn from some professionals. Besides, I kept telling myself, surely I missed the buzz of a restaurant kitchen by now.

The little fishing village was busier than it had been the last time we'd visited. Lots of the café tables were filled with the season's first tourists and I heard American voices, familiar English accents, even a couple of Australians. In the height of summer I could imagine how crowded it must get here.

Leaving Leila to browse in a boutique, I walked round the marina and headed to the little white building with the blue sun umbrellas Raffaella had pointed out. Just as I'd suspected, there was no sign to show this was a restaurant, just a blackboard outside with a few of the day's specials chalked up. I noticed they had a seafood plate with razor clams, fried stuffed sardines, an octopus salad and my favourite, a *spaghetti alle vongole*.

Inside, it was a bit like being in someone's house. There were a few wooden tables and chairs, another blackboard with the same list of specials and a big antique sideboard stocked with plates and glasses. Raffaella was at the far end of the room, cutting paper-thin strips of prosciutto for an antipasto plate.

'Ah, *buongiorno*, Alice.' She smiled at me and I was sideswiped again by the generosity of looks. 'You've come to see us at just the right time. Things are beginning to get busy and we'll be grateful for an extra pair of hands.'

'I can start today if you like,' I offered. 'Just show me what you'd like me to do.'

'No, no.' Raffaella shook her head. 'Today you must eat with us. Tomorrow you can come to help cook.'

'But—'

'I told you this is not like Tonino's restaurant, didn't I? Now where is your very pretty friend? Did you come with her ... yes? Then fetch her and take a table outside in the sun.'

Leila grumbled a bit when I pulled her away from a rack of sparkly dresses in the boutique. She'd only just had breakfast and didn't want to eat again. But sitting beneath a sun umbrella, gazing down at the marina with a glass of chilled white wine in her hand, she began to perk up.

First, Raffaella brought us several plates of antipasto: the prosciutto she'd just sliced along with some salami, barbecued baby squid, roasted vegetables and a basket of crusty bread. Then she came out with small bowls of spaghetti and clams drizzled with fruity olive oil and fresh flat-leaf parsley. Finally we had sardines that had been split open, stuffed with breadcrumbs and tomato, then rolled up and fried quickly. They were served simply with a salad of peppery wild leaves. At no point had we been shown a menu and I was beginning to wonder if the only dishes on offer were the six or seven chalked up on the specials board.

By now Leila was looking stunned by food. 'Please tell her not to bring us any more,' she begged.

But even she couldn't resist the peaches soaked in red

wine we were given to finish our meal. 'Just something to refresh the palate after you have eaten well,' Raffaella said.

It wasn't a big place and by the time we left every single table was occupied. Beside us was an olive-skinned Italian man with a chunky gold Rolex weighing down his wrist. He'd smiled at Leila once or twice and she'd been unable to resist peeking up at him through her hair.

'Might he be your new type too?' I whispered to her.

'No, but he might be my mother's type. She could use something to distract her.'

Raffaella wouldn't let us pay for our lunch. 'We don't want your money,' she told me. 'But come in the morning early. You can go with my husband Ciro to buy the fish and then perhaps come and make fresh pasta for me. Tonino tells me you're very good at it.'

As we were leaving I noticed how the Rolex man stared at Leila again and that she seemed to enjoy his eyes being on her. Male attention never left her feeling exposed or uncomfortable like it did me. Even if a man was unattractive and old, Leila was happy to accept the admiration.

The pair of us might have been tempted to return to the rail of sparkly dresses but the boutique had closed, along with the rest of the shops, and wouldn't reopen until five p.m. I liked how people ate a proper lunch here, rushing nothing, savouring the flavours, and then took their time to digest it. I'd grown so used to London's rush and every minute being so jammed full of things that needed to be done. Life in Triento seemed to be the antidote to that. It was such a relief to be here.

Babetta

Babetta had been trying to remember what she'd been like as a girl. Not strained and anxious like Alice and certainly not all drama and show like the pretty one. She recalled herself as a quiet girl who had known what was expected of her. The youngest of four sisters, she might have stayed at school far longer as there were no more babies to care for. But her father pulled her out when she was thirteen, just as he had the other girls. She could read and write well enough by then, do some basic sums. Soon she would be married with babies of her own so what need did she have for anything else?

Her father kept his daughters close. There were no troubles, no unexpected pregnancies in his family. Freedom for Babetta meant time with her sisters, plaiting each other's long dark hair, laughing and sometimes playing card games. Trips to Triento only happened with their mother or father to accompany them. There was no racing each other around the coast road on scooters the way the young people did today. No standing in the piazza smoking cigarettes and gossiping.

The highlight of the week was Sunday. Mass in the morning then home to eat a good lunch, usually meat or fish if they could afford it. Sometimes her mother would buy a calf's head that had been boned and rolled up and she'd simmer it for a long, long time with onion, celery, carrot and a glass of vinegar. The meat was sliced up thinly and meltingly tender. In colder seasons there would be a soup Babetta loved, made from pig's trotters and winter cabbage from the garden. After eating they would rest for a while and brush each other's hair, until it was time to dress up in their best clothes and walk to Triento along with everyone else.

The *passeggiata* was the same every Sunday evening. Arms linked, the four of them would walk with their mother back and forth along the main street and into the piazza, greeting friends and neighbours, pausing to chat every now and then. This was the way daughters of marriageable age were shown off and a husband found for them. It was how all three of her sisters were paired with the men they ended up with. But for Babetta things happened differently.

Nunzio wasn't a local boy. He had come from further south to work on the road crew they passed when they walked up to Triento with baskets to sell. Babetta knew he was staring her way but was far too modest to look back, even though her sisters giggled and poked her. Finally, he came to the house and asked her father for permission to court her.

After that they were allowed to meet once or twice a week but never without a chaperone. Sometimes they took a walk together and, if one of her sisters was accompanying them, she might look away while Nunzio held her hand.

It wasn't love she felt for him, more curiosity. Aside from her father, Babetta had hardly spent time with any man. She was fascinated by little things: the bristles that grew glossy and dark from his skin, the width of his forearms, the squareness of his hands. She wanted to know what he smelt like, to watch him stripped to the waist and working in the hot sun.

The day he begged her to marry him Babetta had been afraid. He'd come unexpectedly to the barn where she'd been weaving baskets. There had been no time to tidy her hair or wash the sweat from her skin.

Nunzio seemed excited to find her alone, kissing her, pushing and pressing with his body. There was something frantic about it and she had tried to pull away. 'It's all right, it's all right, I want you to be my wife,' he had half-groaned, holding her fast.

She might have preferred to wait, continue the slow courtship another year or two. She was barely sixteen, after all. But there was no refusing Nunzio. When she tried to say, 'No, not yet', he sat beside her holding a rag to his face, crying until she couldn't bear it any longer and, wrapping her arms around him, she said, 'Yes, yes, I will be your wife.'

They had married in a church that was built into the side of a mountain a few kilometres south of them, in Calabria. The altar was in a dimly lit cave, with dripping stalactites above it, and the air felt damp and chill. She had shivered in her pretty dress and had seen the expressions on her sisters' faces. To begin married life in such a cold, strange place didn't augur well for her. But this was Nunzio's family church and she had wanted to please him.

For a year they lived with his family in Calabria but it had been miserable there. His mother was impatient for babies to come and, after the first few months, began prying and prodding. By the end of the year the old woman would barely speak to Babetta but she made her thoughts known to Nunzio often enough.

'You picked a bad one, this one is barren, you should have chosen one of the other sisters,' she would nag, well within Babetta's earshot.

Usually Nunzio was tender but his mother's goading soured his temper and those were lonely days for Babetta. Finally she convinced him it would be better if they lived with her family near Triento. She could go back to making baskets again, save a little money and then maybe when a baby came they might find a place of their own.

It had been a dream that had taken many years to come true and even when Sofia was born things were difficult. Babetta had been a fearful mother. There seemed to be so many ways she could lose this baby that at last her body had given her. Nunzio agreed it was better if she remained close to her mother and sisters. So they'd slept together in the tiny room she'd had since she was a girl, the baby in a cot beside them.

Then old Umberto Santoro had died and they heard the Barbieri family was looking for someone new to care for the gardens of Villa Rosa. There was a decent house that went with the job and, when they saw it, they knew this was their chance.

It was a quiet place with few visitors but for many years they'd had an old Vespa that sometimes the three of them rode, Sofia squashed in the middle. When she looked back Babetta thought how those had been good days. There was plenty of hard work and not much money but still she didn't see how a life could be much happier.

Alice

Raffaella's husband Ciro was a dark, intense man and I saw straight away where Tonino got his looks. There was something quite stern about his face until a smile flashed across it at the sight of a bucket of fresh razor clams or a crate of silver-skinned sardines. Every morning he walked down to the harbour and bought seafood for the trattoria straight from the fishing boats. It was a noisy business, men calling to one another in loud voices, holding up an octopus by its tentacles, showing off a swordfish. Ciro spoke no English but I was certain that, even if he did, he would be too quick and impatient to bother explaining what he was doing as he moved between the boat crews choosing seafood and peeling notes from a roll of cash to pay for it.

He bought much less than I thought was needed and, once we got back to the trattoria, Raffaella explained why. 'The perfect time to cook a fish is within a few hours of it being caught,' she told me. 'See how I press my fingers onto the flesh of this one and it springs back straight away and leaves no dent? So we buy our fish fresh every day. We never serve anything old or from a freezer.'

'But what if you sell out?' I asked.

'Oh, we always sell out. That's the whole point. And once we do then we close up for the day. That's why all the locals eat here.'

Raffaella had greeted us with strong coffee and a dish of home-baked biscotti and now she and Ciro were examining what he'd bought and deciding what to cook with it. Once they'd made up their minds I helped Raffaella chalk up the list on the blackboards. Today there was to be a spaghetti with octopus cooked in a sauce of tomato, olive oil, chilli and parsley, a soup of little sweet prawns, mussels and razor clams, and a linguine with sardines and wild fennel. Raffaella had also bought a few peasant chickens and she was planning to chop them up and make a stew flavoured with rosemary and lemons. From the same peasant's garden she'd taken bunches of herbs and young nettles and yesterday she'd made a paste that we were going to mix with ricotta and put into ravioli.

The kitchen was tiny but Raffaella and Ciro seemed to have some sixth sense and never so much as brushed against one another. They cooked without speaking, knowing which task each should take, Ciro chopping the chickens into portions, Raffaella busying herself with the sauces. As I kneaded the pasta dough I couldn't help wondering about them. How they managed to work side by side each day after so many years of marriage. And what they thought of Tonino and his big city restaurant with all its trimmings.

Once the kitchen was filled with the smells of simmering food and the bulk of the preparation was done, we took a break. Raffaella pulled some pizza bread from the oven and scattered it with rock salt and torn herbs and we ate it with paper-thin slices of prosciutto and a mound of mozzarella so fresh it was still oozing with buffalo milk.

'So, Alice,' Raffaella said. 'Tell me about yourself.'

I wasn't completely sure how to respond. It seemed wrong to admit that I'd fallen into cooking by mistake so instead I told her I'd grabbed the opportunity to work at Teatro but had been finding it much harder than I'd expected.

She wrinkled her nose. 'To me that's not really cooking. Working in a big kitchen, following orders, making someone else's food ... I've never wanted that.'

Where do your recipes come from?' I asked her.

She smiled and went over to the sideboard where she retrieved a tattered old handwritten recipe book. Its pages were frayed and half falling out, the ink faded and smudged in places, but she held it as though it were something very precious.

'This belonged to my mother,' she explained, turning the pages so I wouldn't have to touch the book. 'She was an amazing cook and collected recipes all her life. Many of the dishes we make come from here, others we've come across ourselves or concocted over the years. Every day I learn something new about food. That's why I love it.'

'I'm not sure whether I love food or not,' I was surprised to hear myself admitting.

'Really?' Raffaella sounded shocked. 'But food is so important. In my family it's how we speak to each other, express gratitude, show we care, sometimes even say we're sorry. Good food must be made with love. You can taste it if it's not.'

'Even restaurant food?'

'Oh especially that.'

Cooking with love was a new idea to me but there was certainly nothing stressful about working in the kitchen of the trattoria. Once customers began to arrive, Raffaella moved to the front of house, showing them to their seats and taking orders. I ferried food to the tables, cleared away dirty dishes and filled tall glasses with ice cream or tiramisù for dessert. In the kitchen, Ciro seemed in control. He worked with quiet concentration, occasionally asking me to plate up a dish for him, making himself understood with the pointing and clicking of fingers.

Out in the little dining room and on the terrace beyond it, customers were eating. This was not the refined picking over of plates with knives and forks we saw at Teatro. No one came here to be seen or to socialise. They were solely for the food and they enjoyed it, bending their heads over the dishes, slurping hungrily, wiping up every last slick of oily juice with crusty bread.

Once everyone had eaten and left, we stacked the dirty dishes and Ciro put out some food for us. The fish, as they had promised, was all finished, so instead we had my herb ravioli drizzled in a sauce of crushed walnuts and dressed with shards of pecorino cheese. There was a little of the octopus to taste, some of the chicken stew, a bowl of steamed greens dressed with lemon and olive oil and some crusty bread.

We ate it out on the terrace with a glass of white wine that tasted like apples and Raffaella told me about their lives. She explained how Ciro had inherited a pizzeria in the centre of Triento and for a long time that's where they'd both worked.

'Once the tourists started coming I learned a little English so I could take their orders,' she told me.

'You're so fluent now,' I remarked.

'I liked learning so I kept going. And then Tonino was ambitious and moved to London when he was still so young and I spent a little time over there making sure he was OK. My other son, Lucio, he speaks English as well. It is only Ciro who does not.'

'And what about the pizzeria? Did you sell it?'

'No, Lucio runs it now. I had thought we were going to be retiring early.' She laughed and gestured towards the restaurant. 'This seems to be my husband's idea of retirement.'

'Oh, poor you, having to carry on working so hard.'

'It's not so bad.' Raffaella looked fondly at her husband who was spooning the last of the octopus onto his plate. 'As Ciro always says, if you retire you die. And anyway we only open at lunchtimes and we close all day Sunday because the fishing boats don't go out.'

Once we had finished eating they took me back to their

house. Barely a minute's walk from the trattoria, it was built right into the rock it was perched on. The rooms were cluttered but clean and Raffaella showed me through them proudly, pointing out the sweeping views she had from every window, then took me into a tiny garage where she produced a ratty, ancient-looking moped.

'My old Vespa … it works better than it looks,' she promised. 'It will be fine to get you between here and Villa Rosa every day.'

I was dubious at first as I'd never ridden a moped and there didn't seem to be any helmet to go with it. But heading back up the hill with the wind in my hair was exhilarating. I felt like a real Italian girl as I beeped on the horn at the bends in the road to let oncoming cars know I was there. When I reached the top of the hill I pulled over and looked down at the port. I could pick out the terracotta roof of Raffaella's house and the trattoria, its sun umbrellas all removed for the day. Beyond that was the harbour filled with boats dancing on gentle waves and then the open sea that stretched away into a great nothingness of blue.

I didn't see how anyone could ever be unhappy living in a place as beautiful as this one.

Babetta

For years Babetta's daughter hadn't shown any interest in the gardens of Villa Rosa. As a child she'd played there while her parents worked but she'd never inherited their love of the earth and the things that grew in it. She didn't want hands like her mother's, roughened by work, dulled by soil. Sofia's fingernails were neatly filed and painted. She was careful always to wear a wide-brimmed hat to keep the sun from her face. The garden held no lure for her.

But since the Englishwomen had come, Sofia had taken to visiting more often. She brought a pair of cotton gloves and slipped them on so she could help Babetta in the garden. Not that she did much weeding or planting. She was fascinated by the Englishwomen and peppered her conversation with questions about them. She remarked on their shoes and hairstyles, wanted to know what they did all day and stared at them whenever she got a chance.

Babetta served up the most perfunctory answers. She didn't tell Sofia about the hours she spent shopping and cooking with Alice. In fact, she made a point of almost ignoring the brown-haired girl whenever her daughter was around. And Nunzio didn't say a word, of course. If he'd noticed his wife's growing friendship it hadn't interested him enough to comment.

Sofia followed her round the garden pretending to make herself useful, pushing a wheelbarrow or carrying a basket. She shooed the little puppy away whenever it came close and complained about the ants and flying insects. Babetta wondered how long it would take her to get bored of asking questions.

'So where has the smaller one gone on the scooter today? When will she be back? What is the older one doing down on the rocks? Why is the pretty one typing?'

'I don't know. I can't speak English. How would I talk to them?' Babetta said. 'And anyway, why would I care? I'm just here to work.' And she went off to dig pig manure into the compost, raising a cloud of tiny insects that kept Sofia at a distance.

Most mornings Nunzio came to help. He worked at Babetta's side, taking over the heavier jobs, wordlessly pulling the hoe or spade from her hands. He didn't seem to hear Sofia's questions or care much that she was there. If one of the Englishwomen came past he barely noticed. But he liked the little dog. Babetta had seen him feeding it treats from his pocket and thought he might have half-smiled at the sight of it chasing its tail. Every day he spent less time sitting in his chair and more at Villa Rosa.

Babetta glanced up from time to time at the statue of Christ high above her, so pure and white against the bright blue of the sky, and silently she thanked him.

Alice

The days fell into a pleasant routine. I woke every morning hours before the others and made sure I got to the port in time to watch Ciro shop for fish. Then we sat drinking coffee and working out the day's menu. It wasn't long before I was confident enough to make suggestions of my own and I felt a real sense of pride chalking them up on the blackboards.

Sometimes, once lunch was over and the trattoria closed up for the day, I went with Raffaella to shop for supplies. We drove around the coast and right into the mountains calling on people and buying produce they'd grown. Everyone seemed happy to see us. They'd offer cold drinks and little plates of olives and bring out baskets of wild asparagus they'd gathered, or tender artichokes they'd grown. Sometimes there would be a side of prosciutto and a few skinned rabbits. Or we'd leave with bunches of herbs, bulbs of fennel and bags of blood oranges.

We always ended up back in Triento calling in at the bakery run by Raffaella's sister. She'd go next door to the bar and bring back tiny cups of sugary espresso or slice up bread for us to taste. Whenever we went Raffaella liked to make a huge fuss of the whiskery-faced old lady who sat outside on a bench on sunnier days.

'Silvana is a good friend,' she explained. 'My sister bought the bakery from her years ago but she's forgotten it's no longer hers. She still likes to spend her days here. It's where she hears all the best gossip.'

'How old is she?'

'None of us are sure. But she's been widowed twice and her grandchildren hardly bother with her. So we're her family now.'

Raffaella's sister was a few years younger than her but hadn't aged so well. Her forehead was corrugated with deep lines and the skin beneath her eyes looked bruised and tired. She seemed to do as much talking as she did serving customers. There was even a stool parked by the bakery's counter so people could rest while they chatted to her.

'There's always something happening in Triento,' explained Raffaella. 'Some scandal to get worked up about, a death, a birth or an infidelity.'

'Everybody here must know one another, I suppose,' I remarked.

'Yes, we all grew up together and we have long memories, eh, Silvana? There are people in this town who have hated me since I was a girl. And others who've been my friends for just as long.'

'So did you know Babetta well?' I was curious to learn more about the old gardener.

'Not so well but she's a good woman, of that I'm sure.'

'What's her story?'

'Oh, the usual thing. She married, raised a child and worked hard. That's what women do in places like Triento.'

'But there must be other choices? Did you never want to move? Live somewhere else?' I asked.

Raffaella shrugged. 'I had my parents to take care of. And when they died there was still Silvana. And we had our pizzeria too, of course. Ciro would never have left that.'

Pizzeria Ricci was up a narrow alleyway just off the main piazza. It was a tiny place with whitewashed walls and long benches and it smelt of baking basil and bubbling mozzarella. Raffaella's youngest son Lucio cooked there pretty much single-handedly, and the first moment I saw him stretching dough between his long fingers and humming to himself stayed imprinted on my brain like a favourite snapshot.

I'd expected a younger version of his brother Tonino, sharp-featured and subdued with flashes of arrogance. But Lucio was nothing like that. As we walked through the door he looked up from his work and I saw he had one of those faces that only looks completely right when it's smiling. His nose was crooked where it had been broken when he was a boy, his lips were full, his forehead and his cheekbones high. But when Lucio looked up and smiled his whole face seemed to open up into something delicious.

It took me about five seconds to develop the most enormous crush on him. I was lost, truly I was, and it took me by surprise. Charlie had never made me feel dizzy and silly like this, nor had any of the boys who'd dated me in a desultory sort of way when I was a teenager. I'd wanted to be liked by them but I'd never longed just to sit and stare at them, to watch the way they threw olives on a pizza or drizzled oil and vinegar over a bowl of fresh rocket.

'You must taste some of Lucio's food,' said Raffaella. 'He makes the best pizza, better even than his father's although I'd never tell Ciro that.'

'What's your secret?' I asked Lucio, still unable to stop myself staring.

'It's made with love, of course.' He glanced at his mother and grinned as though sharing a joke.

Lucio made me a pizza with the thinnest of bases, scorched and smoky from the wood-fired oven, covered with a mouth-watering slick of tomato sauce and finished with fresh basil and torn rocket leaves.

'So?' he asked, watching me take my first forkful.

'Oh, the best I've tasted,' I agreed. 'Simple but perfect. Definitely cooked with love.'

'Bite into it, tear it with your hands,' he encouraged me.

'Eat like you're hungry. That's what counts as good manners here in Italy.'

I couldn't, of course. I had to eat the pizza slowly. Not just because I wanted to savour every mouthful but so I could spend as long as possible in Lucio's company.

Just as we were ready to leave, Raffaella came up with an idea. 'Why don't you work with Lucio for a few days?' she suggested. 'You're here to learn, yes? Pizza might not be what you'd cook in a smart London restaurant but still I think it's the perfect food.'

'I'd love to,' I said quickly.

Raffaella nodded as though she'd known I would agree. 'She should come tomorrow, eh, Lucio? You can show her how we make the base and prepare the sauce. Give her all our secrets.'

'Will you?' I turned to him.

'Well, maybe ...' Lucio wasn't smiling as he waved us out the door yet still I held that final glimpse of his face in my mind until morning.

Babetta

Although she would never admit it, Babetta was missing the little English girl. Every morning she left early and barely spent any time at Villa Rosa. Meanwhile, the other one seemed bored. She tapped away on her typewriter as usual and played on the grass with the little dog but Babetta could tell she'd have preferred a different sort of company.

She had known girls like Leila before, beautiful and charming but drawn to mischief. She remembered how her elder sister had been much the same and that her father had breathed a sigh of relief once she was safely married and pregnant. But Leila wouldn't be controlled so easily. Girls today expected more from their lives, wanted excitement and pretty things, and often ended up unhappy … at least that's what Babetta suspected.

She could see Leila now, sitting on the grass, twirling a stick around her head, making the puppy jump for it. That might keep her amused for a little while but soon she would be looking for more. Girls like that only flourished when they had attention.

Once she had finished her work in the garden, Babetta went back to her own house. There she had floors waiting to be swabbed down and paths to be swept.

But first she wanted to cook something special for Nunzio. For days she had been turning over the idea in her mind. She'd killed a couple of old hens that had long since stopped laying and their bones had been bubbling away for hours in a stockpot on the stove. As she tasted the broth from a wooden spoon, Babetta found herself wondering if people were just like a long-cooked stock. As time went by did the flavours of their characters boil down and render into something stronger; some becoming more bitter, some fierier, while others like Nunzio had a melancholy that concentrated into a deeper sadness?

Babetta had decided to feed her husband with dishes that would give him comfort or, if nothing else, bring him a little pleasure. In recent years she knew her cooking had become spare and practical. The pair of them lived on soups of chickpeas flavoured with a little pancetta and tomato. She stretched any meat or seafood as far as she could, heated and reheated leftovers, adding new flavours with bundles of herbs from the garden or a little dried chilli. It was always tasty enough but it was very different from the way she'd cooked as a younger woman. Back then she was always planning the next meal. When they were eating lunch she'd already be thinking about dinner. She prided herself on being able to feed twenty as easily as two, and sitting down to eat as a family – her sisters, their husbands and children, her parents and grandparents – was the most important part of any day.

It was while she was teaching the little English girl to cook a few simple local dishes that Babetta realised she'd lost so much more than she'd thought in the years since her family had died or moved away. Time spent in the kitchen had seemed an extravagance when there were only two of them to feed. And Nunzio hadn't looked like he cared too much what she put in front of him.

But now Babetta wanted to make something special, a meal to savour and remember ... to remind her husband of the man he used to be with flavours from his past.

Alice

There had been moments when I'd caught myself missing Charlie. Curling up alone in bed every night my mind often turned towards him. He'd have loved a summer in Italy; I could imagine him wandering from café to café, and spending hours inside old churches. Of course he'd have read all the guidebooks properly and been able to tell me the history of whatever we were looking at. There would be a list of historic must-sees scribbled in the notebook he kept in his satchel. And in the evenings he'd have found pleasure in sitting beneath the pomegranate tree to roll a cigarette and watch the sun set. Charlie would have loved it here.

But he was spending his summer in London, working long hours. Even if he'd had the time to take a break, Leila would not have welcomed him at Villa Rosa with much enthusiasm. For a while I remembered to send him the odd hastily scribbled postcard and looked forward to getting his letters in reply. And then I met Lucio.

That first day, as I set off to learn to make pizza by his side, my excitement was bubbling away like a sauce on a high simmer. I felt entirely unlike myself. But when I got to Triento I found Lucio's smile missing and his mood oddly edgy. He made a perfunctory offer of coffee and little rum-soaked cakes then busied himself straightening benches and wiping down tables.

'The girl I employ made a bad job of things last night,' he muttered. 'Look at this place, it's a mess.'

'Is there anything I can do?'

'No, no, I'll sort this out, then we can make a start.'

I wondered if Lucio had changed his mind about letting me work with him. For a moment I watched him frowning as he examined the wine glasses, polishing away smudges with a cloth he wore thrown over his shoulder.

'Are you sure you're OK with me being here?' I asked at last. 'I won't get in your way. I can just be an observer if you'd prefer.'

He paused in his polishing and looked at me. 'Eh? No, no it's fine.'

'You're used to cooking alone aren't you?' I pressed him.

He treated me to a half-smile. 'Alone or with my family.'

It was obvious there was some sort of rivalry between Lucio and his brother. Being known for making the best pizza in town could hardly compare with having Michelin stars and being feted all over London, so who could blame Lucio if he resented me being here? Perhaps he'd assumed I was a favourite with Tonino and that's why I'd come.

'Your brother says I have a lot to learn,' I offered. 'I've been having a tough time at his restaurant.'

'Yes, yes, so Mamma says. She also tells me you take food much too seriously, and you're too hard on yourself.'

'She does?'

'My mother likes to help people if she can. So she wants me to show you how to have fun with food, to get excited about it.'

'And you'd prefer not to?'

'I promised I'd show you how to make good pizza and I will.' Lucio remembered to smile. 'Perhaps we'll even have some fun just as Mamma says, eh?'

It all came so easily to him. He'd been handling the dough since he was a boy and was deft enough to put on a show, throwing it in the air and spinning it between his fingers. In comparison I was desperately clumsy. I made holes as I stretched it, created the oddest shapes, even dropped it on the floor once or twice. In no time I'd grown to hate the yeasty smell and the shreds of dough peeling from my hands like dead skin. But most of all I was furious that such a simple food had made me look like an idiot in front of Lucio when I'd wanted so much to impress him.

While his pizza emerged deliciously blistered and scorched from the wood-fired oven, mine came out pear-shaped and lumpy. Time after time I got it wrong. Finally I was aware Lucio had stopped trying to help me and was struggling not to laugh.

'It's not funny,' I snapped. 'I can't do it. I'm useless. Perhaps I should just give up.'

'No, no, you'll get it in the end. I'm laughing because my mother is right. You take it all so seriously. It's fine to waste a bit of dough, Alice. And it's OK if your pizza is a little thick or not quite a perfect circle. You're still learning.'

'But I don't like getting things wrong,' I admitted.

None of us do.' Lucio cuffed my shoulder with his hand. 'Let's take a ten-minute break. We can come back later and finish off.'

He took me over to the bakery and we sat on the bench with Silvana, all three of us sipping at dainty cups of coffee he'd bought at the bar next door. As they passed by, people nodded and smiled, some calling out a greeting, others stopping to chat. Already there were faces I recognised, the man with the chunky gold Rolex who'd stared at us over lunch, a couple of well-dressed older women who often ate at the trattoria. Once they'd walked away Silvana whispered snippets of gossip about them and Lucio translated them for me.

After a short while he suggested we should return to work. 'Do you feel strong enough to go back to the dough yet?' he asked, grinning at me.

Despite myself I started to laugh. 'I'm completely terrible at it, aren't I?'

Lucio shrugged. 'People think pizza is easy. You can buy it everywhere. In London I think you can even get it delivered in a box. But there's a lot of bad pizza around and many, many people who are completely terrible at making it. You're not going to be one of them, I promise you.'

As we walked back through the market stalls and across the piazza, my heart sank a bit at the thought of more humiliation. But instead of wrestling with the dough, Lucio showed me how to set up what most chefs grandly call their *mise-en-place* and he referred to as his 'pizza stuff': the oils, vinegars, sauce, seasonings and other ingredients he would need to have close to hand once the place opened and service began.

For Lucio simplicity was the key. His pizza wasn't cluttered with toppings. There were no chunks of pink ham clashing with tasteless pitted olives, and certainly no signs of any pineapple. Customers could choose between a pizza loaded with shaved prosciutto and torn rocket, or one with seared baby squid and garlic. There was a simple pizza of anchovy, capers and fresh tomato, or a richer one with baby artichokes and melted mozzarella cheese. Lucio changed his pizza toppings with the seasons and served them with nothing more than a simple salad of leaves dressed with oil and lemon.

Every evening he opened at five p.m. and the place was soon bustling with tourists and locals. The young girl he'd hired as his waitress almost had to run to keep up with the orders. Lucio was in his element. A much noisier cook than his brother, he often paused in his work to call a loud greeting to a regular, or to berate the poor waitress if she was too slow and make a big show of delivering a pizza to the table himself.

I tried to stay out of his way, helping by filling the odd bowl with salad leaves or restocking the *mise-en-place* if

I could see supplies of something were running low, but mostly I just watched.

The place stayed busy until about ten thirty. Once the last customer had left there was still the cleaning to do and Lucio had to make a list of all the things he needed to buy the next day so we weren't finished until well past midnight. If I'd been in London this was the time I'd have headed out to unwind over a couple of vodkas with the rest of the kitchen crew. We did a lot of heavy drinking in odd bars at strange hours. But nowhere in Triento would be open so late and I couldn't imagine how Lucio managed to bring himself down from the buzz of cooking each night.

'It's a beautiful evening,' he remarked as he locked the door of the pizzeria behind us. 'Would you like to come for a drive with me?'

'Yes, OK,' I said, just as casually. 'Where will we go?'

Lucio had a tiny Fiat he managed to squeeze down the narrow alleyway and into the piazza. Its tyres squealed when he took corners too quickly which he almost always did. We drove up the mountain, around a series of hairpin bends, past a small settlement with an open-air chapel and then up towards the summit. My seat belt was jammed and the hand-strap missing, so I clutched the edges of the seat and tried not to squeal as Lucio slid into the bends.

'I'm taking you to Jesus,' he shouted over the tortured whine of the engine, and I hoped he didn't mean it literally.

The steep, winding road finished at an empty car park where Lucio couldn't resist ending the ride with the flourish of a handbrake turn. 'We're here,' he told me, pulling the key from the ignition. 'Come and see our Jesus.'

He took me past a couple of souvenir shops, closed and shuttered for the night, and then up a flight of stone steps towards the statue of Christ, illuminated against the night sky. It was only then I realised quite how amazing it was, like the one in Rio de Janeiro, only more modern and possibly not quite so tall. I was surprised to see it wasn't looking out over the sea as I'd imagined, but instead it faced the mountains.

'That's strange. Why does it have its back to the coast?' I asked Lucio.

'It was built in the sixties,' he told me. 'Mamma says there was some big fight over who was going to pay for it. The fishermen refused to give any money so Jesus turned his back on them. He was the loser in the end, though, he got the dull view.'

Lucio was standing so close to me now that I could smell the sweetness of freshly-baked pizza bread on his clothes and a very male muskiness from a long night spent sweating beside the wood-fired oven.

'I've always loved the view from here,' he told me. 'It's spectacular in the daytime but I like it best at night when the sea is black and all you can see are clusters of light from the fishing villages along the coast.'

'It's beautiful,' I agreed.

'And the stars look so clear from here,' he went on. 'After all those hours stuck in the pizzeria I like to come and remind myself how big the sky is.'

'You never see stars like this in London,' I remarked.

He nodded. 'The sky is destroyed by city lights. How do you stand living there, Alice? Pizza in boxes, no sky ... what a terrible place.'

'There are some good things about it,' I insisted, although right at that moment I couldn't think of any.

'And you work for my brother,' he added. 'That can't be an easy life?'

I wasn't sure how much I should say. 'Not really ...'

'I cooked with him when we were boys, you know,' Lucio told me. 'We learnt to make pizza together.'

'What was he like back then?'

'Just the same as now, I suppose – always dreaming of

something bigger, always ambitious and always totally certain that his way was the only way.' Lucio gave a dry little laugh. 'No wonder you find cooking so stressful.'

'Oh I like it,' I assured him. 'I like to cook. I'm just not so certain how much I like a cook's life.'

He nodded. 'Fair enough.'

'What about you?' I dared ask. 'Do you love to cook?'

He looked at me, holding my gaze, and for a moment he reminded me of Tonino. 'I think cooking is the most intimate thing you can do for someone,' he said softy. 'I make something for you with my hands and then you put it inside your body. What could be more intimate than that?'

I swallowed hard. 'Nothing,' I managed.

'But there's a lot of nonsense surrounding food, I think,' he went on, unaware of the effect he was having on me. 'People want to talk about it, write about it and make a big fuss. They arrange a tiny mound of it in the middle of the plate and make patterns all around from different coloured sauces. What's the point of that? It's not art, it's only food. So cook it, eat it, enjoy it, *e basta*.'

There were lots of things I wanted to ask. I was curious about his past, his family, what he'd done and what he'd like to do. But instead I stood beside him silently staring out at the view, breathing the same cool night air and reminding myself I had an entire summer to get to know him.

There really wasn't any rush.

Babetta

Babetta saw the confusion on Nunzio's face. He had taken his usual place at the table expecting her to serve him a cake of yesterday's rice reheated in the oven, or a simple bowl of spaghetti with olive oil and garlic. Instead, Babetta placed a steaming dish of *tortellini in brodo* in front of him. She had made the little pasta dumplings herself, stuffed them with a mixture of pancetta and Parmesan and served them swimming in her delicate chicken broth. Nunzio breathed the flavours for a while before lifting his spoon to taste it.

He cleaned the bowl and looked at her, asking with his eyes for more. But Babetta shook her head and instead brought him the second course she had prepared, an osso buco cooked for hours in onions, red wine and tomatoes until the meat had softened and shredded and the sauce had thickened around it. Nunzio stared at the plate as though he didn't recognise the things on it.

'Eat, eat,' Babetta urged him. He took a mouthful, then another and soon had the bone in his hands and was sucking the marrow from it, grunting with effort and pleasure.

Once they had finished eating they rested for a while, letting the food digest and the heat of the day pass. Babetta put her chores out of her mind and lay listening to her husband's breathing whilst in her head she ran through plans for dishes to please him with tomorrow. Perhaps some red onions stuffed with pecorino cheese, a piece of swordfish belly braised in rich tomato sauce, or even a fricassee of lamb flavoured with minced sage and cooked with artichokes.

Lulling herself with thoughts of food, Babetta drifted into a doze, her head tipping from the pillow and resting lightly against Nunzio's shoulder.

Alice

Eventually I did get better at making pizza although I never could spin it with the same confidence as Lucio and it never tasted quite so good. I worked with him on busy weekend nights and during the week spent my days at the trattoria cooking seafood with Raffaella and her husband.

There was hardly any time left over to hang out at Villa Rosa. Although the weather was warmer and the lido had opened up, I'd only been swimming with Leila once or twice. I kept promising to go the next day but then I'd get busy in one of the restaurants, or start helping Babetta in the vegetable garden – which had stretched to triple its original length and was yielding things for us to eat in the way of herbs and leafy green vegetables. It was such a pleasure to pick the food myself then cook it while it was still fresh that I didn't mind missing out on lazy days at the beach.

I could tell Leila was growing bored, even with the little dog Sky constantly running around her feet. She was still tapping away at the book she claimed to be writing but it never seemed to hold her interest for long. I suppose I should have known she'd come looking for me and, when she didn't find me at the trattoria, follow me up the hill and discover me kneading dough at Lucio's side.

She looked so very beautiful that day. Her skin had tanned to gold from the hours she spent lazing in the sun and she'd gained a little weight that softened the sharp angles of her face and suited her. I heard Lucio give a long, low whistle as she made her entrance.

'So this is where you've been, Alice.' Leila sauntered behind the counter to peer at the jars of fat black olives and salted capers that Lucio kept there. 'You're a pizza maker now, are you?'

I wished she wasn't looking so perfect, that her hair had been left unwashed or her summer clothes weren't clinging in so many of the right places.

'I've just been helping out a bit,' I said, introducing them casually. 'Leila, this is Lucio.'

'Hi.' She smiled at him. 'Pleased to meet you.'

'I'm pleased to meet you too.' Lucio sounded like he meant it.

'Hey, Alice, I came to tell you I'm going to leave for Rome in the morning.' Leila took a seat at the bar. 'My friend Caroline has been nagging me to get there.'

'Oh, OK,' I nodded at her. 'But you'll come back, won't you?'

'Probably ... although I might see if I can pick up some waitressing work in one of the tourist places where it won't be such a problem that I don't speak much Italian.' She smiled at Lucio again. 'Unless you need a waitress here.'

'He doesn't,' I told her.

'Shame.' Even her regret sounded flirtatious. 'Anyway, Alice, I was hoping you'd take the afternoon off and spend some time with me since it's my last day.'

I glanced at Lucio. 'Well I ...'

'Why don't I take an hour off too?' he said, to my dismay. 'Things are pretty organised here. There's time to drive up to the statue and show your friend the view if you'd like.'

Usually I didn't mind men preferring Leila. I didn't care about attracting their attention, almost liked being over-looked. In London there had always been Charlie hanging around in the background and he'd been enough for me. But now I resented Leila's grabby beauty and the way she used it so carelessly. I didn't want to be her little brown shadow. Not if it meant Lucio would stop noticing me at all.

Nevertheless I squashed myself obligingly into the back seat of his Fiat so Leila could have the front. And I tried not to care as she threw back her head to laugh at the madness of his driving and he showed off even more as a result.

It was the first time I'd seen the view by day and it really was something special. The mountains behind us were burning off to brown in the hot summer sun but the sea below shimmered and the old fishermen's cottages seemed to be almost tumbling down the slope towards it. I could see the spires of many churches, the pattern made by Triento's narrow alleyways and the way the small town seemed to tuck itself into the folds of the land.

Once we'd had enough of picking out landmarks, the three of us walked round the base of the statue and then down an overgrown path that led through the ruins of an old settlement.

'This is where Triento used to be,' Lucio told us. 'In the old days this part of Italy was full of bandits so they built that first town high on the mountain where they could more easily defend themselves.'

I noticed how he and Leila seemed to have paired up. There was only enough space for two to walk abreast along the narrow path and I found myself either several steps in front of Lucio or just behind him. It was Leila who stayed by his side.

Even when we stopped at the little bar beside the souvenir shops she seemed to manoeuvre herself between us. She was talking in a too-loud voice, putting on a show that Lucio seemed to be enjoying.

'What a shame you're leaving for Rome tomorrow,' he kept saying to her. 'It will be getting hot in the city, you know. Better to stay here by the sea where the air is fresh and cooler.'

Back at the pizzeria, it was me who made lunch while Lucio sat outside lighting Leila's cigarettes and filling her glass with Prosecco.

As I drove the heels of my hands into the pizza dough, I couldn't help resenting her. Did she have to take every man? Couldn't she leave just this one for me?

Leila was too caught up to notice if I was a little off-key. She stubbed out her cigarette and then she and Lucio shared the pizza, eating from the same fork.

Later that night at Villa Rosa, I watched her throwing bright silk dresses, little embroidered purses and slippery underwear into her suitcase and listened while she talked about Lucio.

'If only I'd discovered him weeks ago when we first got here. He's a little young for me but *so, so* much in need of a good time don't you think ... what a shame, he would have been such fun.'

'Oh well, there'll be more like him in Rome, won't there?' I said lightly.

'More pizza makers with long, lovely fingers? Oh maybe.' Leila smiled and snapped shut the locks of her suitcase. 'If there aren't then I can always come back, I suppose.'

Even though it made me feel guilty, I found myself hoping she'd find something to make her want to stay in Rome.

Babetta

The showy one drove off early one morning and didn't return but Babetta wasn't sorry. She wouldn't miss the clatter of the typewriter breaking the silence of a perfect morning, or the way the girl had of arranging herself, lying on the wall of the terrace to smoke a cigarette, spreading out her tangle of dark hair if she flopped down on the grass.

Life at Villa Rosa settled into a more peaceful routine without her. Each morning Babetta and Nunzio began their work in the garden while it was still cool. Often Aurora would bring them coffee when she woke, sometimes even a basket of bread and some pomegranate jelly. She would dress in a wide-brimmed straw hat and pale overalls stained with bright slashes of blue, and on fine days Nunzio would help her carry her painting equipment down onto the rocks where she stayed for hours making her pictures.

Once the sun grew too hot, Babetta liked to disappear into her kitchen. Soon onions were turning golden in hot olive oil, chicken stock was coming to the boil and there was a risotto of asparagus or radicchio on its way. Nunzio seemed to know when it was time to come inside. He would take his seat at the table, hungry for what she'd cooked, scooping up the last of every meal with a heel of crusty bread.

The dishes she made changed each day: a spaghetti of bitter greens and anchovies; a casserole of salt cod and roasted peppers; a scaloppine of veal with mozzarella and prosciutto. And while it pained Babetta to be spending more with the butcher and the fish man, the sight of Nunzio with his head lowered over his plate and the change on his face by the time he'd finished eating, always made up for the money that was gone.

Despite all her efforts he still lived in his silence and still spent hours every afternoon sitting in the old cane chair. Babetta missed the sound of her husband's voice. For a while she had returned his speechlessness with a stubborn quiet of her own but soon she understood there was no point in it. He may have run out of things to say but still she had plenty of words left for him. So she chatted as they weeded the gardens, talked nonsense mostly, told him she thought there would be good crops this year because the weather was perfect for growing, remarked on how quickly the tomato plants shot up after a day of warm rain. There was no way of knowing from Nunzio's face how he felt about all this chatter. Perhaps he'd have preferred no noise but the whirr of crickets and the call of birds.

When their daughter Sofia visited he came alive a little, allowing his cheek to be kissed and raising his hand to wave goodbye. But even for Sofia there were no words.

And then one morning Babetta woke a little late. When she went down to the kitchen she found her husband already there, busy grinding the beans for coffee.

'*Buongiorno* Nunzio,' she greeted him as always, rubbing the sleep from her eyes.

To her surprise he looked up and gave her the sketchiest of nods.

'*Buongiorno* Babetta,' he said in a hoarse, unpractised voice and then he fell silent again and went back to making the coffee.

Alice

I never admitted to anyone how I felt about Lucio. Perhaps I felt self-conscious or even a little silly to have fallen for him like a teenager. But I kept it a complete secret. As far as Leila knew, once I got home to London I'd be picking up where I left off with Charlie. My relationship with him had been drifting on in the same old way for ages now and neither of us seemed to feel any need to change things: we spent our Sundays together then returned to our workday lives with no pressure to see each other again until the next weekend.

The whole arrangement drove Leila insane. Her theory was that I'd settled for Charlie because I was scared of other men after what had happened to me.

It was true that I didn't trust so easily. Maybe that was a big part of Lucio's appeal. I'd cemented myself so well into his family by the time we met: his mother was my friend, his brother was my boss and even his father seemed fond of me. It was OK to be with Lucio.

Once he got over his initial prickliness at having a stranger in his kitchen, Lucio and I had fun together. When we weren't working, he'd scare me half-senseless with a drive round the coast, or we'd go down to the port to eat salty fried potatoes and drink cold beer. As the summer developed I waited for our friendship to change and deepen. Some days he'd pinch my cheek to say hello, others he'd link arms with me as we walked through the piazza. But those faint beginnings of familiarity never became any bolder.

Other girls might have been more obvious, signposted

their affections. But I'd never been that way – not before the stranger who'd burst in on my life and certainly not afterwards.

So I worked and waited. I learnt how to spot the freshest fish and haggle with the men who caught it. I developed a heavy hand with a bottle of olive oil and knew which peasant grew the best green beans and which the tastiest tomatoes. When I walked through Triento the locals stopped to say '*buongiorno*' as though I belonged there. I even began to look at Aurora's sky paintings and see something different in every one of them. But I never made any headway with Lucio.

'Tell me about your childhood,' I said to him one afternoon as I shredded prosciutto for that night's pizza. 'Did you always know you'd be a cook?'

'In my family there was no other choice. It's what we did,' he said almost ruefully. 'Other kids might go out to play once they'd finished school. We came here and helped Papa.'

'Did you mind?'

'Tonino never minded but I'd do everything I could to sneak away. I drove my father mad.'

'And your mother?'

'I think she knew there was time enough for making pizza. She used to turn a blind eye if she saw me slipping away. And Tonino always could do the work of two boys. He was obsessed with food even then. My parents always expected big things of him.'

'But your mother is always saying she wishes he'd get married and have babies,' I said, remembering Raffaella's confidences as we drove around the countryside seeking out fresh vegetables. 'I think she'd prefer it if he wasn't so ambitious.'

Lucio laughed. 'Every Italian Mamma wants grandchildren. Mine is no different.'

The unasked question hung between us for a moment until Lucio volunteered the answer. 'Mamma is just as frustrated with me. Almost every day she asks whether I've found a girlfriend yet and nags me to get on with it.'

'So will you?' I sounded coy.

'I've known the girls in this town all my life.' Lucio pushed his knuckles into the dough he was kneading. 'There's no one special here for me. But like Tonino I'm not in any hurry. It's only Mamma who is.'

'Do you think you'll move away from Triento like your brother has? Go and work in Rome or London?' It was something I'd been wondering since we'd first met.

'Why should I?' Lucio sounded irritated.

'Well, I don't know ... for the experience? And to meet new people, I suppose.'

'You're a new person and I met you standing right here by my own pizza oven,' he pointed out.

'So you're happy here then?'

'What you're really asking is if I would prefer to be like Tonino.'

'Well ...'

'You think I should want the same things as him?'

'No ...' I could see he was annoyed.

'But I'm not Tonino, am I? And yes, I'm happy enough here.'

Lucio went back to kneading his dough, the conversation finished. We worked in an uneasy silence that night. And once everyone had left and the pizzeria was closed up, he didn't ask me to take a drive with him in his Fiat to the top of the mountain or to one of the deserted stony beaches where we could stare out at the dark sea and come down from the stress and busyness of the night.

Instead, Lucio went off alone and I returned to Villa Rosa feeling disappointed and wondering if I'd really got to know him at all.

Babetta

Life hadn't turned out how Babetta expected. As a girl she'd never imagined there would be a time when she wouldn't be surrounded by the clamour of family. In her parents' house they'd lived crammed together. Always someone was arguing, shouting at a child or creating a background hum of noise and chatter. Even when she and Nunzio had come to this place her family liked to wander in and out as though they too were living there.

Slowly things had changed. First her grandparents had died, next her parents. Then one by one her sisters moved away. The eldest went to Rome, another followed her husband to America, the youngest moved to London. All were looking for a better life. Only she and Nunzio had stayed in Triento, the two of them with their little girl, living as they'd always done.

Babetta missed the sound of people. The radio in the kitchen was rarely turned off but the babble of strangers never entirely filled the silence. It was so easy to run out of reasons to speak, even in their younger days. Often she'd saved snippets of thoughts to pass on to Nunzio or talked too long about little things that had happened during the day. She knew he only listened when he wanted to please her.

The silence had crept over them both once Sofia left. Some days they might only exchange a few words over the dining table or in the garden. Once Nunzio retired from the road crew, they'd had all day to spend together. The more time there was, the less there seemed to be to say.

Babetta never grew used to it. She found herself talking to the statue on the mountain, to the green lizards that sunbaked on the rocks, even to the seedlings she set into hollows of earth. The sound of her own voice soothed her, especially once Nunzio gave up on words altogether.

He had always been such an uncompromising man. '*Buongiorno* is dead' he'd said to her that morning and she'd known he meant it. Nunzio simply hadn't seen the point of talking any more. He'd stopped pretending to be interested.

Babetta watched him carefully all through that quiet time. She noted the things that pleased him: the little dog, the flavours of certain dishes. And she wondered what else might tease him from his silence. Each morning she was encouraged when he returned her greeting of '*buongiorno*' in his gruff voice. She waited for more words but they didn't come. Still Babetta stayed hopeful.

Alice

It seemed I was running out of time. Leila had sent a postcard covered in her spidery handwriting and blotched with coffee stains. She'd had enough of the city and was catching the train back to Triento.

For the next few days I made every excuse I could to join Lucio in his pizzeria, but still there was no change. We remained nothing more than friends.

There were some moments I felt hopeful. One lunchtime he took me a few miles along the coastline to a restaurant that was famous for its pasta. We ordered our meals, handed back our menus and then found ourselves sitting across the table from each other with nothing to do but talk.

Lucio asked me questions he'd never bothered with before. Where did I grow up? Did I have a boyfriend? So I told him all about the dull little town I'd been in such a hurry to escape, I even told him about Charlie.

'He's not a proper boyfriend any more. More of a habit really,' I explained. 'Usually we see each other on Sundays when we're both at a loose end.'

'Do you cook for him?' Lucio asked.

I thought about it and realised we only ever ate take-aways or cheap curries at the local Indian. 'No, never,' I admitted.

'Then there's definitely no future in it,' Lucio said with certainty. 'If you don't care to prepare food for each other then you don't care enough.'

'Do you think so?'

'Look at my parents. They don't just package up something from the trattoria and take it home for dinner. Every night one cooks for the other and then they sit down at the table to eat together. I've always thought that's how they keep hold of their love.'

'They're still crazy about each other, aren't they?' I'd watched Raffaella and Ciro in the trattoria and, although they weren't a couple who touched and kissed a lot, hardly even murmured an endearment, it was obvious.

'Yes, completely crazy about each other even after all these years,' he agreed.

Then the waiter appeared with the food and it was easier to eat than talk. The pasta was good, a rotolo of spinach and ricotta for me, a spaghetti with sardines, fennel tops and lemon zest for Lucio.

'Mmm, this is incredible,' I said. 'A joy to eat.'

'They make it to order,' Lucio told me. 'No bagging it up in portions and cooking it later like I expect you do in London.'

'We can't do things any other way in Teatro. The place is so busy. But the pasta there is still good, I think. All the food is. That's why the place is doing so incredibly well.'

'And my brother Tonino, does he even cook any more?' Lucio's tone was scathing.

'Not really,' I admitted. 'He cooks when he's creating a new dish but the rest of the time he's more like a general quietly ordering his army about.'

Lucio moved his spaghetti round with his fork but didn't take a mouthful. 'I suppose his chef's whites stay clean till the end of the night?'

'Yes, quite often they do.'

'What's the point in that? It's not cooking.'

I tried to change the subject. 'This pasta really is very good,' I repeated, adding, 'I remember when I was a kid we ate tinned ravioli … and the worst thing is I actually quite liked it.'

Lucio didn't care to be distracted. He was still brooding about Tonino. 'For some people it's always about the prize,' he said bitterly. 'They want a big success and then when they get it they start looking for the next one. My brother doesn't care about food any more, all he cares about is succeeding.'

I wasn't sure what to say but that didn't seem to matter. Lucio wasn't interested in listening.

'I always imagined he'd be the one to take over the pizzeria and I'd go off and do other things,' he went on. 'But Tonino left home as soon as he could. He moved to Rome, then on to Paris, then London. He never stayed anywhere for long because he was in such a hurry to better himself. And it was me who had to remain here and look after the pizzeria.'

I'd stopped eating now and could see the waiter casting concerned looks in our direction. 'What were the other things you wanted to do?' I asked Lucio.

'Oh, I had ideas, plans but when Tonino left I forgot about them. None of that matters much now. It's a good life I have here. I'm happy enough with it.' Lucio stabbed at his pasta and began eating again, but fiercely as if he wasn't getting much pleasure from the flavours.

Still his moods always could change in an instant. By the time we'd finished lunch and were eating ice creams on the beach any storminess was forgotten. We rolled up the legs of our trousers and let the waves wash over our feet, laughing as the ice cream melted down the cones and ran over our fingers. Lucio even linked his arm through mine as we strolled along the paved promenade beside the beach.

The following weekend Leila came back to Villa Rosa. She was wearing new clothes and her hair had been cut into a bob. The first thing she did was grab the puppy and tear around the garden with him. Then she suggested we go to the pizzeria.

'In Rome I didn't find anything as good as the pizza you made for me there,' she said. 'My friend Caroline kept trying to make me eat local specialities like tripe and roasted suckling pig. God, it was awful. What I'd love is a simple little pizza with tomato and basil on it. And just a drizzle of olive oil ...'

'But I've told Lucio I'm not going in to work tonight,' I countered. 'Why don't we stay home and I'll cook something? There are beautiful tomatoes ripening in the garden and loads of fresh basil. I could make a pizza for you here.'

She frowned. 'No, I think I'd rather go out. I'll see if my mother wants to come too. She could do with a break from painting, I expect.'

Lucio seemed delighted to see the three of us. Even though the place was busy and he was working alone, he came out from behind the counter to kiss us all on both cheeks. He didn't seem to linger over Leila but, once we sat down, he did glance over at our table a lot. And he sent us special treats. Some baby squid he'd cooked quickly in the wood-fired oven. Some thinly sliced zucchini dressed with lemon and oil.

Leila had seated herself so she could watch him working. She ate more than usual, finishing every last scrap of her pizza. Aurora too tucked in with relish. But I didn't share their hearty appetites. I made an effort because it was Lucio's food and I didn't want him to think I wasn't enjoying it, but I almost had to force myself to swallow.

As I struggled on through my meal, I thought how good mother and daughter were looking. You could see in Aurora's face what Leila would become. She had a sort of wistful, edgy beauty, with a tousle of coppery-tinted hair and a wardrobe filled with floaty clothes. I thought about my own mother, not bothering to touch up the grey in her hair because where did she ever go to get noticed; spending her life in stretch trousers so her body could spread in comfort; rarely bothering even with a slick of lip gloss. And I felt like such an outsider. I wasn't like these people. I didn't belong with them at all.

Lucio came out from behind his counter once more when we left. He took Leila's hand as he kissed her goodbye. 'So the city was too hot like I said, eh? You've come back to us.'

'Yes, you were completely right.' She smiled at him. 'It was boiling hot and awful in Rome. I can't wait to go to the beach for a swim first thing tomorrow.'

'A morning swim sounds good,' agreed Lucio. 'In fact, perhaps I'll join you. Alice, will you come too?'

I shook my head. 'I told your parents I'd work in the trattoria in the morning. I don't want to let them down.'

'So just the two of us then?' he said to Leila.

I wanted to scream but I didn't say anything to Leila, didn't even hint at how I felt. What was the point? Lucio wasn't interested in me. Nothing had happened between us.

Over the next week or so I sort of edged myself out of the picture to make way for Leila. There was no point in trying to prevent what was going to happen but still I didn't have to watch it. So I spent more hours in the trattoria, got there early and left as late as I could. The rest of the time I pottered about the garden with Babetta or cooled off in the rock pool below the house.

And a few nights later, when Leila didn't come home, I knew exactly who she was with.

Babetta

Babetta had grown used to watching. She had become good at it. The past years with Nunzio had taught her to see the tiniest shift in a person's expression, to sense how they were feeling. So although she and Alice couldn't speak to each other and she had no idea about the girl's life beyond this place, she could tell she was unhappy. Babetta had seen it from the very beginning. There was something fragile in the girl, something that had been broken and never mended properly. She wondered what had happened to make it so.

For a while she thought she had noticed a new lightness in Alice, especially after the other one left. Her face had opened into a smile more often, even the way she walked seemed freer. But now her showy little friend was back and Alice seemed to be living life through gritted teeth. Babetta had noticed how she invented tasks in the garden to get away, even once or twice coming over to help Nunzio in their little plot. The two made an interesting pair. Her husband hardly moved, while Alice never stopped. And yet to Babetta it seemed there was something they shared. A certain sadness. A giving up.

She watched the girl as she gardened. Some days she brought her into her kitchen for tall glasses of freshly squeezed lemonade and little bits of whatever she'd been cooking. But Alice seemed listless. She smiled and nodded but never scooped out a second taste of a particularly good sauce or cared what had gone into it.

Babetta wanted to help. She tried to think of a way the

girl might find some happiness. As they worked together she searched her mind, certain there was something she could do. And then it came to her. She remembered a place that was sadder even than Alice. Perhaps it might help to take her there, to somewhere dark and grim so she could see what lay at the end of the path she was following.

It took a little persuasion to get her on the scooter. Alice was confused by this sudden insistence on an outing, and reluctant to leave the garden. But finally she agreed and, hopping on behind her, Babetta pointed out the way. It was a longer drive south than she'd remembered and she felt a little shaky as trucks thundered past on the winding coast road. But she found the place all right, the façade of a church set into the rock, the low-roofed chapel in the damp cave. There was a steep slope and then a flight of stone steps to get inside but Babetta was strong and her old legs carried her up.

'Wow, this is amazing.' Alice was gazing round in wonder at the wide chamber with its dripping stalactites and ornate altar. Nothing much had changed since Babetta had been married there all those years ago and it still seemed like the most desolate place for God to choose to be. But Alice liked it. She was touching the walls, moist and cold just like the skin of a snake, and exclaiming at the statues.

Babetta dipped her fingers in holy water, crossed herself and went to kneel in front of the altar. She was glad there was no priest here today, no one to interrupt her prayer or try to take her confession. She closed her eyes and asked God to help the girl. Her prayers had been answered before and she hoped they would be this time but Babetta knew you had to be patient. She had prayed for years for a child, it was all she'd wanted and at long last there had been Sofia. But Babetta's God was the type who granted wishes only when he chose to. He was like Nunzio, quiet and brooding and occasionally he surprised you.

Alice kneeled beside her, but awkwardly, as though it was something she hadn't done for years. She raised her eyes to the roof of the chamber instead of closing them and she didn't fold her hands in prayer but still Babetta was certain that was what she was doing. And she was pleased. Two voices instead of one might hurry God along.

Alice

I didn't want Leila to realise how upset I was because it wasn't her fault really. Men liked her, she enjoyed them and there was nothing wrong in that. What hurt me was knowing that Lucio was no more than a distraction, someone amusing to carry her through the last few weeks of summer. Once we were back in London she'd forget about him.

I tried to stay out of her way. There was always something to do in the garden and Babetta seemed to like me helping her. She kept taking me into her house and trying to ply me with little treats, cold drinks and morsels of food. Some days she even followed me to the rocks and watched while I swam in the deep, natural pool. It felt like she was looking after me.

Things came to a head the day Babetta made me go to that strange church in the cave. Leila spotted us coming back together and was hurt she hadn't been asked along.

'I'd have liked to have seen it too,' she said when I explained where we'd been and how amazing I'd thought it was. 'We could have borrowed my mother's car and all gone there together.'

'Sorry, but I had no idea where she was taking me,' I said. 'It's not difficult to find though. I'll draw you a map and you and your mother could go together.'

'Why don't you take me?' Leila insisted.

'Because I've been already. If your mother doesn't want to go then get Lucio to take you.'

'Alice what's going on?' Leila looked thoughtful.

'Nothing. What do you mean?'

'You've been weird since I got back from Rome. It's almost like you resented me being here. And then after Lucio and I—' Suddenly it dawned on her. 'Oh hell. You liked him didn't you?'

I didn't say anything at all.

'Oh hell, hell. He's the first new man you've really liked since you were attacked and I've gone and stuffed it up for you.'

'No you haven't,' I said quickly. 'There was nothing to stuff up.'

'But you liked him?'

'Yes,' I admitted.

'I'm so sorry,' Leila covered her mouth with her hand. 'God, I'm stupid. I didn't even think …'

'Why would you? I never said anything. And aside from that Lucio wasn't into me at all. It's not your fault, Leila.'

'He likes you so much though. He talks about you all the time … misses having you in the pizzeria … he's hurt that you haven't even dropped by lately. He really, really likes you.'

'But not the way I like him.'

'No, I suppose not.' Leila tried to grab a strand of hair to chew but it was too short now so instead she sort of fluttered her fingers through it nervously. 'I'll break off with him right away. There's no need for him to know why. I can just say it's been fun but now it's over.'

'Don't do that,' I said with some effort. 'What's the point?' Leila looked a bit sick.

'He was never really important to you, was he?' I said softly. 'Just someone to have a good time with?'

She nodded. 'But you know, Alice, he might not be what you think he is. He's moody, kind of immature, his world's really small …'

156

'Yes, I know all that.'

'And you still like him?'

I nodded. 'But it's pointless me liking him.'

'Did you ever tell him how you felt?' Leila wondered.

'Do you think it might have made a difference?'

She tried to chew her hair again. 'I don't know, to be honest.'

'It doesn't matter anyway. It's too late now. Let's just forget about it, hey?'

Leila wanted hugs then and lots of reassurances we were still friends. We sat up late that night drinking red wine and talking. She was full of chatter about the things we'd done at college and the wild nights out we'd had those first few years in London. She laughed too hard and drank too much.

As Leila talked on, I looked around at the courtyard: the riot of bougainvillea growing over the terrace, the crazy old ceramic picture tiles and the leafy pomegranate tree encircled by its low wall. I remembered thinking how difficult it would be to feel miserable in such a beautiful spot.

I'd learnt a lot since then – about food, about growing it and cooking it. But most importantly I'd learnt how it was possible to be unhappy just about anywhere, even a place as entirely perfect as Villa Rosa.

PART II

'The thing about working a lot is that you never have a chance to worry about things that have happened or things that are going to happen. It forces you to live in the moment.'

Dave Hughes, Australian comedian

Alice

I'd never much liked the order and hierarchy of Teatro's kitchen, the wearing of formal chef's whites and calling out, 'Yes, chef' like a robot when an order came through. But now I was longing to get back to it, hoping the discipline of that sort of cooking might help stave off how I was feeling. If I worked hard, I reasoned, then perhaps there wouldn't be time to think.

Despite everything it had been sad to leave Triento at the end. I'd enjoyed being close to the sea and the earth, feeling the sun on my skin and taking salty swims on calm, hot days. I knew I'd miss the layers of blue in Aurora's wide expanse of sky, but the biggest wrench of all was saying goodbye to the people I'd come to care about.

Lucio had been especially surprised when I went to say my goodbyes to him one afternoon while Leila was busy writing.

'You seemed to love it so much here,' he said. 'I thought you might want to stay.'

'I do love it but I need to go back to my own life.'

'We've hardly seen you these past few weeks. And now you're leaving.' Lucio sounded genuinely sorry. 'When will you be back?'

I shrugged. 'I'll have to see what happens.'

'You'll come back soon,' he said with some certainty. 'A month or two in London and you'll be ready to look at the sea again and eat a decent *spaghetti alle vongole*.'

'I'll be busy so I won't have time to think of this place

much. And if it's *spaghetti alle vongole* I want then they have it at Teatro. Actually, Tonino flies Venus clams in from some place near Venice. It tastes as good as it does here, I promise you.'

Lucio's face fell into a frown. 'Give my best to my brother,' he said. 'Tell him we're doing well here. Our telephones are working, our mail is arriving. There would be no problem if he wanted to get in touch.'

I didn't want to get caught up in his squabble with Tonino or prolong saying goodbye. So, quickly kissing him on both cheeks, I left before he could see how upset I was to go.

It was the same at the trattoria when I said goodbye to Raffaella and Ciro. They made such a fuss, thanking me for all my hard work, then opening a bottle of Prosecco and toasting my future.

'Back to a real restaurant kitchen, not just our little family one,' said Raffaella. 'Tell our son we know how busy he is but still it would be nice if he called every now and then.'

We all hugged and then they stood waving at the door of the trattoria until I was out of sight

It wasn't until I said goodbye to Babetta that I found myself in tears. She was old, so near the end of her life and I knew it was unlikely I'd see her again.

When she understood I was leaving she insisted on giving me a jute bag filled with just-picked vegetables and then patted my cheek with her soil-scoured fingers.

'*Arrivederci e buona fortuna,*' she said, and suddenly there were tears wetting my face. I scrubbed them away awkwardly with the back of my hand.

'*Buona fortuna* to you too. And *grazie ... grazie* for everything,' I surprised myself a second time, putting my arms round Babetta's thick little body and giving her a fierce hug.

And now I was back in London with all its bustle and noise, breathing fume-laden air and trying not to waste too much time missing Villa Rosa. This was my life and I had to get on with it.

My first day back at the restaurant was a shock. I'd been worrying that it might take time to get up to speed, that new dishes would have been added and I'd have to learn them quickly or someone else might have taken over the pasta station and I'd be demoted back to prep. But the changes I found were much greater than that.

As I was putting on my chef's whites I heard the sound of a new voice. It was raw and loud, cutting through the usual low hum of conversation as the evening shift came in.

'Come on, guys, you've been here two minutes already. You wanna get paid for the whole shift? Then get to work.'

'Who's that?' I hissed at Mario the salad guy.

'New head chef,' he hissed back.

'Where's Tonino?'

'Opening another place in the City. He's busy setting it up. So now he's calling himself the executive chef and this guy Raoul is in charge of the day-to-day running of Teatro.'

'What's he like?' I buttoned my chef's whites hurriedly and crammed on my hat.

Mario stood back to let me go through the door first. 'You'll see soon enough,' he said.

It was amazing how much one person had changed the atmosphere of the kitchen. It had been such a quiet place to work, almost factory-like, and the loudest sounds were the clanging of pans and the slamming of oven doors. All of us were aware of the customers and the clear view they had of us through the big sheet of glass. We were on our best behaviour.

But Raoul didn't care who was watching. Or perhaps he did care and was determined to put on a performance. He was a little man, puny in the way of someone who'd spent far too many years taking drugs and working in intense heat. He'd come from some New York restaurant, a pricey French place, and he clearly thought Teatro needed shaking up. All night as we cooked he kept up a noisy repartee with the other guys in the kitchen. There was cursing, lots of insults and crude jokes flying round, slang I'd never heard before they all seemed to think was hilarious. The kitchen had become a testosterone-charged place, and I noticed a couple of the women who'd worked there had disappeared, to be replaced by guys I didn't recognise.

Raoul didn't just shout, he also threw things, knives mostly, and he hated the waiters, all of whom were looking shell-shocked. He hadn't bothered to learn any of their names. Instead they had to answer to what he'd made up for them – Pigface, McShit, that kind of thing. And Raoul had his own New York kitchen slang that it seemed we all had to use now.

'Hey, Alice, get your *meez* sorted,' he yelled at me halfway through the first night, and someone had to explain that he meant my *mise-en-place*, my set-up of ingredients.

It was disorientating, like arriving home and finding the place inhabited by complete strangers. A lot of the guys seemed to be following Raoul's lead, their voices had got louder, their language coarser. Some had even started tossing their knives around like cheap Hollywood cowboys and Raoul encouraged them, whistling appreciatively if someone managed a particularly good throw and catch.

'Shit,' I whispered to Mario the moment I had a chance. 'The guy's a psychopath.'

'Yup,' was all he said in reply.

My relief at finding myself back working the pasta station faded fast. Right from the moment I walked into his kitchen it was clear Raoul had it in for me.

'So you're Alice, eh?' he drawled at me. 'I've heard *all* about you. Let's see what you can do.'

At first Raoul never singled me out openly. But if he had a chance he'd bump into me and throw me off balance while I was carrying something heavy. He'd jog my elbow then call me clumsy if I dropped my pasta tongs. Sometimes I'd notice him looking at me in a way that made me suspect he'd been saying, or at least thinking, something crude. It was really creepy.

I tried to have a word with Nico the sous-chef but he wasn't interested. 'What do you expect, Alice? You come back from living with Tonino's family in Italy, you're the little favourite. Of course you're going to be given a hard time. Tough it out or leave. It's up to you.'

'I wasn't living with his family ...' I tried to argue but Nico couldn't have cared less.

We were still cooking Tonino's menu so I knew sooner or later he'd have to come back from his new place in the City to give it a tweak. He couldn't afford to take his eye off Teatro, let it go downhill. And surely when he saw how this guy Raoul was behaving he'd sort him out?

In the meantime I tried to follow Nico's advice and tough it out. I shouted 'Yes, chef' obediently and, ignoring the cursing and crudity, tried to keep my head down. It seemed the only way to survive.

Babetta

Nunzio had offered her one word. 'Gone?' he'd said when he saw Aurora driving away, her car full of bags, her daughter beside her and Alice sitting in the back.

'Gone,' Babetta had agreed. She'd thought of the garden with its rows of vegetables and no one there to pick and eat them now.

'The dog?' Nunzio had asked, surprising her again.

'He must have gone with them, I suppose.'

Nunzio shrugged and poked out his lower lip as though he didn't much care but Babetta could tell a current of feelings had rippled through him.

And later, when he saw Aurora driving back, her car empty and her expression a little wistful, Babetta thought she saw the beginnings of a smile on her husband's face.

'I expect she's dropped them off at the train station,' she said to him. 'Perhaps she and the little dog are going to stay.'

At that, Nunzio filled his pockets with something from the kitchen, found his spade and wandered over to Villa Rosa. Babetta saw him ten minutes later, the dog sniffing at his hands for treats as he wandered round the garden. He seemed peaceful, untroubled. Babetta was glad for him.

She didn't share his calm. The morning's departure from Villa Rosa had left her feeling uneasy. All the worries that had settled down while the girls were there, stirred up again. There was still no word on whether she and Nunzio could stay in their little house. Aurora never mentioned it.

She watched them working in her garden, ate what they grew, let Nunzio fetch and carry for her and was pleasant enough whenever they met. But she never offered any payment and Babetta had no idea what she was planning.

Picking up her broom, she went to sweep the paths of Villa Rosa. Now was not the time for slacking. Very soon more leaves would be falling from the trees, fruit ripening, the garden bolting and running to seed. In autumn, more than any other season, she and Nunzio could prove their worth.

Alice

I avoided Leila as much as I could. It wasn't all that difficult because both of us were working long hours. She was desperate to earn some money so she could take more time off and finish her book. Her mother had pulled the plug on her irregular allowance and so she was having to pull double shifts at the brasserie and was coming home exhausted.

When we did spend any time together it seemed all Leila wanted to talk about was Villa Rosa.

'I'm missing my little dog,' she'd say quite often. 'Do you think we should plan to go back for Christmas? My mother would love to have us there.'

'You go ... I'll be working,' was always my response.

Leila remained uncrushed. 'Oh well, no need to decide now. Let's see how you feel closer to the time.'

Neither of us mentioned Lucio. There didn't seem to be any point. But somehow he was always there between us.

The first Sunday we were back in London I caught up with Charlie. There was something reassuring about the sight of him, armed with his *Guardian* and his ancient Penguin paperbacks, unchanged by the summer that seemed to have altered me so much.

'I missed you,' he told me as we lay together wrapped in his slightly yellowed sheets, surrounded by dusty stacks of old *Rolling Stone* magazines. 'Did you miss me?'

'Um, yes I suppose.'

I tried to describe Villa Rosa, tell him about Babetta's

garden and the chapel in the cave, but already it felt like the past and best forgotten.

'I wish I'd been able to spend a couple of weeks with you,' Charlie said wistfully. 'Maybe next time, hey?'

'I don't know if there'll be a next time,' I told him. 'I've learnt the things I went to Triento to learn. Perhaps I'll go somewhere different next summer.'

'Maybe we should try Spain then?' Charlie seemed keen for us to make long-term plans. 'Or Portugal? I've heard it's beautiful there.'

'Maybe.' There was no harm in dreaming, although I was sure it would never happen

That evening, as we walked to the cheap Indian place down the road for a curry, I thought about Lucio and his insistence that to care about someone meant cooking for them. He'd had such a brilliance about him, a noise and dazzle. In comparison Charlie seemed sort of damped down. So I tried to push Lucio from my mind and focus on the man I was with.

Charlie still hadn't given up on his plan for us to live together. Every now and then he brought it up and I dismissed the idea. But that night, as I ate my spicy *balti* and enjoyed the change it made from Italian food, I let him talk on.

'My mate Dave has a ground floor flat in Highbury with a little back garden. He's leaving at the end of the month and it's coming up for rent. You'd like that, wouldn't you? It's not far from the tube and you could grow vegetables and stuff there like you did in Italy.'

'I suppose ...' He'd piqued my interest.

'Aren't you over living with that drama queen Leila? It must be great not having to pay any rent but let's face it that's not going to go on for ever.'

'I know that.'

'So you'll come and see Dave's place then? If we get in

really quick before it's advertised we'll be sweet.'

It wasn't that I was particularly keen on the idea of renting a place with Charlie, more that I wanted to get away from Leila. And living by myself still didn't seem like an option. I wasn't ready to sleep through a night alone, didn't trust that some man with a knife mightn't somehow get in no matter how many locks I had on the windows and doors.

So I went to see the flat and was pleasantly surprised. It had quite a big garden, definitely space for me to have a vegetable plot in the summer. There was even a bit of a lean-to that could be turned into a rough glasshouse so I could raise tomato seedlings in pots. It wasn't far from the Highbury swimming pool and while that wasn't quite the rock pool below Villa Rosa, it was better than nothing. And if I lived there I wouldn't have to see Leila and be reminded of Lucio almost every day.

'It's great,' I told Charlie. 'I think we should take it.'

'Really?' He seemed excited.

'Yes, but there are a few conditions.'

'Oh yeah.' Now he sounded dubious. 'What?'

'Well, for a start I don't want to see that little box with the engagement ring in it,' I told him in a stern sort of voice that I only ever managed with Charlie. 'I'm moving in with you but that's not a step towards marriage.'

He didn't quite keep the disappointment from his face. 'Fair enough,' he said.

'And the other thing is I don't want to go back to spending time with your family. No Christmases with them or weekends. They've never really liked me much and that's fine.'

'OK, what else?' He looked hurt which made me feel bad.

'That's it, I think.' I looked round at the kitchen with its scrubbed pine table and French doors onto the garden.

'This place will be perfect for us so long as we can both keep working and paying the rent.'

I didn't give much thought to the realities of living with Charlie, seeing him every day, sleeping next to him each night, tidying up the trail of mess he couldn't help leaving behind him. Mostly I focused on how nice it would be to have my own little patch of earth in the middle of the city. I could sit there peacefully, a cold beer in my hand, after a night working in the increasingly fraught kitchen of Teatro.

When I told Leila I was moving out, she seemed sad but unsurprised. She was lying in the bath, soaking in bubbles, and I took her a glass of wine then sat on the edge of the tub to talk to her.

'But Charlie's not the right one for you,' she told me as she rubbed shampoo into her hair. 'I don't know why you're settling for him.'

'He cares about me.'

'I care about you too, Alice,' Leila said in a small voice.

'Yes, I know that. But it's time I moved on.'

'But we'll still see each other all the time, won't we?' she asked, and then slid her head under the water to rinse off the shampoo and saved me from having to answer her.

A short while later Charlie and I moved in to the new place. It felt exciting to be making a fresh start, furnishing the little garden flat with things I'd chosen instead of always living with someone else's stuff. I bought loads of equipment for the kitchen: a food processor, a set of pans and a big deep Le Creuset casserole. As I arranged it all on shelves and in cupboards, I decided it was time I started cooking for Charlie.

Babetta

Autumn had always been Babetta's favourite season. There were those who preferred spring for its delicate vegetables and berries. Others longed for the heat of summer and the wanton sweetness of stone fruit. Babetta didn't mind either but it was autumn she loved best of all. This was the season of ripening, of picking and preserving whatever couldn't be eaten. Of the nuttiness of *cime di rapa*, the leafy green turnip tops with their tender buds. At the bottom of her garden there were monstrous pumpkins and at Villa Rosa the trees were heavy with pomegranates. Autumn was Babetta's reward for all the hard work she'd put into the garden.

Already she had jars set out, waiting to be filled with sauces, syrups and jellies. Some of the preserves would go to Sofia, lots would be sold and a few she'd add to the store in her cupboards. Babetta liked knowing they were there to stand between her and hunger.

This year she planned to give a share of her preserves to Aurora, since much of the fruit they'd been picking came from her garden. She was trying to work out just how much would be fair when she saw the Englishwoman appearing at her front gate.

'Babetta? Babetta? Are you home?' she was calling.

'Signora?' Babetta stepped out onto her terrace and shaded her eyes. 'Come in. I was just about to make some coffee. Can I offer you a cup?'

'That would be lovely.' Aurora came up the path, the

little dog at her heels. 'Actually, I've come to ask if you wouldn't mind doing me a favour?'

'Of course. What can I do?'

'I have to go back to London for a few weeks to get ready for an exhibition of my work. I wondered if you'd be able to take care of Sky for me while I'm gone. He's a good boy. I'm sure he won't be any trouble.'

Babetta looked down at the dog. It wagged its tail and panted up at her. 'He can stay with us,' she said, trying to disguise her relief that it was the animal the Englishwoman had come about, not the house.

'Oh, that's fantastic, thanks. He won't miss me too much, hopefully, with you and your husband for company.' Aurora paused. 'Oh and there's one more thing.'

'Yes?' Babetta asked tentatively.

'The work you've been doing in the garden? If things go well in London then perhaps we can come to a more formal arrangement. A regular sum like you used to get from the old owners. You've been doing such a good job.'

Babetta tried not to let the relief show on her face. 'Thank you.'

'You're welcome to take the produce you've grown at Villa Rosa, of course. Perhaps you can sell it? Alice told me the woman who runs the trattoria she worked in buys fresh vegetables from people all the time.'

'Raffaella Ricci, yes, I know her.'

'Well I'll call and suggest she drops by then, shall I? Oh, and I'll bring Sky over with his bedding and his food bowl on Sunday. Thank you so much. I really appreciate this.'

Once she'd gone, Babetta went to look for Nunzio. He was down near the chicken coop, turning the compost with a pitchfork.

'The Englishwoman is going back home and she's leaving her dog here with us for a few weeks,' she told him.

He thought about it for a moment, then nodded and went back to turning the compost.

'I have enough do to round here, especially at this time of year,' she persisted, 'so I thought you might be in charge of feeding it and taking it for walks.'

He looked again. '*Va bene,* I'll feed him. I'll walk him,' he said brusquely.

It was by far the longest sentence he'd managed in such a long time and Babetta felt tears starting in her eyes. She brushed them away quickly with her hand and went back to the pans that were bubbling with sticky sweetness in her kitchen.

Alice

I never thought I'd be thrilled to read a bad review of Teatro, especially not one from the *London Evening Standard's* fearsome Fay Maschler. Thankfully, it wasn't the food she'd taken issue with but the service. The wait-staff had been in a brittle mood that night, thanks to their tormentor Raoul. It might have been OK had Teatro been a mid-range restaurant but at the prices our customers were paying they expected slick service, not snippiness. There had been shouting in the kitchen, some knife throwing, a few pans chucked around, Raoul demonstrating his famous trick with the tea towel where he flicked it so hard at the waiters that it cracked like a whip. Fay Maschler had missed none of it.

'Tonino is going to freak,' I told Charlie. 'He'll be back at Teatro so fast he'll leave scorch marks. That lunatic Raoul is deep in the shit.'

'She liked the food though ...'

'Yeah, but it's not just about the food. For Tonino everything has to be perfect. The fact that no one in the dining room recognised her will be enough to send him into a tailspin. No, he'll be back and then let's see how long Raoul lasts.'

What I didn't expect was that Tonino's reappearance would make things worse for me. He was there the very next day, just as I'd expected. By the time I got in he'd spent hours holding a tense post-mortem with the senior staff. Everyone in the kitchen was subdued, especially Raoul, and I couldn't wait to see what was going to happen.

I tried to eavesdrop on a hushed conversation that was taking place near the walk-in as I set up my *mise-en-place*. A couple of bookings had cancelled for that evening and by the sound of it Tonino was certain the review was to blame. Risking a glance over at him, I saw how the furrow in his brow was too deep for a man of his age. He looked tired rather than angry. Word was the City restaurant was going over budget and his backers weren't happy. Tonino had a lot of problems.

When he noticed me glancing over, his expression changed. He smiled briefly and, once he'd finished his conversation, came over.

'So, Alice, how was your summer in Italy?'

It felt like the entire kitchen had switched their antennae my way. 'Brilliant, thanks, chef,' I said, aware everyone was listening.

'And my parents, how are they?'

'Good. I loved working for them in their restaurant. And I helped your brother too in the pizzeria.' Now people were openly staring at us.

Tonino frowned. 'I didn't send you to learn how to make pizza, Alice ... I hope you haven't been wasting your time.'

'No, I learnt a lot. Thanks for setting it all up for me. I really do appreciate it, chef.' Even the chastened Raoul was looking our way and I wished Tonino would hurry up and move on.

'No problem.' He patted me on the shoulder just to make sure everyone knew for certain I was in favour. 'We'll have a proper chat some time about what you cooked while you were there. I'd love to hear all about it.'

For the next couple of nights Tonino paced around the kitchen, keeping an eye on every single detail. He put in appearances in the dining room, going from table to table, shaking hands. It was something he'd always avoided but now he must have thought it was important to show his face.

The third night there was no sign of him. The mood in the kitchen was muted but still once or twice Raoul managed to come past and give me a shove. I thought he might have whispered a couple of insults too, the word *puta*, perhaps, but so softly that I couldn't be sure.

In the weeks that followed Tonino took to dropping in unannounced and for Raoul and his cronies it became a cat and mouse game. How much could they get away with when he wasn't there? How quickly could they tone it down when he arrived?

The loutish behaviour escalated and I noticed there was a lot of unnecessary foot traffic in and out of the walk-in. At first I thought they'd stashed some alcohol in there but then I began to suspect it was something more than that – cocaine probably. Raoul could seem especially wired at times and he'd always had a habit of sniffing a lot.

Not that I said anything to Tonino. By singling me out he had given Raoul all the excuse he needed to step up his little war on me. He was much more open about his shoves and insults now. Sometimes they even raised a laugh.

So I cringed the next time Tonino came in and made a point of calling over to me. 'Hey, Alice. Don't forget you still have to tell me all about your trip to Italy.'

'Sure, chef,' I nodded, without looking over at him.

'Oh, and there's something I've been meaning to tell you. Your friend Guyon is back in town. He has a job and is doing OK, I hear. I thought you might want to look him up.'

This time I raised my eyes from my work. 'Really? Thanks,' I said gratefully. 'I will.'

The relief was huge. Guyon was exactly what I needed right now. It would be unfair to overload him with my problems when he was fresh out of rehab, but still I couldn't wait to tell him about Raoul. Surely he'd have come across chefs like him? I could make him laugh with my stories and see if he had any advice.

I couldn't wait to see him again.

Babetta

The shutters of Villa Rosa were closed against the sun and the house looked blank-faced and unfriendly, just as it had for most of the years Babetta had lived beside it. But now there was a deeper sadness about its emptiness. It had been abandoned.

As she worked in the garden Babetta missed the sound of other people, the clinking of their dishes echoing from the kitchen, the swell of their voices, even the clatter of a typewriter to break up the monotony of the summer-long buzz of crickets. She tried to stop her spirits from sinking, to remind herself she still had most of what she wanted, but a sort of lethargy seemed to have taken hold of her. Everything took longer and seemed harder, she needed to rest more, felt new aches, seemed clumsier. Autumn's onset became a worry and for once she began to wonder if her daughter was right. Perhaps she had grown too old for this life.

As Babetta felt age squeeze her, it seemed to loosen its grip on Nunzio. He worked longer and later, harvesting the pomegranates from the trees, lighting fires to burn spent crops, sweeping the paths clean even though there was no one but her and Sky to walk along them.

The little dog had pushed its way into every part of his life. While he ate, it stood beneath the table, its head pressed against his leg, hoping for titbits. It slept on a pile of old rugs at the foot of his bed and woke when he did. Wherever Nunzio went, it stayed at his heels.

Babetta watched how he was with the creature, constantly reaching down to stroke its head or feed it something from his fingers, muttering to it beneath his breath while he worked. Sometimes he would stop to smile as it skittered after a leaf or chased away a bird. And when he rested in his cane chair, it seemed content to rest with him.

One afternoon her husband was sitting in the shade of a tree to escape the heat with the dog collapsed next to him panting. Babetta saw how he held out his hand to be licked and then rested his arm across the animal's shoulders.

For a while she watched the two companions, so close, so peaceful together. And despite herself, Babetta felt jealous.

Alice

I found Guyon working in a vegetarian café in Covent Garden, one of those places set up to do lunches for office workers. The food was quite simple: big salads full of fresh herbs and pulses, a couple of soups, a few sandwiches and cakes. It was the sort of thing he should have been able to knock out without even trying but as soon as I set eyes on him I could tell he was struggling.

Guyon looked vulnerable, beaten up by life. It was shocking to see him like that, as if a curtain had been drawn back and the room inside didn't look the way I'd expected. Still, when he spotted me, he managed to haul his old self back somehow. For a moment or two he was the Guyon I knew.

'So, little Alice, are you still on the road to becoming a top chef then?' he said with a wobbly grin.

'It's a rocky, dangerous road full of potholes,' I told him.

It was pretty obvious to me that Guyon needed help. There were piles of vegetables to be chopped, huge white bowls waiting to be filled with food and it wasn't that far off lunchtime. Almost automatically I washed my hands and pitched in, dicing onions, carrots and celery to make the base for a soup. Guyon looked surprised but didn't comment.

'I told you working at Teatro would be tough, didn't I?' he said as we cooked together. 'If you're going to have a successful career in a top kitchen you have to really love food. Be obsessed with it even. Otherwise it would be an unbearable sort of life.'

'Yes, but it's not the food that's unbearable.'

As I hacked up butternut squash for the soup, I regaled him with tales of Raoul. Just confiding every barely-veiled insult and surreptitious shove made me feel much better. The soup was bubbling and I was busy grating beetroot for a raw energy salad by the time I managed to stop talking about it.

Guyon hadn't said much up till then, just nodded a lot as though he'd heard it all before.

'What am I going to do?' I asked him.

'Well, the obvious thing is to leave, surely? There are plenty of other kitchens in town. There's no reason you have to stay in that one.'

'But then Raoul will have won.'

'It's not a competition, Alice. Anyway, he's already winning if he's making you this unhappy. So get out of the place. I don't know why you've stuck it out for so long. You're a determined little thing, aren't you?'

The trouble was Teatro was the only link I had left with Tonino's family and I wasn't quite ready to let it go. I didn't want to admit that though so I stayed silent for a while, busying myself stirring crushed peanuts through the grated beetroot and adding finely chopped red onion that had been soaked in lemon juice until it had plumped up and turned pink. With fresh coriander sprinkled on top, and a dressing spiked with chilli I was quite pleased with my creation.

'Surely Raoul has to get sick of tormenting me?' I said eventually. 'If I stick it out, prove myself, then he'll have to give me a break.'

'Perhaps ... I doubt it though. Once a bully always a bully.' Guyon took my beetroot salad and put it out on the counter next to the food he'd prepared. 'Why don't you see if you can get into the kitchen of this new place Tonino is opening?'

'Nah, he's already told everyone he's not going to take staff from one to the other. Teatro is the flagship. He doesn't want to weaken it with too many changes. He came and gave us all a little pep talk and said that very thing.'

'I bet he did. I expect the review in the *Standard* spooked him. Bad timing, that. He'll have a lot riding on this new place. Needs Teatro's reputation to bring people in.'

'Actually, Tonino looks terrible, completely knackered,' I confided. 'I wonder if he's regretting trying to open a second restaurant?'

Guyon gave the soup a stir. 'An ambitious man like him? He wouldn't have been able to help himself. I've seen this so many times before. The first restaurant is a big success, they think they've got it cracked so they open another and then another until they have an empire.'

'But if they're not careful surely the whole thing can come crashing round their ears.'

'Exactly.'

'God ... I hope that doesn't happen to Tonino.'

'I hope so too. He can be an arrogant sod at times but he was good to me when things were at a very low point.' It was the first time Guyon had come close to referring to his stint in rehab.

'I know he was,' I said in a soft voice, and then risked a question, 'What about now? How are you?'

'Yeah, OK.' Guyon didn't seem ready for this conversation.

'Are you feeling better? Stronger?' I persisted anyway.

'Not really, Alice.' It sounded like it cost him to admit it. 'Not all that much stronger at all.'

I didn't want to see Guyon fall back into drinking but could think of only one way to help. So early every morning, before the counter staff arrived, I turned up at the little vegetarian place. I never explained why I was doing it and Guyon didn't ask. We worked together side by side like we had in the prep kitchen at Teatro. Sometimes he criticised the way I'd chopped something, or insisted on adding an ingredient to one of my dishes. I didn't mind. To me it was a sign he was regaining his confidence.

The long hours I was working didn't bother me either. If my hands weren't busy preparing food and my brain not tied up with the next chore I felt kind of edgy. It was as though working hard was the only thing that held everything up. It meant I didn't have the energy to worry or the time to plan ahead. Work filled my whole world and I didn't mind.

Better that, I thought, than to leave it hollow and empty.

Babetta

Babetta's kitchen was filled with pomegranates – baskets of them overflowing with the waxy fruit Nunzio had been picking all week. The very sight of them exhausted her. She almost wished they'd been left to fall and rot.

Last autumn the trees had given them easily as many pomegranates. She'd spent hours cutting them open and squeezing out the juice then produced jars of rich red jelly and syrup. It hadn't been so difficult.

Only a year had gone by since then but Babetta felt she'd aged a decade. The thought of the work waiting to be done sent her out to Nunzio's empty cane chair on the terrace, where she sat for a while watching her husband who was stacking wood ready for winter, the dog close by as usual.

Babetta tried not to think of the pomegranates or the energy required to score their leathery skins with a sharp knife, pull out the fleshy seeds and squeeze them dry of juice inside a muslin bag. She wished the job were finished, that the juice had been boiled with sugar and lemon until it had thickened and was already poured into clean jars and stacked up in her storecupboard.

The sound of a car coming down the hill was a welcome distraction. For a moment Babetta wondered if it were the Englishwoman, back so soon from London, and she worried what Nunzio might say when she asked for her little dog back. But this was a different car, darker and smaller, and the woman who climbed from it was a little older and much more beautiful.

'*Ciao*, Raffaella,' Babetta called out, rising from her chair.

'*Ciao*,' Raffaella called back, stopping to pat the dog before coming up the path. 'Your English neighbour phoned me. She thought there might be some produce to sell. Told me you've been growing vegetables all summer and now there's no one here to eat them.'

'Yes, there's plenty. Come and see.'

Unlocking the gates of Villa Rosa, Babetta led the way to the terraced garden with its neat rows of leafy green vegetables and herbs rippling slightly in the breeze.

'Oh you've grown *cime di rapa*, I'd love some of that.' Raffaella exclaimed. 'And chicory, parsley, radicchio. How much can I take?'

'As much as you want, *cara*. Most of it will only go to waste.'

Babetta fetched some baskets from the house and helped Raffaella fill them with the herbs and vegetables she'd chosen. 'It's a treasure trove,' she was murmuring appreciatively. 'Ciro will be thrilled. He's sure to send me back for more.'

It was when they were wandering back up the path that Raffaella noticed the trees had been stripped of pomegranates. 'Now that's a big job,' she said. 'I remember doing it myself once. What do you do with all the fruit?'

Babetta sighed. 'It's in my kitchen waiting for me. Usually I make jars of pomegranate syrup and jelly. This year I don't seem to have the strength for it.'

'Pomegranate syrup,' mused Raffaella. 'Excellent to glaze a piece of pork, to baste a goose or roasting chicken.'

'Good for all those things,' agreed Babetta.

'I got that from my mother's recipe book,' Raffaella explained. 'The one she left to me when she died. But it's a while since I've had any pomegranate syrup to cook with.'

'If I ever get round to making it I'll remember to save you some,' Babetta promised.

Raffaella turned to her. 'Why don't I help? I'll work in return for a share of the syrup.'

'Really?' A little of the burden eased from Babetta's shoulders. 'Would you mind?'

'I'd like to. We'll take turns cutting and squeezing the fruit.'

'It's a messy job,' Babetta warned. 'Be sure to wear old clothes.'

'Yes, yes, I remember. Nothing stains like fresh pomegranate juice.'

She had expected Raffaella to forget her promise. But a couple of days later there she was, dressed in old overalls and ready to work, unfazed by the sight of so many baskets filled with fruit. She even half-smiled when she saw them and cradled the first pomegranate in her hand before cutting into it with the sharp knife Babetta had given her.

'So beautiful,' she said. 'The skin glows as though it's been polished by hand. I never liked the juice though. I found it too bitter to drink on its own.'

'That's why I make the syrup,' Babetta agreed. 'Even though it's much more work.'

They made a good team, Raffaella cutting the fruit while Babetta pressed it for juice. She noticed how Nunzio steered well clear while there was a stranger in the house. Now and then she thought she heard him whistling for the dog but was too busy squeezing the red flesh and straining its juices into a bowl to worry about him.

As they worked, they chatted, Raffaella speaking about her sons, her longing for at least one of them to marry and have children, her hopes that the restaurants they'd worked so hard for would be passed down through the family. In turn, Babetta talked about the past, the precious letters she so rarely received from her sister in America, the

ways Triento had changed and the ways it hadn't. Talking
and working all afternoon long they emptied the baskets of
pomegranates until all they had left were cast off piles of
rind and drying seeds and tall jugs of saved red liquid for
Babetta to simmer and thicken.

'All that fruit won't boil down to much,' warned
Raffaella.

'Every year I say the same thing,' agreed Babetta. 'Still,
there'll be enough to last us till next autumn and that's the
important thing.'

'Tonight I'll talk to Ciro about how we'll use it in the
trattoria.' Raffaella smiled. 'Once, many years ago, I
cooked a duck with pomegranate syrup, blood oranges and
sweet onions. Perhaps I'll try that again.'

'It sounds delicious.' Babetta couldn't remember the last
time she'd eaten a meal that someone else had cooked. 'I'd
love to taste a dish like that.'

'Why don't you come to eat with us then?' Raffaella
encouraged. 'You and Nunzio could use the old Vespa I
lent to Alice. It's still over at Villa Rosa somewhere. And it
wouldn't cost you anything. You can pay us in vegetables.'

'Nunzio wouldn't come,' Babetta said regretfully.

'Just ask him. Perhaps he'll say yes.'

Babetta thought about Nunzio. His trousers were held
up with an old piece of cord and his hands were ingrained
with dirt. A crushed old hat rarely left his head and it had
been years since he had strayed more than a few metres
from home. There was no way he would go to eat on the
terrace of a restaurant as tourists walked by. No chance it
would ever happen.

Alice

Tonino kept singling me out for special attention and Raoul carried on hassling me. It occurred to me that I was an idiot trying to stick it out, especially as by far the best part of my day was spent whipping up salads and soups at the vegetarian café. I loved the freedom of throwing together my own combinations of seasonal ingredients, cooking by taste rather than rote. Cooking with love, I suppose, just like Lucio had said I should.

But taking a permanent job in a little café seemed a defeat. I worked for the hottest chef in London, was on track for a career at the top. Walking away would be madness, I insisted, whenever Charlie nagged me about the hours I was putting in and the frayed, emotional state he found me in on the rare occasions I was at home.

'So you really think you want to be a top chef?' he asked me one Sunday night. 'Is that your ambition? What about family, kids? You probably can't have both.'

'I'm still in my twenties,' I pointed out, as I slumped on the sofa, TV remote in hand, flicking through channels. 'I can't think that far into the future.'

Charlie looked sad. 'The thing is I *am* thinking about the future. I want to be married and have children one day. I'd like to do those things with you but ...'

'Didn't I tell you not to even talk about marriage? I made that completely clear when we moved in together.'

'Yeah, I know that.'

'So?'

Charlie took the TV remote and punched the mute button. 'How long are you going to keep punishing me for that one mistake I made ... that one stupid infidelity?' he asked.

'I'm not punishing you.'

'It seems to me that you are. Why can't you forgive me, Alice? What's holding you back? I'd love to know.'

'You dumped me and then I was raped.' I could hardly bring myself to say the word. 'That was hardly just an infidelity, not exactly a one-night stand.'

'Then maybe we go for counselling, or therapy, or whatever it is people do to get over things like that.' He said it quite gently. 'You know, Alice, we're both getting older and we've been together a long time. It's time for us to move forward with our lives.'

'What does that even mean?' I asked, my tone scathing. 'Move forward? That's just some dumb thing people say.'

'It means I want us to start thinking about the future. Not just marriage and babies but who we are and what we want. I need for us to plan a life together.'

This was exactly the conversation I hadn't wanted to have with Charlie. I couldn't believe he'd managed to railroad me into it.

'And what if I say I'm perfectly happy with the way things are and don't need to do any planning or get over anything?' I asked.

'Then there'll have to be some changes.' Charlie sounded regretful.

'What sort of changes?'

Looking uncomfortable, he stared at the silenced television.

'Charlie?'

'Well, OK ... if it turns out we don't want the same things from life and that you're not prepared to make any effort ... it would make sense to—' He stopped then tried to start again. 'It's not what I want but …'

Suddenly it dawned on me what was happening. 'Charlie, you're dumping me,' I said.

'No I'm not.'

'But you're giving me an ultimatum?'

'I'm asking you to think about what you want from life, that's all. And if it turns out we want different things then yes, maybe we should go our separate ways. It might be best for both of us.'

My first reaction was fury. 'Oh, for God's sake, I've got enough to deal with right now without this.' Grabbing the remote, I turned the sound back on.

Charlie shrugged and retreated to our bedroom to read or listen to music. Once he'd gone I started to feel more sad than angry. For years I'd relied on our relationship and now it looked like I was going to lose it unless I agreed to marriage. And how could I do that when I knew my head had been so easily turned by the show and glitter of a man like Lucio? The TV series I'd been watching was some sort of comedy but still I was crying.

The next night at work Raoul seemed to pick up on my more sensitive mood and started on me right from the beginning of the shift.

'Bit down in the mouth, Alice? Got your period have you? On the rag, eh?'

As always I kept my mouth shut.

'See, that's why women don't make top chefs,' he announced to the rest of the kitchen. 'Up and down with their hormones they are. Inconsistent.'

He glanced at me to see if he'd got any sort of reaction. Trying to keep my expression blank, I focused on putting together my *mise-en-place*.

'Just look at the top chefs in the world right now. All men, right?' he went on. 'Women can't cut it. Don't know why they bother trying. They don't belong.'

No one risked speaking up, especially not Sarah the pastry chef who liked to give Raoul the widest berth possible and seemed relieved I was the one bearing the brunt. Somehow I managed to stay quiet too. But I was getting really tired of putting up with this.

Later that night I cleaned up and got out of the place in record time. By then I'd pretty much given up on going drinking with the rest of the crew so I went straight back to the flat and tried to unwind with a bottle of beer and a copy of the morning's newspaper that Charlie had left open on the kitchen table.

He'd circled a big review of a gallery opening. Next to it were images of three or four paintings, all of a familiar view. Layered slabs of blue fell towards solid blocks of islands and the always-moving sea. This was the work Aurora had completed over summer. Some of it I recognised, some she must have painted after I left. It was interesting to see what her brush had made of the scenes and I wished she'd painted other things too ... Babetta crouched over her vegetable beds, Nunzio pushing his wheelbarrow, the strand of pomegranate trees and the pink-washed house beyond it. Perhaps the art critic was thinking much the same thing when he looked at them. The work was technically brilliant, he wrote, but it was time Aurora moved on, reinvented herself.

There was no photo of Leila but I knew she'd have been there at the opening, supporting her mother. And even though it had been my choice not to stay a part of their lives, it was impossible not to feel some regret.

I drank my beer and stared at the blue-sky paintings, listening to the rumble of Charlie snoring in the bedroom. I'd let go of Leila and now it seemed I was about to lose him too. How much more could I mess up my own life?

Babetta

There was a sense of satisfaction in seeing the rows of pre-serves mounting up in her cupboards, so many full jars that Babetta was sure she would soon run out of space. Every time the pomegranate syrup caught her eye, she thought of Raffaella's invitation to go and eat at their little trattoria down at the port.

She knew she could ask her daughter to take her. Sofia would be thrilled to eat a meal out, to make it obvious her mother knew the restaurant owners and have an excuse to wear her smartest clothes and her most uncomfortable shoes. But Babetta had a picture in her mind of Nunzio sitting across a table from her right at the harbour's edge. She could see a white tablecloth and linen napkins, a carafe of red wine and cutlery that had been polished till it gleamed. She could taste the marriage of duck and pomegranate and imagine the expression on her husband's face as he enjoyed it. Three or four times a day she took to breaking from work and staring up at the statue of Christ on the mountain, wondering how she could make it happen.

One morning she even went and found the old Vespa that Alice had used during her stay. She wheeled it out round to the front of the house where Nunzio could see it.

'Look,' she said to him. 'What do you think?'

He shrugged and glanced down at the little dog and then up at the scooter.

Babetta nodded as though he'd spoken. 'Yes, you're right. That might be a problem. I'll see what I can do.'

It had been many years since she'd woven a basket but Babetta's fingers hadn't forgotten. She worked at night at the kitchen table after Nunzio had taken the dog upstairs and they'd both fallen asleep. The first few she made didn't seem sturdy enough, the shoulder straps were too long or too narrow, the basket itself not quite the right size. But, fuelled with slices of crusty bread spread thickly with pomegranate jelly, Babetta kept weaving until she was completely satisfied with her work.

When she showed him what she'd made, Nunzio seemed uncertain. Still, he agreed to slip the woven knapsack onto his back and didn't complain when she lowered the little dog Sky into it.

As for the creature, it didn't mind. It was close to Nunzio and that was all that seemed to matter.

Babetta didn't suggest going anywhere on the Vespa, not for a while. Nunzio was happy to amble round the garden, the dog at his heels, and she was content to watch.

Raffaella came twice a week until the vegetable beds had been thoroughly plundered. She raised her eyebrows when she saw the Vespa still sitting beneath the pomegranate tree in the centre of the courtyard.

'Have you used it yet?'

Babetta shook her head.

'Tell your husband to start it and take it up the hill. The thing is ancient. If it's left sitting around too long it'll only seize up.'

Nunzio simply nodded when she repeated what Raffaella had told her. Later that day she spotted him tinkering with the old scooter and then saw him roaring up and down the hill, the little dog running behind him. He did the same thing every couple of days, putting the dog in the basket on his back if he thought it was too hot or too tired.

When Raffaella came to collect her final haul of vege-tables she noticed the Vespa had been moved. 'Oh good, you got it going,' she exclaimed. 'Perfect timing. I tried out the duck dish the other night and it was delicious so we're putting it on the menu tomorrow. I'll reserve a table for you, shall I?'

'Oh, I don't think so ...' Babetta began.

'I got the ducks from old Angelo Sesto. He's been fattening them up for me. They'll be perfect. You mustn't miss them.'

Awkwardly, Babetta shook her head. 'Nunzio won't come,' she said. 'It's no use trying.'

But Raffaella simply chose to ignore her. 'I'll reserve the table, Babetta,' she repeated. 'We'll be waiting for you.'

Alice

The night I lost it completely was the most unexpected thing. Raoul had been fairly quiet that shift, only one or two cracks of the tea towel in my direction, and then all of a sudden he came past, put his palm down flat on my buttock, grabbed a big handful of flesh and squeezed it hard.

'Getting a bit lardy aren't we, Alice?' he remarked.

I happened to be holding a long-handled fork at the time. Without thinking I wheeled round and jabbed it towards him. He was quick on his feet, jumping clear, otherwise I'm certain I'd have stabbed him.

There was this awful frozen moment of silence while we both processed what had happened. Then Raoul said gleefully, 'You are so very, very fired. Don't think being Tonino's little friend will help you now. Even he's not going to let you get away with this.'

'You can't fire me because I quit,' I said.

'Is that so? Well get out then. And don't bother coming back.'

I changed out of my chef's whites as quickly as I could. As I bundled them up and shoved them in my locker the tears came. Now I really did have nothing left.

No one could quite meet my eye as I walked out past the kitchen for the final time. I hailed a cab and went straight to Guyon's little flat in Maida Vale. By then he'd finished work and was sitting over an open bottle of red wine. I didn't comment on his drinking, just let him fetch me a glass and joined him.

'Maybe I should try doing something else. I don't think I'm tough enough to cook,' I told him as I gulped down the alcohol.

He clicked his tongue. 'Tonight you can get drunk, tomorrow you should buy the newspaper and start looking for another job. Not all head chefs are like Raoul. You'll find a good kitchen to work in.'

'But do you think I should go to see Tonino? Explain what's happened? I feel like I've let him down.'

'I wouldn't bother. Just make a fresh start. Forget about him.'

'What if Raoul bad-mouths me all over town and I can't get a job?'

'I managed to get work after everything that's happened with me. All you did was try to stab the head chef.' Guyon started to laugh. 'God, I wish I'd seen it.'

'There's a part of me that wishes I'd actually made contact,' I admitted. 'Honestly, I don't know what happened. I've never done anything like that before in my life.'

Guyon was a good friend. He put the word out among a few people he knew and before long I had a job in a French restaurant in Covent Garden. It specialised in pre-theatre menus and late at night was often filled with actors. They drank a lot, didn't eat much and hardly ever settled their bills so it wasn't exactly a huge surprise when the place closed within a couple of weeks and I found myself unemployed again.

I might have been tempted to crawl into bed and throw the blankets over my head for a few weeks but I was frightened things were about to come to a head with Charlie and then I'd be jobless and homeless, which didn't bear thinking about. My mother was really worried and kept telling me I could go home and stay with her but it was the very last thing I wanted. She lived her life in over-heated

197

rooms, on a schedule dictated by the *TV Times*, and took her opinions directly from the pages of the tabloid press. By the end of a weekend together we'd almost always had a big fight about something.

So I jumped at the chance of a temporary position at a spaghetti place near Holborn. The chef had gone home to his sick father in Italy for a few months and I was left in charge of his menu. It was only a cheap and cheerful place but I really enjoyed cooking there. Yes, I was boiling up dried pasta instead of freshly made, and then drowning it in red sauce rather than letting its own character shine through. Yes, the risotto was pre-made then 'finished' when an order came in. The bread and desserts were bought, not made on the premises, and the seafood we served up all arrived frozen. There was nothing flash about any of it. But it was fun.

I was back to holding life at bay with hard work and feeling like everything was under control again. I didn't let myself worry about what might happen when the permanent chef came back, and I skirted round Charlie, acting as though there'd never been any talk about our future, carrying on as normal.

Then one night I got home late and found him sleeping on the sofa, a couple of suitcases stacked beside him.

'Charlie.' I shook him awake. 'What do you think you're doing?'

'I'm leaving you first thing in the morning, Alice. I'm really sorry.'

'Don't do this. Please. I need you.'

'Yeah, I know you need me. But do you care about me?' And he turned his face to the back of the sofa and closed his eyes.

He spoke to me again just as I was on my way out the room. 'Oh, and your mate Guyon called. He said to tell you he's booked himself back into rehab. Wants you to go and see him first thing about a job somewhere. Maybe your career's about to get back on the up and up, Alice.'

Babetta

To Babetta it seemed like a miracle. Although Nunzio was as hushed as ever, his attention divided between the dog and the food on his plate, everything else was as she'd imagined. The day was a still one with the first bite of winter in the air. The crowds of tourists had thinned and the two of them were the only ones hardy enough to be eating outside. Raffaella had given them a table near the water's edge. There were no menus, no decisions to be made. Food and wine was brought and placed before them, and then Raffaella slipped away without speaking.

It had been easier than Babetta expected to coax her husband to this place. She'd dressed him in musty clothes that had lain for years in their old dresser and although he'd seemed a little confused, he had been compliant. Then she put the woven knapsack on his back, placed the dog in it and steered him towards the Vespa.

It felt like a real freedom to be riding the coast road, Nunzio in front and the dog safe between them. He hadn't seemed to care much where they were heading. Silently he'd followed her directions until they'd arrived at the port. There he'd been more anxious, fussing with the dog's collar and struggling to attach its lead, but still he'd allowed himself to be herded towards the trattoria.

If Raffaella had behaved differently things might not have continued so well. But she didn't bother with a greeting, made no sort of fuss at all. Just showed them to a table and left them in peace.

And now Nunzio was eating the duck, relishing the sweet-sour flavours of the dish, a sly hand darting beneath the table every now and then so the dog could taste it too.

Each time the restaurant door opened, Babetta heard the hum of conversation rise. All around the harbour there were groups of people enjoying the gentle autumn sunshine, walking side by side, stopping for a while to exchange a few words with an acquaintance. Sitting at their table outside the trattoria, she felt a part of things, yet separate from them.

The flavours of the food Raffaella had brought seemed unusually intense and the sip or two of wine she'd taken had gone straight to her head. Babetta ate as slowly as she could, knowing each rich mouthful took her a little closer to the moment this rare and perfect day would be over.

Alice

The timing was perfect for me in a way. Guyon was checking himself back into rehab before his drinking got out of control. He seemed really positive about the decision, buoyant even. But he needed a chef to fill in for him at the vegetarian café for a few weeks, someone who wouldn't try to pinch the job while he was out of town, and I was the obvious choice. I could work days there and nights at the spaghetti house until the Italian chef came back. My time would be so jammed full I'd barely even notice Charlie had moved out. It was exactly what I needed.

Still, it was harder work than I'd expected, coping with stuff like ordering and costing out meals. None of it had been part of any job I'd held before and I blundered along, hoping things would come right in the end so long as I focused on not wasting anything and bought cheap, seasonal produce. I thought a lot about Tonino, the planning that went into his menu, the careful budgeting and setting of prices. But this was only for a few weeks so how much damage could I do? As long as the food was good and the customers went home happy then I'd have done my job properly.

In many ways it was a lonely time. There were lots of people around me but none who cared to hear the thoughts in my head, no one to share my worries or random ideas. Leila, Charlie, Guyon ... they'd been my family and now I was having to survive without them.

From Monday to Friday my life followed the same

crushing, relentless routine. Up early to prep at the café, a busy lunchtime and then I'd clean and plan for the next day. As soon as I'd finished I'd jump in a cab and speed to the spaghetti house in Holborn to do the same thing all over again. By the time I made it home late every night I was exhausted and, with only a few hours for sleep ahead of me, longed to fall into bed.

Extra locks had been fitted on the doors and windows of the garden flat but still I didn't much like being there alone. Before I went to sleep I had to check every room, inside the wardrobe and beneath the bed. Every breath of wind through the trees in the garden woke me and every police siren set my heart banging. As soon as things calmed down at work there would be time to find another place to live, somewhere high up with several flights of stairs and multiple locks between me and strangers. Until then this flat would have to do.

Weekends weren't great because I had too much time to fill. The vegetarian place was closed, leaving me with empty hours to get through before I could go to work at the spaghetti house. I bought *Time Out* and circled exhibitions and movies but never bothered to go to any of them because I'd have felt awkward alone, surrounded by couples and families. Instead I stayed home and played around with food, preparing pizza dough the way Lucio had shown me, or making fresh pasta parcels filled with pumpkin and goat's cheese. Not that I ever ate much but making it comforted me.

The one person I couldn't get out of my mind on those long, empty days was Tonino. I regretted the way things had ended at Teatro, especially as I knew I'd be wearing all the blame for it. Who would dare tell him the truth, after all? No one wanted to rile Raoul and risk becoming his new target. Even the waiters, who hated him, wouldn't want to be involved.

For all I racked my brains I couldn't see how I could get near Tonino to explain what had actually taken place. I wasn't welcome at Teatro, nor could I turn up at Palio, his new place in the City, and hang round hoping to bump into him.

I'd saved an article I'd found in one of the Sunday colour supplements that had been published when the new restaurant had only just opened for business. They'd photographed Tonino in chef's whites in the kitchen but the shot that interested me most was a small inset picture of him as a boy. He looked so skinny and serious next to a rounder, smiling Lucio. Sitting between them was Raffaella and I thought I recognised the bench they were on as the one outside the bakery in Triento's main piazza. Every time I pulled out the clipping I felt a bleak sort of nostalgia.

When the spaghetti house chef came back to reclaim his kitchen my evenings were suddenly just as difficult as the weekends. I should have used the free time to find some-where better and cheaper to live but all my energy seemed to have been used up. Enervated, I spent hours lying on the sofa flipping through recipe books, once dozing off and waking an hour or so later with my head resting gently against a photo of veal chops and new potatoes.

In the end it was Tonino who came to me. He appeared at the vegetarian café in the middle of a Monday afternoon when I was chewing on the end of a pencil, trying to come up with some semblance of a plan for the rest of the week's meals.

The familiar sight of his face was so welcome that I grinned as he strolled into the kitchen and then leaned against the counter as though he owned the place.

'I've fired Raoul,' he said abruptly and then was silent, waiting to see how I'd react.

'So have you come to offer me my job back?'

'No.'

'Then why?'

'Why did I fire him?'

'No, why did you come?' I noticed his eyes flicking over my set-up, taking in everything with a couple of glances.

'Well, actually I came to see if you would like to have dinner with me.'

'What?' The question was so unexpected.

'If you're not doing anything this evening then I'd like to take you for dinner.' Tonino sounded oddly formal. 'We've never talked properly about your summer in Italy. And tonight I have some time so it seemed like a good opportunity.'

'Where would we go?'

'Teatro, of course.'

'Why?'

'Alice, these are not appropriate responses to a dinner invitation.' Tonino sounded amused. 'One does not say why and what. One says yes or no. Which is it?'

'Erm ... well, yes, I guess. I'll come for dinner.'

'Very well then. I'll reserve a table for seven. Don't be late.'

'And will you tell me about Raoul?' I asked eagerly. 'Why you fired him?'

He half-laughed. 'I'd have thought of all people you would know.'

After that it was impossible to concentrate on stuff like orders and budgets. Instead of doing sums I tried to imagine myself sitting in the dining room of Teatro, with Tonino opposite me, making conversation as familiar waiters rushed to serve us and my old co-workers cooked our food.

It seemed like the strangest idea and yet I was impatient for it to happen.

Babetta

Winter had always been an empty time for Babetta, driven indoors by wind and rain while the garden fell to its hands and knees around them. There was little to do but chop wood, keep the fire stoked and simmer warming soups and stews on the stove. But this year things were different.

Even though Villa Rosa remained closed and the storms hit the coast as hard as they ever had, Babetta couldn't remember a winter like this one. It was all thanks to the Vespa that Raffaella had insisted they keep. The battered old machine had opened up a world to them again.

Babetta still didn't feel confident enough to ride the scooter alone but on finer days Nunzio could be persuaded to drive her up the hill to Triento, even once or twice taking her to church on a Sunday, although he skulked outside while the priest heard her confession.

Always the dog was between them, snug in the basket on Nunzio's back, so she couldn't wrap her arms round his waist as they curved along the coast road. Still she felt much closer to her husband as he brought them nearer to the world he'd spent so many years isolated from.

Nunzio seemed to enjoy the trips up to Triento or down along the coast to Calabria and the bigger towns that lay a few more kilometres away. Some days he even came to find her, the dog already in the basket on his back and she had to rush to change her headscarf and make herself presentable.

Often now when the butcher arrived at the gates in his

van or the fishmonger came, she sent them away without buying a thing because her kitchen was already full of food she'd bargained for at the market.

People in Triento smiled when they saw them, the old man and his wife with the dog trotting at their heels. Some stopped to pat the little creature and the waitress at the corner bar always had a dish of water ready for it. Nunzio rarely said much but he didn't mind stopping in the street while she exchanged a few pleasantries or a morsel or two of local gossip.

They only stayed in Triento for half an hour or so, long enough for Babetta to take a taste of life. And she was always happy to come home again, to work in her kitchen, making something delicious for Nunzio while he dozed in front of the fire she'd stoked for him.

When the wind was wild or the rain heavy they stayed at home. Babetta busied herself mending old clothes and making pasta that she spread over the kitchen to dry while she took an afternoon nap. She dreamed of spring, the warming of the earth in her garden, the return of the Englishwomen. She dared even to dream of going back to the trattoria down by the harbour and trading her own fresh picked vegetables for Raffaella's wonderful food.

Perhaps she had worries too that life was not supposed to go this well, that something bad was waiting round a corner. But Babetta refused to let them into her mind as she lay beside Nunzio, listening to the rhythm of his snoring and waiting for winter to come to an end.

Alice

I'd been expecting some sort of revelation, for Tonino to explain the real reason he'd issued this dinner invitation. All evening as we ate together I waited but it never came.

Being in Teatro as a customer was like walking into a different world. There was a brief taste of my old life in the heat and clamour of the kitchen as I walked past it to get to the dining room. Casting my eyes sideways, I saw a few familiar faces as well as some I didn't recognise, all working with that fevered concentration I remembered.

Our table was at the far end of the restaurant and Tonino made sure I was seated with my back to the glass wall of the kitchen. Once there, surrounded by the towering wine bottles reflecting the candlelight back at me, it was amazingly easy to forget about all the effort being made elsewhere. I lost myself in the luxury of starched white linen and shining crystal and in the little rituals, the opening of my menu, the tasting of the wine, choosing a fresh-baked roll from a basket.

There were new dishes to choose from as Tonino liked to keep the menu fresh. But I spotted old favourites too and I wondered who was working the pasta station now.

'Why don't I order for you?' Tonino asked, although it wasn't really a question.

'That would be good,' I agreed, setting my menu aside.

He chose quickly, rattling the orders off without seeming to consider them much. Little dumplings of potato with a wild herb sauce, mushrooms with a purée of beans, peppers cooked with almonds, a salad of porcini and truffles, roasted rabbit. There was more food than we could possibly finish but I knew that wasn't expected. It was a matter of tasting and appreciating for Tonino, not filling up without restraint.

'So how is Palio going?' I asked once the waiter had disappeared to the kitchen with our order.

Tonino made a face as though he'd swallowed something bitter. 'There are still some teething problems. It's twice the size of this dining room, you know, and the clientele is very different. There were many things I hadn't anticipated. Still, we're getting there.'

Remembering how I used to call out endless obedient 'Yes, chefs' to Tonino, I felt almost honoured to be sitting with him now, listening to his problems.

'Who is head chef here now?' I asked, hoping to steer the conversation back towards his showdown with Raoul.

'I promoted Nico. He's doing a fantastic job,' was all he said.

'So things have settled down in the kitchen then?' I continued to probe.

'Don't worry, Alice, you'll get a good meal.' Tonino smiled at me. 'Nico knows what he's doing.'

'And what about Raoul?' I pressed him.

'Gone back to New York, I think. More his kind of place.'

It was ages later that I found out what had happened. I bumped into one of the line cooks on the street and he told me all about Tonino dropping in for one of his surprise visits and finding Raoul snorting coke with Nico in the walk-in. Apparently his rage was molten and terrifying. And Tonino was such a softly spoken man, so economical with words and movements; very un-Italian really, so to see his fury transform him was shocking for everyone.

Raoul didn't even bother to argue when he was told to

get out and not come back. As for Nico, he was reduced to begging for his job, promising almost anything to be allowed to keep it. And then Tonino amazed everyone by promoting him, saying he was relying on Nico to keep the kitchen straight and run it exactly how he would himself.

Judging by the food, the ploy was working. Of course, we were only ever going to get the best. There is a heightened sense of tension when an executive chef eats in his own restaurant. Everyone is on their mettle. And with a boss like Tonino, who demands perfection every time, the pressure in the kitchen must have been unbearable.

But the food was beautiful. As I tasted it, here in the dining room Tonino had practically designed himself, I appreciated his genius more than ever.

'So no more Raoul then,' I said as the *amuse bouche* was brought over.

I wondered if Tonino was going to admonish me for losing my cool with him, tell me I was wasting my time and talents cooking dhal soups and cauliflower curries in the vegetarian place. But he didn't even mention it. Instead all we talked about was Italy, the food I'd cooked and eaten there, and what I'd thought of the small town where he'd grown up.

'It's difficult to believe it's only a few months since I was there,' I said.

'You should plan to go back again in spring,' said Tonino. 'I'm sure my parents would appreciate some help once the tourists start arriving.'

I shook my head. 'When Guyon gets back I'll have to find a proper job. I can't afford to take another summer off.'

'Oh well, another year, maybe. I don't suppose my family will be going anywhere.'

Spending time with Tonino was completely unlike being with his brother. He was so quietly spoken I had to lean halfway across the table to hear him over the buzz of the restaurant. And he didn't smile or laugh nearly as much. Life was a serious business for him and eating the most important thing of all. I'd always known he was driven but spending an evening with him, stuck on this little island of a restaurant table, the differences between him and Lucio were so apparent I could understand why they'd never got on.

Through the starter and the main course we talked about inconsequential things. I kept expecting Tonino to get to the point but we ended on cheese and coffee, with the conversation still meandering.

At one stage he slipped off to the bathroom, leaving me alone, and I tried to decide whether I found him attractive or not. It was almost impossible to know what he was thinking, which gave him a certain allure, and I found his quiet intensity compelling. But I wondered if there was something cold about him, something removed. It was as though the shutters were always half down and ready to be slammed closed completely.

We said our goodbyes on the street as Tonino put me into a taxi.

'That was very nice,' he said. 'We'll have to do it again soon.'

I smiled and agreed with him, all the time wondering what on earth it was Tonino wanted from me.

Babetta

Nunzio died before spring. One clear, sunny morning Babetta found him in the cane chair, still and cold, the little dog at his feet. She put a blanket over him and went back inside, moving about the house, doing her chores as though he were only sleeping. At lunchtime she cooked and put his share in the oven like she might have if he were busy working in the garden and would be in to enjoy it later. But then she heard the dog whimpering out on the terrace and the sound seemed to wake her.

Taking a key from the hook behind the door, she walked slowly to Villa Rosa. There had been no reason to go inside the house once the Englishwoman left and she felt like an intruder. But the key had been left in case of emergencies and Babetta decided this must count as one.

To her the place felt chilled and damp. Dust had settled over magazines and books, dead flies lay cast on the window sills. Babetta found the phone and, dialling the number Sofia had written down for her, readied herself to say the words aloud.

After three or four rings, she heard her daughter's voice. '*Pronto*,' Sofia said with her usual energy.

Babetta took a deep breath. 'Your father is gone,' she said, and waited for the sound of wailing to begin.

In the end it was Sofia who took care of everything. She organised for Nunzio's body to be moved to the chapel of rest and planned out the funeral. She wrote a list of things that needed to be done, forms to be filled in, certificates granted, payments to be made, and efficiently ticked them off one by one. She cooked for them both and tidied the house.

Robbed of all her usual concerns, Babetta felt lost. She took to sitting in Nunzio's empty cane chair beneath the blanket that still smelled of him, searching through her memories to find the ones that pleased her most. It was best to think of the times when Sofia was young and Nunzio had taken them to the beach and played with her in the water, lifting the child when the waves came lashing up, making her scream with delight.

Babetta reached down and rubbed her hands through the dog's coarse fur, taking comfort from the warmth of its body. Her mind conjured up an image of Nunzio, stripped down to his swimming trunks, tanned and firm from his work on the road crew. The pair of them had never thought much about the future then, never imagined how soon they would be old.

And now, as she stared out at the view her husband had so often trained his eyes on, Babetta still couldn't bring herself to think about what lay ahead. So she spent the empty hours stroking the dog and kept her mind attached firmly to days gone past.

It felt safer to stay there.

Alice

I was pleased when Guyon emerged from rehab looking chipper and ready to get back to work. It did leave me in a tricky position, though, unemployed, living in a flat I couldn't possibly afford and with endless unspoken-for time stretching ahead of me.

I found myself thinking about Charlie a lot. He hadn't called since the morning he'd walked out and I was feeling hurt. Several times I'd rung his office and left messages but none were returned.

This was the exact same treatment I'd meted out to Leila so I could hardly complain. For weeks after I'd moved out of the Maida Vale flat there had been phone calls from her, half-formed plans to catch up for drinks that I'd conveniently forgotten, coffees, breakfasts and lunches I'd cancelled. In the end Leila had given up on me and now it seemed Charlie had followed suit. I only had myself to blame but still, in my lonelier moments, I couldn't help reflecting on what I'd let go.

When Tonino called and asked me out to dinner a second time there seemed no reason to refuse. He suggested we eat at Palio this time and I was curious to see how the place had turned out.

There was no real reason to dress up for him. Tonino was used to seeing me in chef's whites and a deeply unflattering hat, after all. And yet still I found myself buying a little black dress I couldn't afford and a pair of shoes with delicate straps and improbable heels.

Even as I got ready, spending longer than usual fiddling with my hair and make-up, I wondered what on earth I thought I was doing.

When I stepped into Palio I was glad I'd made the effort. The whole place smelt of wealth. The dining room was shaped like a shell, just like the main piazza in Siena, apparently, and the walls were covered in hyper-real images of that city's famous horse race. Just standing there felt like being in the middle of an amazing pageant with bright costumes and fluttering banners. It was dramatic and impressive and at the entrance I faltered for a moment. Again I had that feeling of not fitting in, despite the protective shell of my expensive dress and shoes.

Then I saw Tonino over by the bar, his arm raised to attract my attention. He greeted me with a kiss on both cheeks and I could sense people were watching us. Sleek young women, well-fed bankers, impeccably dressed wives, all wondering who on earth this ordinary brown-haired girl might be and how she'd ended up with the city's star chef.

Leafing through the menu as I sipped the cocktail Tonino had procured for me, I realised just how bold a move Palio had been. This was his take on northern Italian cuisine with lots of grains like polenta, gamey pheasant dishes, creamy soups of chestnut and pancetta. This wasn't the food he'd grown up with. He seemed to have made a conscious effort to steer away from the staples of the south, the pasta, light tomato-based sauces and the seafood. The menu at Palio was far richer – just like the clientele.

Tonino watched my face carefully as I read through the main courses but didn't make any comment. Once more he chose what I would eat, not bothering to enquire about my likes or dislikes, and again I didn't argue.

I was beginning to wonder what we'd find to talk about over another long evening of eating and drinking but he seemed to have fixed an agenda this time. As the first course arrived he raised the subject of his brother Lucio and kept hammering away at it until we'd finished with cheese, coffee and *panforte*.

Tonino seemed determined to wring out every detail he could – what Lucio looked like these days, what he was cooking, what he was planning.

To begin with I was grateful for the free pass to talk about the man I'd been so obsessed with. I answered all his questions at length, describing the days Lucio and I had spent together and even some of the conversations we'd had.

But then it dawned on me that this rivalry between the brothers went both ways. It seemed to me that Tonino was constantly looking over his shoulder, fearing Lucio might be gaining on him, worrying he might catch up. And I was concerned that I might have said too much.

I tried to find other subjects to steer the conversation to, bringing up the restaurant business, Guyon's current state of health, anything we had in common, but Tonino wasn't finished yet.

'So you were together a lot, you and Lucio,' he observed. 'There were outings, lunches, shifts at the pizzeria. Who suggested you should work there in the first place?'

'Actually it was your mother.'

He raised his eyebrows. 'Ah yes, Mamma. Always keen to put a pretty young girl into the path of one of her sons.'

'I'm sure it wasn't like that,' I said quickly. 'She thought he'd be able to teach me some useful stuff.'

'But all my brother knows about is how to make pizza, and a talented young chef like you could pick that up in less than half a day. I'm sure that's not why you ended up spending so much time with him.'

He raised an eyebrow at me and I realised he suspected some sort of affair between me and Lucio. 'Oh no, really there was nothing …' I began but then felt awkward and shut up.

Tonino gave me a languid smile as if it didn't really concern him and then smoothly changed the subject.

'You know it's still early. Why don't we head back to my apartment and have a couple more drinks?'

He saw the expression on my face and smiled again, more patronisingly this time. 'Just a drink or two, Alice, and then I'll put you in a cab and send you home. You're quite safe with me, you know.'

The laughing way he said it made me feel gauche. I realised I was always expecting the worst of men, even when they'd done nothing to deserve it. And anyway I did trust Tonino. He was conceited and high-handed yes, but I judged him as being essentially decent.

Without waiting for my consent, he had my coat brought over and asked the waiter to hail us a taxi. Sitting in the back I was careful not to brush against him. I barely even met his eyes. Yes I trusted Tonino but still I didn't want to send out any of the wrong signals.

It turned out he had a loft apartment down near the river. It was a fancy place with exposed bricks, a wall of windows and a view over London's lights. Every space was so ordered and clean it looked as though he was expecting an interiors magazine to turn up for a photo shoot any minute.

The first thing he did was pour a couple of big shots of Laphroaig. 'Thirty years old, Islay single malt,' he said as he handed it over. 'I take it that's OK?'

'Yes thanks,' I said, although I wasn't a whisky drinker.

It was cold outside but still Tonino wanted to sit on the terrace. He brought me a rug and said he thought the single malt would do the rest of the job of warming me up.

'I love this view,' he told me as we sat shoulder to shoulder staring out into the night. 'There are days I'll spend sixteen hours or more buried in a kitchen and never get to see the sky, so it does me good to sit out here.'

'I miss the sky too sometimes,' I said wistfully. 'Especially looking at it from the house where I stayed near Triento. That sky was something special.'

He said nothing for a moment and then, leaning over, brushed his lips against mine so very, very gently it barely counted as a kiss.

'Sorry, Alice, I know I said "just a drink" but I couldn't help it.' Tonino was smiling, but not in the languid, slightly patronising way he had before.

'That's OK.' Flattered, I smiled back and then added softly, 'We both taste of whisky.'

'We taste of good whisky and that's the important thing.' Tonino leaned in again and kissed me properly this time.

And I closed my eyes, let my head fall back and didn't complain.

Babetta

The days blurred into a big mess of nothing for Babetta. She was no longer aware of the weather or the seasons. Sometimes she'd sit out on Nunzio's cane chair for hours and then realise she was wet through, the little dog shivering in the rain beside her. She supposed this was what mourning was made of. Yet she'd never felt like this before, not when her grandparents had died, or her youngest sister, or her parents. This was a different kind of emptiness.

Raffaella came to the house quite often. She piled rugs over Babetta on chilly days and left food in her kitchen. Sofia was there too several times a week, a good daughter, concerned about her mother. She filled the silence with words Babetta didn't want to hear.

'Now will you think about moving, Mamma? You can't stay here alone. It's too isolated and anyway there are far too many stairs. Soon you'll be too old to manage them so better to move now while you still have your health.'

Her daughter meant well. She couldn't understand why anyone would prefer this quiet place to the colour and life in town. Nor could Babetta properly explain it. She liked Triento, was attracted to it like a glittery thing, but this was home, as it had been for many years, and she wasn't ready to leave it.

'I'll be OK,' she insisted. 'And anyway I'm not alone. See, I have the little dog.'

She pointed at the creature that always seemed to be

at her heels, although she never fed it treats or showed it much affection.

Sofia snorted derisively. 'Some use that dog will be if a hoodlum decides to break in and beat you up just like you read about in the newspapers.'

'I never read the newspapers,' Babetta replied stubbornly.

'Fine.' Sofia was exasperated. 'Just like you hear about on the radio then.'

'I'm not frightened here. I never have been.'

'But you won't be allowed to stay anyway. Without Papa you can't handle the gardens next door. That rich Englishwoman with the fancy handbag will evict you as soon as she hears he is gone.'

'I don't think she will,' Babetta lied.

'At least come and see some apartments that are for rent in Triento?' Sofia begged her. 'There is an agency in town. I went by and got some information. I think you'll be surprised at how nice some of the places are. Modern appliances, easy to keep clean, a short walk to the market ... wouldn't you like that?'

'I'll have a look,' Babetta agreed grudgingly. 'But there's no rush. I'm not moving anywhere until I have to.'

'So I will make some appointments with the signora at the agency?' Sofia pushed on.

'Yes, yes, do whatever you like.' Babetta didn't want to think about it. She just wanted to sit and stare out at the sky.

Alice

That night with Tonino was unexpected in every way. I don't remember any awkwardness, no fumbling with my clothes as he removed them. Nor do I recall any discussion of what we were about to do. It was a new dance and Tonino had taken the lead. I was just following the steps.

The whisky must have helped blur the edges a bit. I'd had three or four by the time we moved inside, dazed from the cold and the kissing. First I followed him onto the sofa and from there to the bedroom as though I had no say in the matter. Neither of us spoke. By the time I wondered if this was really what I wanted, it all seemed too inevitable to stop.

Afterwards he fell asleep almost straight away and I lay awake trying to imagine what was going to happen next. Would there be a dry, embarrassed conversation in the morning and an insincere promise to call? Would he want to do this again? And if he did, would I?

There was a part of me that felt triumphant to have finally broken free of Charlie and allowed another man to touch me. I suppose my vanity had been stroked too after so many years playing second fiddle to Leila. But as I turned to look at Tonino's dark head on the pillow my main feeling was incredulity. This didn't feel real.

I must have fallen asleep eventually. In the morning I woke to find myself curled into the curves of Tonino's body, one of his arms trapping me gently. I tried to shift but he didn't let go so, giving up, I settled back into him.

If I hadn't been so lonely then I might have been stronger. Instead, over the next few months I allowed myself to be taken into Tonino's life. I never told anyone about our nights together, not even Guyon. In the mornings I got up early and went to help out in the vegetarian café as always but Guyon never had a clue I hadn't come from my own place.

On his advice I'd signed up with a temping agency so most nights I'd be working in some kitchen or other, mostly round the West End. And when I was finished I'd go back to Tonino's place and often find him sitting on the terrace with two tumblers of whisky, waiting for me to join him.

There was a quiet strength to Tonino. He knew exactly what he wanted and worked slowly and methodically until he got it. Restaurants, money, acclaim, women; his approach was the same. He was steady and made me feel protected, watched over. Most of all he was gentle.

No one knew about us, I was sure. We were both careful never to let our affair leak into the rest of our lives. If his phone rang, I never answered it. Most of my stuff was kept in my garden flat, even though I rarely slept there. And, just like that first night together, neither of us ever discussed what would happen next.

I thought I was happy. There were things I loved about Tonino, like the rolling sound of his accent and the way he sang Italian songs tunelessly as he threw a simple pasta dish together for us on Sundays. I liked listening to him talking about food and home. And I was grateful for the fact I never had to spend a night alone unless I really wanted to. Even though I didn't feel any fierce sort of emotions, like I'd had for his brother, I couldn't help settling for the comfort he offered.

A couple of years after that first night we'd spent together, he suggested I move in with him. There was no romance, no sense that our relationship had deepened into something more serious. Tonino was purely practical. 'It's crazy you paying all this money in rent when you spend most of your time here,' he told me. 'Just think of the saving you'll make.'

He even bought me a mobile phone so I wouldn't have to use the one in his apartment. We were living together and yet still keeping our connection a secret. It seemed ridiculous but, as he explained, he had his reasons.

'You know how my mother can be about wanting me to settle down and give her grandchildren,' he said lightly. 'I don't want to give her yet another reason to nag me, especially as my family are so fond of you. It would only make things difficult. And we are fine as we are, hey, Alice?'

I didn't really mind the secrecy. It meant I didn't have to come clean with Guyon and somehow I sensed he'd disapprove of my affair. Plus, I was happy to avoid any awkward meetings between Tonino and my mother or any need for me to get tangled up with his public profile. It was easier for us to remain together but separate. It meant we could steer clear of reality.

I didn't even move in with him in the true sense of the word. None of the kitchen stuff I'd bought was unpacked. Why bother, since Tonino already owned everything we'd need? All the art on the walls was his, all the furniture, everything. I just sort of slid in and pushed my belongings into nooks and crannies: a few clothes in the wardrobes and drawers, a few CDs beside the stereo. No one who walked in and looked around would ever guess I was living there.

Not that Tonino ever invited people over. His public face was for the restaurant only and closing his front door was his retreat into privacy. Even within the apartment there were parts of him he kept hidden. I'd never realised he was such a big reader, for instance, until I found the books stacked in a cupboard. There were novels, most of them literary, thick tomes about history and art. Up till then I'd thought the only books in the place were the ones about food that were neatly arranged in the kitchen.

Tonino showed himself to me slowly, piece by piece. It was a tease that kept me interested, kept me wondering. And gradually I forgot it was the other brother I'd wanted. I took the easy way and stayed with his one.

Babetta

Almost immediately Babetta regretted agreeing to look at apartments in Triento. Sofia acted swiftly, making a string of appointments with the signora from the rental agency and Babetta spent a wearisome day being shown through pokey rooms in aged stone buildings.

'This one would look so pretty with some red geraniums here on the window sill,' Sofia said brightly. 'And with some pretty curtains and cushions to brighten it up, don't you think? Or what about the other one with the little terrace? Perhaps you could even grow some herbs there.'

'It was too shaded. It would never see the sun,' Babetta replied.

'Don't be so negative about every place we see, Mamma. Nowhere is going to be perfect.'

Babetta didn't tell her daughter she'd stood on that terrace and looked up at the sky and all she'd been able to see was a tiny square of blue, no bigger than a handkerchief.

'I just didn't like it,' she said stubbornly. 'And I don't like this one either.'

'Well you have to live somewhere.' Sofia was losing her patience. 'The signora has set aside a lot of time for you today, you know.'

'I didn't ask her to,' Babetta said stubbornly, and looking up she saw that here the sky was just a ribbon winding between the narrow alleyways lined with old dwellings.

'My mother has lived in the same place for many years,' she heard Sofia telling the signora from the rental agency.

'It's going to be hard on her making a move.'

The woman, briskly confident in her suit and losing patience also, simply nodded. 'One more place and then that is all I have for you,' she said. 'Triento is small and people are saving their places for holiday rentals these days. There isn't much available for those who have lived here for years.'

Babetta didn't like the last place either, even though Sofia found much to admire: a modern kitchen, a shower, bath and bidet, a slice of a view over the piazza. 'This is the nicest yet I think, Mamma. A little more expensive than the others but still I think we should take it. You have plenty of savings. You can afford it.'

'I'll think about it,' said Babetta.

'So close to the market and the bread shop, see? You'll be able to go and chat to old Silvana every day, keep up with the gossip.'

Babetta thought she wouldn't care for an old woman's talk of other people to be filling her ears day after day. 'I'll think about it,' she repeated.

And now she was back in the cane chair, the sky stretching over her and down to the horizon. She knew Sofia was right and sooner or later she would be made to move away from here. Still, it was almost spring and she would plant her garden as always, put tomato seedlings against the wooden stakes Nunzio had sunk into the ground, dig manure in around the artichokes, sow the rucola seed in the most fertile soil. And perhaps if she were very lucky there might be one last season of her own vegetables.

Alice

I think by now I'd realised I was never going to be a top chef. Even though Tonino kept insisting I had the talent, I knew what was missing was the drive. The places I preferred temping in were the ones that reminded me of Raffaella's trattoria – little neighbourhood bistros with small menus and friendly staff. I'd stopped caring about stretching myself, wasn't worried about learning. I'd even eased up on the hours I worked.

My days were free because Guyon had stopped needing me. His drinking was under control and so was his job at the vegetarian café. And the fact I had no rent to pay meant I didn't need to worry too much about gaps between temping jobs. There was a lot of empty time these days but I was more at ease with it. Hours were frittered away reading the books I found in Tonino's cupboards or playing around in his kitchen. At one point I took a cake decoration course and discovered I had a flair for it. But I didn't have the urge to take it any further, couldn't see myself icing wedding cakes for a living. I couldn't see myself doing anything, really.

One morning I was idling over a newspaper in a coffee bar in Covent Garden when I spotted a photograph of Leila in the review section. Like me she was beginning to look a little older, fine lines radiating from her eyes where there had been nothing but smooth skin a few years before. As I stared at the picture I had a little stab of missing her. And then I turned my attention to the article beside it, a review of the novel she'd had published. It was called *Soul Sisters* and the reviewer loved it. He said it was fresh, original and smart, and that she was a new talent to watch out for. What confused me was that I had a clear memory of Leila telling me she was writing a story about a dog but there was no mention of any animals in the reviewer's précis of the plot. He said it was about two girls, thrown together as students, who fall out when one sleeps with the other's boyfriend and then take years to find their way back to each other.

I reread that review at least three times, shocked and angry that Leila had taken our story and used it without asking. Yes, she'd changed our names and a few facts but anyone could see it was based on the two of us.

There was a bookshop just along from the tube station so I went straight there to see if they had Leila's novel in stock. I found a big stack of them, the newspaper review already clipped out and displayed beside it. Slightly resentful to be putting money in her pocket, I bought my copy, then hailed a black cab and headed straight back to Tonino's place. Reading in a car has always left me feeling queasy but still I couldn't resist starting on the first chapter as we drove.

Leila wrote the way she spoke; coy, funny and always with an undercurrent of drama. As I raced through her book that afternoon I saw how clever she'd been, snipping fragments from our lives and then quilting them together with other ideas and memories. It wasn't our story exactly but the characters had nearly everything in common with us.

For instance, both the girls in the story were fatherless, just like Leila and me. She was well aware that my dad had walked out when I was a kid and gone to have another family with a woman he preferred to my mother. I'd told her many times how once I'd hit my teens he barely bothered sending Christmas or birthday cards. And in turn she'd told me how her father was a married man Aurora had enjoyed a brief affair with and never even told she was pregnant.

I'd always suspected this lack in our lives was one of the few things Leila and me had in common and, reading her book, it seemed she agreed. It was what pulled her characters together, bonded them firmly, even though one was bohemian and wild, just like her, and the other rather ordinary and working-class like me.

By now I'd stopped feeling angry and was, if anything, intrigued by Leila's interpretation of our lives. When I got to the bit where she slept with my boyfriend, I felt a flare of indignation. And then towards the end, when Leila brought her characters together again, I was almost tearful.

It was dark by the time I turned the final page and I was in that dreamy, slightly removed state you get into when you've spent hours reading in a silent room. It was difficult to decide how I felt. Part of me thought Leila had been wrong to steal our story. Hadn't she realised I'd be bound to read it? I wanted to call her, ask what she'd been thinking, but making contact would rumple up my life again. So I closed the book, pushed it into one of Tonino's anonymous little cupboards and decided to forget about it.

And then my messy old life came crashing in on my smoothed-over new one a second time, just a couple of weeks later. I was walking down Long Acre in Covent Garden, mindlessly window-shopping, when I spotted someone familiar coming towards me. Gingery hair, far from handsome, sucking on a cigarette ... 'Charlie!' I called out.

He looked up and smiled. 'Hey, Alice,' he said, as though we'd only spoken yesterday.

'What are you doing here?' I felt ridiculously happy to see him again.

'Took a day off work. Just having a mosey round some music shops. What about you?'

The two of us were damming up the busy pavement, forcing the crowd to flow around us. 'I'm just pottering around too. Shall we have a quick drink?' I asked impulsively. 'There's a little pub down that alleyway.'

'All right then. I'll buy you a beer if you like,' Charlie agreed.

Nothing about him seemed to have changed at all. There was the same old style of rucksack over his shoulder stuffed with second-hand books and newspapers, the slightly worn clothing, the clunky Doc Marten shoes.

'It's been ages, hasn't it,' I said as the barman filled our glasses. 'I did try to call you a few times but ...'

He interrupted me. 'I needed a clean break from you, Alice. It would have been too hard otherwise.'

'I understand. Sometimes that's the only way to put an end to things, isn't it?'

For a while we kept the conversation on safe ground, talking about work mostly. Charlie had been given a couple of promotions and his career in the film business was forging ahead. He seemed surprised that mine had stalled so completely. 'Perhaps if you hadn't been so driven when we were together things might have been different for us,' he said wistfully.

'You don't regret it though, do you? Leaving?'

'Things have worked out OK,' Charlie said simply.

He reached into the inside pocket of his jacket and produced a laminated photograph. It was of a pretty, dark-haired woman holding a newborn baby, her cheek resting gently on the top of its head.

'Are they yours?' I asked.

He nodded. 'We don't have much history yet, me and Mary. No things she blames me for, no transgressions, not yet. But we do have Grace. Lovely, isn't she?'

'Both of them are lovely.'

'It could have been you, Alice.' The way he said it made me feel slightly sorry for this dark-haired Mary.

'Well, I'm in a relationship too,' I retaliated quickly. 'I'm living with Tonino Ricci, the chef from Teatro, remember him?'

As soon as the words were out I regretted them. What I had with Tonino had been so carefully measured out, and calling it a relationship, talking about it to Charlie broke the spell and made me realise the whole arrangement was far from normal. A sham of a thing really. I'd known that all along, of course, I'd just managed not to think about it.

'So is he the man you think you'll have children with?' Charlie asked as he tucked his precious photo safely back in his pocket.

'Yes,' I said, clinging to the fiction. 'I think he might be. When the time is right for both of us he might be.'

PART III

'Do you ever get a sense of detachment from your own life? So often I do something like put my key in the door and can't quite believe it's my door and my life.'

British socialite Sheherazade Goldsmith.

Alice

Over the next decade or so Tonino built an empire and his name became known well outside the circles of London's fine diners. This was the era when chefs stopped being people who cooked and became something more: celebrities with multiple restaurants, recipe books and endorsements, with lives lived above the line. Tonino embraced all that far more than I'd ever thought he would.

When he started making really serious money he bought a big house just outside a pretty Hertfordshire village and eventually I retreated to it. It was like a storybook version of an English country home, aged red brick with ivy growing over it and a vast walled vegetable garden. With time on my hands I started working the soil just like Babetta had taught me all those years ago. I used up many hours digging well-rotted manure and compost into the soil and planting out seedlings. The climate was colder, of course, so I raised my tomatoes in a fancy glasshouse Tonino had built for my birthday. Each spring I reclaimed more of the garden for cultivation, planting fruit trees and berry bushes, making the land useful again.

Sometimes my mother travelled down on the train but she felt awkward around Tonino and only liked to stay if he was busy working. So yes, I spent a lot of time there on my own but I'd given up minding too much. The house was fitted out with strong locks and an alarm system and there were a few friendly people in the village, a couple of pony-club mums who were always up for a coffee, old people who swapped cuttings with me. I felt safe enough living there. In the spring and summer I worked long hours in the garden, the autumn was for bottling and preserving what I'd grown, the winter for dreams.

I stayed out of Tonino's spotlight. When the press came down to write about his wonderful organic garden they photographed him wearing gumboots as he dug for potatoes or filled baskets with produce and fresh-laid eggs from our chickens. Any reporter who looked closely might have noticed those gumboots of his were barely worn, that there was no telltale crescent of soil beneath his fingernails. But they took home the story they wanted, the top chef's idyllic country life, the home-made pickles and preserves that were sold in the local farmers' market, the peas he picked to make them a lunch of *pasta e piselli*, the baking sourdough bread that scented his kitchen. What they didn't know was that an hour or so after they'd headed back to the city he would follow them, because even on a Sunday afternoon Tonino had a schedule to keep. And I was left to spend another week in my garden.

There was nearly always something that needed doing – weeds breaking through, trees to be pruned, seedlings to raise. Sometimes in winter it was a treat to put on smart clothes and go into London to meet Tonino for lunch in one of his many establishments, like the organic café he'd opened in Belgravia where there was a shelf stacked with jars of my own carefully-labelled preserves for sale.

By then, of course, people knew about us. Guyon had found out soon after I moved to the country and, once he'd got over being amazed, had been as disapproving as I'd expected.

'Why Tonino, of all people?' he'd asked me.

'I don't know ... it just happened,' I admitted.

'I expected more than this from you.' He was exasperated

with me. 'What about your own ambitions? Have you just given up?'

'The thing is I'm not sure I ever really had any ambitions,' I admitted. 'What I had was this sense that I had to live every moment, squeeze life dry. But you can't really do that, can you? Maybe the real secret is to be happy with what you've got instead of always striving for something else?'

'Everyone has to have goals though, don't they?'

'Well, I suppose I do. This year's goal is to put in an asparagus patch and also I might grow some more tomatoes and make a bottled sauce for Tonino to sell in the café. Is that enough?'

'You're slow-cooking your life then,' Guyon observed. 'Down there in the country you've got everything on a low simmer and all the time in the world.'

He sounded scathing but I thought the idea of a slow-cooked life was rather comforting.

'And what about the future?' he nagged me.

'I don't know,' I admitted. 'But then who does?'

I didn't mention that my relationship with Tonino was as lacy as ever. Incredibly his family still hadn't been told about us. He tended to keep them at arm's length, discouraging them from London visits by saying he was much too busy to spend any time with them and, if he did go back to Italy, I stayed home in England with my garden.

Tonino was tender in the short amount of time he had available for me but I had no idea what he got up to when we were apart. What I did understand was that for him the future held only more work, more success. Despite the pressure his mother had always put on him there was never any talk of marriage and babies. I suppose I'd never realised I wanted either of those things until it dawned on me I wasn't going to get them.

There were some parts of my life Tonino didn't have a

stake in. I don't just mean the garden, my friends in the village or even the time I spent with Guyon. There were other things I did and never bothered to mention.

Twice a month I caught a train to London and met up with Charlie. Usually we went to Regent's Park Zoo or one of the museums, anywhere equipped with stuff to keep the kids amused.

Charlie had two of them now, Grace and Mia, pretty little girls with hair he struggled to plait as neatly as their mother could. Things hadn't worked out for him and Mary and they'd split when Mia was still a baby. Every other weekend Charlie had the girls and he seemed desperate to jam the time with activities. His satchel was stuffed with colouring books and Barbie dolls these days and he knew the words to songs that never got reviewed in the *NME*. In most other ways he was still my Charlie, though, still the person I felt most at ease with. And I liked the idea of this secret time I had with him.

We stayed in touch by e-mail and it always gave me a little lift when I found a new message from him. Often I'd find myself turning on my laptop just to see if he'd been in touch. Usually he'd recommend a book he thought I might like or a movie I shouldn't miss out on.

From time to time I let myself pretend his girls were mine. I'd tidy up their hair or not bother contradicting someone who referred to me as their mother. They called me Aunty Alice and when we were crossing a busy road they always put their hands in mine. Sweet little girls. I felt more envious of Mary for having them than I ever had of her and Charlie.

If Tonino had known about the time we spent together he'd most certainly have been jealous. It would have put a few dents in his gleaming male pride. Even though there was nothing going on except a friendship, I didn't see the point in creating a problem, so Charlie and me had an agreement that he wouldn't phone me.

When I answered my ringing mobile one wet Sunday morning and heard his voice it jolted me. 'What do you want?' I hissed at him.

'I've just got the newspapers and there's an obituary for Leila's mother,' Charlie told me. 'She died of some rare blood disorder no one knew she had. Sorry, but I just thought you might want to know.'

After I'd got him off the phone I sat on the edge of my bed feeling a numb disbelief that someone who had been so alive could be gone. Aurora, with her love of the sky and her quiet generosity seemed an especially shocking loss. Perhaps it was because I hadn't seen her since that Villa Rosa summer so had never watched her ageing. Or maybe it was that she'd been so very much like Leila. But I felt as though the ground was shifting beneath me and things I'd thought were certain couldn't be trusted any more.

'Who was that?' Tonino asked in a morning-groggy voice. We'd been having a Sunday lie-in and he was still half asleep.

'Just a friend to tell me Leila's mother has died. I can't quite believe it.'

'Go and Google her,' he suggested, his eyes still tight shut. 'See if it's true.'

I did what he suggested and found there was already a couple of news stories up, linked to the fact Aurora had a high profile in the art world and Leila was well-known for her best-selling books. Looking through them I had a sense I ought to do something. Leila was alone now, so surely the least I could do was send a card or letter.

Half the day was spent trying to compose my note to her, while outside the rain sluiced down the windows and kept me away from the garden. Bored with watching me,

239

Tonino took the train back to London while I wrestled on with corny phrases and well-worn condolences. Most likely Leila would get sack-loads of mail and mine wouldn't even be read but still it seemed vital to get it right.

In the end I wrote down a series of memories from that blue-sky summer: watching Aurora at her easel down on the rocks, trying to coax her back to the house to eat a little pasta, drinking limoncello with her as the sun set. I signed my name at the bottom and went to post it before I changed my mind. Although I had no idea where Leila was living I'd found an address for her literary agent on the Internet so hoped the note might be forwarded to her.

About a month later the reply arrived. It was scrawled in black ink in her familiar spidery writing and when I read it I could hear Leila's voice in my head.

Dear Alice,

How wonderful it was to get your letter. I've been so weighed down by my own and other people's grief, so emptied out by it all. And then there are all the practical things that have to be done when a person leaves the world. So I can't tell you what a relief it was to sit for a few moments, read your letter and just remember. For me there's never been a time quite like that summer, even though I've been back to Villa Rosa very often since.

Oh yes, Villa Rosa, I have to decide what to do about the place. Sell it, rent it out, keep it … I just don't know. I keep wanting to ask my mother's advice. Once I even dialled her mobile number. Silly isn't it?

You used to feel like a sister to me, Alice. Now I'm on my own and I need a sister badly. Would you come back? Would you come to Villa Rosa and help me decide what I should do with it? I have other people I could ask but for some reason it feels more like the proper ending if it's you. Please say you'll come.

With love of course,
Leila.

It took me by surprise, that letter. I'd expected something more guarded. After all, hadn't I treated Leila so badly all those years ago? There had been times, especially in the early days, when I'd thought about calling her but my pride had got in the way. And then she wrote her books and got famous and it was too late. If I'd made contact then she'd have thought it was only to latch on to her success.

Now Leila had offered me a way to connect with her again but to take it would mean going back to Triento, and I wasn't sure if I could do that.

There were so many reasons to turn her down: the complication of Tonino's family being there, the craziness of going so far to be with someone I hadn't seen for over ten years, the work in my garden that always held me to the house. But I found myself wondering if to go would be the right thing.

Perhaps I was bored and could see my life needed to be pushed off-course. Maybe it was simply that I still missed Leila. Who ever really knows why they do anything? But I found myself fetching my laptop, typing in the e-mail address I found at the top of Leila's letter and sending her a one-line response. 'OK, I'll come.'

Villa Rosa

Someone had opened up the gates of Villa Rosa and pushed back the shutters. There was the sound of a radio chattering inside the house and a bucket with a mop outside the front door. This was just a hasty tidy-up. There was no time for the place to be woken properly, for walls to be painted and ragged wood to be smoothed again. Only the worst of the dirt would be tackled, floors swept and sluiced, dull surfaces polished clean.

'Where does all the dust come from?' Raffaella's voice rang out from an upstairs bedroom. And then a few moments later, 'Never in my life did I think I'd end up cleaning this house again. *Porca la miseria*, when am I going to learn to say no to people?'

Once she'd put fresh sheets on the beds, Raffaella came downstairs and stood in the doorway, surveying the ruin of the garden. There were long days of work to do here and she wasn't the one to tackle it. Still, there might be time to weed the flowerbeds nearest the house or put out some pots of marigolds along a wall to brighten the view.

'It's a shame,' she said to herself. 'A real shame.' And then she picked up her mop and bucket and went to tackle the kitchen floor.

When she'd agreed to make the place ready for the English writer she'd thought it would only be a matter of a few hours' work. She was happy to do her a favour. But Raffaella had forgotten what neglect does to a place, how time settles like dust over empty rooms, how mould and damp grow over empty spaces.

She was beginning to wonder if something about this house invited abandonment. Yes, its face needed colour, its tangled garden a good combing out. But even if it were made pretty again would anyone care for it?

Villa Rosa had barely changed since Raffaella was a girl. She had come here the first time, newly widowed and wondering what life had left for her. Most of her days were spent cooking for the American who built the statue of Christ on the mountain and she remembered how she'd been dazzled by his looks and importance. In the end, for both of them, Villa Rosa had only been a staging post, a sweet spot between one life and another. They'd passed through it just as everyone else seemed to.

Raffaella thought the place deserved better, an owner who would spend summer after summer here, letting the days unravel. As she swabbed the grime from the kitchen floor and considered if she might have time to tackle the oven, she wondered what lay in store for it.

Alice

It was a relief to see Villa Rosa again. I'd been imagining how it might have changed in the years since I'd been there but the minute I glimpsed the house through the open gates I knew it was the same.

I'd flown to Rome and taken the train south and then a taxi from Triento's railway station. As the driver threw his car around the angles of the coast road I kept my eyes fixed on the view. Leila would be waiting for me at Villa Rosa but I tried not to think about her. Instead, I studied how the cliffs fell back in layers and the way the rocks had been forced into jagged shapes by the waves. I looked out at the expanse of sea and up at the wide-open sky, set my eyes on all the things I'd missed about the place.

As the taxi pulled up I cast a glance towards Babetta's old place. She'd been such a lovely old woman and I wondered what had happened to her. Surely she was gone after all these years. If so, I hoped her ending had been a gentle one.

And then there was Leila coming out of the house to greet me, waiting beneath the pomegranate tree while I fumbled with my euros for the cab fare. She looked beautiful but brittle.

'*Ciao, bella*,' she called out. It was a little rally of the old Leila but she couldn't keep it going for long. Sadness had squeezed the colour from her. As she handed me a glass of limoncello and steered me onto the terrace, she said in a barely-there voice, 'For remembrance sake.'

Leila looked worn out. Her skin was sallow, her dark

hair shot through with wiry strands of grey and scraped back roughly from her face.

'I'm so sorry,' I said. My words seemed feeble but what else was there.

She turned to me. 'Sorry for what, exactly?'

'For your loss ... and for letting you down.'

Leila looked thoughtful. 'I think we should get this over with now, don't you? Then maybe we can forget about it. So tell me why, Alice. What made you drop me like that? Turn your back on me? Was it just the thing with Lucio?'

I'd known this question would be coming and still I didn't have an answer ready. 'I'm not sure,' I said awkwardly.

'You must have understood how important you were to me?' Leila wasn't in the mood to pull punches. 'How much I needed our friendship.'

I stared at her, appalled, wishing I'd left this business with Leila in the past with all the other messy things I didn't want to think about.

'But still you dropped me,' she said sadly.

'I know ... I'm sorry.'

'You don't have to keep saying that. All I want is to understand why.'

I fiddled with my glass of limoncello, trying to come up with a way to explain it.

'Tell me why, Alice,' she pressed in an off-key voice.

'I suppose what I thought was that if I couldn't have Lucio, then you shouldn't have me,' I admitted in the end.

'So you were punishing me?'

Ashamed, I nodded. 'I guess so. And by the time I realised how stupid I was being it seemed like there was no going back.'

'After my first book was published I was certain you'd get in touch.' Leila sounded wistful. 'That book was our story ... my letter to you, in a way. But maybe you never read it?'

'I read them all, the books, the newspaper and magazine interviews,' I told her. 'Everything, really.'

'But still you never called.'

'By then you were doing so well and I didn't think I'd matter to you any more.'

Leila gave a harsh little laugh. 'My mother didn't understand it, you know. She thought I must have done something terrible to you. I explained about Lucio but she couldn't believe it was only that. She kept asking, what else, what else? It had to be entirely my fault, she told me, because Alice isn't like that.'

Each new thing Leila said left me feeling a little worse. 'Why did you ask me to come here?' I asked. 'Was it just to have this conversation?'

'No, of course not.' She reached out and touched my elbow, her fingers cold from the ice-filled glass. 'As I said in my letter, I felt like we were sisters. And now I'm by myself; my mother has gone; I have lots of lovers but no husband, no family at all. So I need a sister. I really need a sister, Alice.'

'And you chose me? You can forgive what I did even though I found it so impossible to forgive you for Lucio?'

'Yes,' she said simply.

'It will never be the same though. We're different people now.'

'Of course we are.' Suddenly she smiled. 'What you don't know is that I call Charlie from time to time to find out how you are.'

'You don't even like Charlie,' I protested. 'You always hated me being with him.'

'Oh, I don't know, maybe I've mellowed.' Leila shrugged. 'But he's been very useful helping me keep track of your life over the years.'

It was a shock to hear they'd been talking behind my back. 'So I assume you know I'm with Tonino now?' I asked.

She nodded. 'Yes. Although Charlie doesn't think you're happy. He says you're with him because it's easy. He's got quite a lot to say about it, actually.'

I'd forgotten how you can't ever fool the people who know you, how easily they can strip away the newly-decorated, reconstructed bits and expose the flawed parts hidden beneath. I didn't like it much.

'I live in a beautiful house and please myself how I fill my days,' I said defensively. 'Everyone should have my problems.'

Leila smiled again. 'Never mind that now. Have another drink and then we should go inside and eat. Yes, I've cooked for you, although I can't promise you'll think it's up to much.'

Only as the mood between us softened did I have a chance to look around me properly. That's when I saw how faded Villa Rosa was looking. The house itself needed painting and in the terraced gardens beneath us unpicked artichokes had flowered into purple thistles and an unruly rabble of tomato plants had self-seeded at will.

'How sad,' I remarked. 'Babetta would have hated to see her vegetable garden growing wild like this if she were still around.'

Leila gave me a sharp look. 'Babetta? But she hasn't gone anywhere. Actually I'm not sure what I'd have to do to prise her out of that house next door.'

'Really? The old lady's still alive?' I couldn't believe it. 'But she must be about a hundred by now?'

Leila laughed. 'I've no idea how old she is and she isn't telling. All I know is she rides that Vespa round the coast road like a madwoman. She's famous for it. She even puts the old dog Sky in a woven basket on her back. It's quite a sight.'

'You're kidding, right?'

Leila shook her head. 'No, I wish I was. You should go over and see her. She'll be so pleased.'

The thought that Babetta had been here all along was somehow reassuring. Maybe we weren't all so changed by time after all.

Once the sun had sunk into the sea and the pink light faded from the sky, we went inside to eat. Leila had prepared a light supper – tender fillets of white fish she cooked in foil with capers, olive oil and lemon, a salad of peppery rocket leaves and a basket full of bread she'd warmed in the oven.

'This is great,' I told her. 'Simple but delicious.'

She wrinkled her nose. 'I can't take the credit for it. Raffaella told me what to do.'

'Raffaella?' Again I was surprised. 'Do you see her often?'

'Yes, she comes over here a lot. She sort of adopted Babetta after her husband died. It's entirely her fault the old lady rides that Vespa.'

'So what's Raffaella like these days?' I asked, unable to hide my curiosity. 'Still beautiful?'

'Oh yes,' said Leila. 'But then I think she will be until the day she dies.'

I stared down at my empty plate. 'I'd like to see her again.'

'I'm sure Raffaella would be keen to see you too since you're living with her son.'

'But she doesn't know about that?' I asked quickly.

Leila looked awkward. 'Um, yes, she does. And it's my fault actually. After Charlie told me, I mentioned it to Raffaella in passing. I hadn't realised it was supposed to be some big secret.'

'I don't get it. If she knows about us then why has she never said anything to Tonino?'

'Hurt, maybe? Or furious? Hard to tell with Raffaella. By all accounts she and Tonino don't speak much. She says he's too busy running his businesses to call her.'

I nodded. 'That would be right.'

It was tempting to ask about Lucio, impossible not to wonder if he was still making pizza, still handsome ... still single. But I couldn't bring myself to admit I'd been thinking about him. So instead I steered the conversation back to safer ground, asking Leila to tell me more about Babetta.

'My mother agreed to let her stay in the house in return for looking after the dog and the garden,' Leila told me. 'These days she's too old to do much more than keep the paths clean. She spends at least an hour a day sweeping and I think she pretends not to see the mess the rest of the place is in. We've never dared get someone else in to sort it out, though. She'd have made such a fuss.'

'I'll do it,' I offered. 'Well, I'll give it a good tidy up while I'm here. You'll have to pay someone to maintain it in the longer term, though. Gardens are headstrong. Left alone they tend to do their own thing.'

'Would you really have a go at it?' Leila sounded relieved. 'It's defeated me completely. Just knowing that it's out there going feral makes me want to hide indoors.'

I laughed. 'Yes, I know that feeling.'

Things were easier between us after that. Leila fetched a platter she'd covered in cheese, shelled walnuts and thin slices of fruit and put it on the table between us. It was pleasant sitting there, picking at the cheese and chatting. I felt my spirits lift.

But then I remembered all the things beyond the gates of Villa Rosa that I still had to face: Raffaella's anger, Lucio's charm. So many complications. Better to hide myself away here amongst the long grass and the straggling weeds for as long as I possibly could.

Babetta

Babetta had decided to wear black for the English artist even though they weren't in any way related. The woman had been good to her, so some mark of respect seemed called for. And the old dark dresses she'd worn for Nunzio still fitted well enough. A stitch or two here and there, and they would see her through. She knew young people didn't bother with the proper customs of mourning these days but that was no reason she should change the way she had always done things.

As she shook out the dusty black clothes, Babetta hoped this would be the last time she would wear them. There were so few people left she cared for now. Only her daughter, the precious twin granddaughters who had come only with the help of doctors, and Raffaella who felt almost like family. Surely all would outlive her?

Not that Babetta felt close to her own ending. True, her body ached more each year, her bones had settled and her back become a little hunched as though it were always bent over a patch of earth that needed weeding. But ever since Raffaella had coaxed her onto the Vespa, she had begun to feel like there was a younger woman living inside the well-worn body. A woman who liked to go without a helmet so she could feel the wind whip at her hair, who rode the scooter as fast as she could for the sheer joy of it. A woman who felt so much freer than before.

The ways her life had changed surprised Babetta. It seemed to have filled up with little pleasures. Most mornings she rode down to the port and spent an hour or two at the trattoria playing at being some help to Raffaella. She might slice a little prosciutto or set up a few tables but mostly she drank coffee and ate whatever Ciro put in front of her. He liked to try out new dishes and she was always happy to give him her opinion.

In the afternoons she swept the paths of Villa Rosa clean of leaves and enjoyed the way the weeds had colonised the garden. Once her fingers might have itched to tug them out but now Babetta saw no point in it. They would only fight to grow again. And there was a beauty in their vigour, in the way they tangled up and spread so fast, an undeniable lushness.

Now and then she planted out a few seedlings and forgot about them. Weeks later she'd find them twining with the weeds; there would be tomatoes to pick even if the plants hadn't grown straight and tall, bunches of herbs to gather and give to Raffaella. The garden might have run wild but still it surprised her with its fruitfulness.

Once she was satisfied the paths were clean, Babetta liked to ride her scooter up to Triento. Most days she would drink a coffee at her favourite bar and then go to sit on Silvana's bench outside the bakery. The old woman was long gone, taken by the harshness of a long winter, but still people stopped to rest on her bench, and swapped stories and gossip just as they always had. Babetta had been surprised how much she enjoyed becoming a part of it.

The world was changing so fast, or so it seemed to her. People wanted things they'd never needed before. Yet Triento wasn't so different from the way it had always been. Babetta saw the same faces behind the market stalls and in the *salumeria*, aged and lined but still familiar. People cooked the dishes they'd always made, found joy in the same places. Spring meant the *festa*, fireworks, music and gypsy stalls. In summer the beaches still drew their crowds. In winter everyone stayed close around their fires. Life followed much the same rhythms.

And when it ended there were still a few old ones left to dress in black and mourn the loss properly.

Alice

For a moment I was disorientated. I didn't recognise the whitewashed walls or the faded old quilt I'd pulled over me. It took a few seconds before I remembered I was back in Villa Rosa, in the same room I'd slept in all those summers ago.

Leila and I had stayed up late the night before, drinking and talking. We'd emptied a couple of bottles of the local red wine but it can't have been strong because I'd slept well and woken without a dull thud in my head.

Coffee was the first thing I needed, thick and strong the way the Italians liked it. Then I knew I ought to call Tonino. He'd been furious with me for coming here. To him it had seemed like I was breaking some unspoken promise. What he was going to say when I told him his family knew all about us, I couldn't imagine. It seemed easier to deal with the whole mess once I got back to London.

Leila was still in bed and the house quiet and shuttered. I moved softly about the kitchen, careful not to wake her as, judging by the bruises beneath her eyes, her sleep had been hard to come by lately.

Once I'd had my coffee, I slipped out of the house and through the gates of Villa Rosa. Leila had amused me with her tales of Babetta racing round the coast road on the old Vespa and I was eager to see the old woman again.

Perhaps there's a point when you stop ageing. So many years had gone by since I'd last laid eyes on her, but Babetta barely seemed touched by them. Her skin was more wrinkled, I suppose, her body slightly stooped, but her smile lit up her face when she found me on her doorstep, just as it always had.

I heard the old dog Sky barking in the kitchen, too lazy now to bother getting out of his basket. Babetta led me through to her low-ceilinged living room and offered me a seat next to the fire she'd already banked up with logs to take the edge off the chilly spring morning.

She muttered something I didn't quite catch in a language I still couldn't understand and disappeared from the room. When she came back it was with a tray of coffee and a dish of sweet biscuits she must have baked herself.

For a while she chatted to me in Italian while I kept smiling and nodding as though I understood. Then she beckoned for me to follow her out onto her terrace and down the steps into her garden.

The ancient Vespa was parked beneath a lean-to that had been roughly built from corrugated iron. Babetta pulled it out and gestured that I should take the seat behind her.

I tried to refuse, shaking my head in an exaggerated fashion, but she patted the ripped leather seat insistently. '*Andiamo, andiamo*,' she said, and I remembered how difficult it had always been to argue with her.

We jerked away and sped up the hill so fast the engine screamed but if Babetta heard me protesting she managed to ignore it. Determinedly, she kept going, cars and lorries hooting their horns as they whistled past and the view just a blur as the scooter rattled over the uneven coast road and then dipped down towards the port.

Only when we eased to a halt could I catch my breath and look about me. Not much seemed to have changed down here. I saw the same ramshackle fishing boats moored among the sleek yachts, the same boutiques and cafés lining the harbour and, at the far end of the point, Raffaella's trattoria with its sun umbrellas fluttering outside, but red now instead of blue.

Babetta began to herd me along towards it, pulling my arm and nudging at me with her shoulder. I was reluctant, of course, but there seemed no way to argue. So I let her steer me at the red umbrellas, knowing this meeting had to happen sooner or later.

'Raffaella!' the old lady called out as we drew nearer to the trattoria. 'RAFFAELLA!'

'Ohhh, Babetta,' I heard Raffaella shout back from inside.

Already there was the sweet smell of frying onions leaking from the door and cartons of artichoke buds stacked beside it. Raffaella came out, wiping her hands on a cloth and smiling. When she saw me, she blinked once or twice and then seemed to regain her composure.

'Alice,' she said. 'Is it really you?'

Raffaella was, as Leila had promised, still very beautiful. Her hair had turned grey but she wore it long enough to touch her shoulders, her skin was even-toned, her figure girlish. There was nothing of Tonino in her – he'd taken his quieter looks from his father.

'Yes, it's really me,' I said, still hanging back several steps behind Babetta as though I feared I wouldn't be welcome.

Smiling now, Raffaella came forward and kissed me on both cheeks, calling out for Ciro to come and do the same. And then there was an awkward moment as we stood looking at each other.

Unaware of the tension, Babetta filled the silence with a volley of excited Italian.

'She's saying she brought you here because she needs me to translate for her,' Raffaella explained.

'What does she want to tell me?' I asked.

'That she lost her husband Nunzio a long time ago and now she's alone. That she wonders what you've been so busy with and why you have stayed away from us for so many years. She wants to know if you're happy, married, have children? What shall I say to her?'

'No, I'm not married ...' I faltered for a moment. 'And no, I don't have children.'

Raffaella frowned. 'I know that,' she said in a way that was meant for me alone. 'But I don't understand it.'

'It's just how it is,' I told her. 'There's no real way to explain it.'

'But don't you want those things? Is that it?' Raffaella persisted.

'I ... Tonino ...' I began uncertainly, and then Babetta saved me by interrupting with another great lahar of words. She patted my cheek as she spoke as though I were still a young girl.

'She's glad you're back,' Raffaella translated, 'because it's spring, a busy time in the garden, and she hopes you'll stay and help her. So tell me, how long are you staying? For the whole summer again?'

'I'm not sure,' I said. 'I'll stay for as long as Leila needs me. But I hadn't thought that would be the whole summer, no. I have my own garden to take care of now.'

'I'd like to see it.' Raffaella fired me a meaningful look. 'But we'll talk about that another time. For now, why don't you come inside because it looks like it's about to rain. I can offer you a drink and some biscotti Ciro made this morning. Come, come.'

Nothing inside the trattoria seemed to have been altered. It still felt like stepping into someone's home. We sat at a table near the kitchen and, while Ciro cooked, the three of us waited out the squall. After a bit I couldn't resist edging into the kitchen and was happy when Ciro smiled and nodded at me, lifting the lids from the pans so I could breathe the savoury steam of the sauces bubbling away inside them.

'You are still a cook,' Raffaella said when I returned to the table.

'Not really. I don't work in restaurants any more, haven't for ages.'

'Yes, but you are still a cook. I see that.' Again she shot me a look that I knew was meant to mean something.

It was a relief to leave the place when the rain stopped, even though another trip on Babetta's scooter lay ahead. This time she drove with less urgency, even turning her head from time to time and babbling words at me, seemingly not caring whether they were understood. I heard Raffaella's name once or twice and Lucio's too. And every time she mentioned him she seemed to make a tutting sound. But I had absolutely no idea what she was saying.

Leila was up and about when we got back to Villa Rosa. I busied myself in the kitchen making a big bowl of spaghetti for the three of us to share using up some spicy sausage I found in the fridge.

As we ate Leila tried to speak to Babetta in Italian that was so halting even I understood a little of their conversation. It seemed they were talking mostly about the old dog. But then Leila's eyes welled with tears and she began dabbing at them with the serviette I'd left beside her plate.

'What is it?' I asked, thrown by the sudden shift in mood.

'Did you wonder at all why Babetta's all dressed in black, even her headscarf?' Leila asked.

'No, not really.' I'd assumed all ancient Italian women dressed in dark colours.

'She's just told me that those are mourning clothes in respect for my mother. Oh, Alice, this old woman has found a way to grieve for her and meanwhile I can't even believe she's gone. What am I going to do?' Leila dropped her head into her hands. 'How am I going to face this all alone?'

'I'll stay with you.' The promise was rash but I meant it. 'For as long as you need me, I'm here.'

Babetta

Babetta watched the little English girl tearing at the garden, working as though she were releasing a pent-up fury at everything that grew in it. She pruned back the overhanging branches, brutalised the mess of climbing plants and tamed the rabble in the vegetable gardens. While she hadn't asked for any help, Babetta was there to pile the waste into a pyre on a lower terrace of the garden. She might have found a way to live with the overgrowth but she wouldn't be sorry to set a match to it.

The other one, Leila, stayed out of the way most of the time. Babetta knew she was at the kitchen table, tapping away at her computer keyboard, the dog at her feet. That's how she had spent the past few weeks, only breaking from work to walk down to the rocks or lie on her bed if it were raining. Babetta had noticed how she too had taken to wearing black. Her skin looked even paler against it.

Tonight, once it was dark, both girls would come to watch her light the pyre. She had piled dried sticks around it so the flames would catch but once they reached the greener branches they would throw up sparks into the night sky. The smell of smoke would settle into hair and clothes. And their faces turned to the fire would burn, even though their backs stayed cold.

Afterwards they would eat together as they had almost every night. Perhaps Raffaella might come to join them and bring little tastes of delicious things left over from lunchtime at the trattoria.

In all the years she'd spent alone Babetta had grown out of the habit of watching people's faces, and yet still she sensed a change in the little English girl whenever Raffaella was around. Nothing obvious, just a stiffening of the shoulders, a firming of her expression as though she were bracing herself for something.

Tonight, when the fire caught and the four of them stood round it, there would be light on all their faces. Babetta thought she would try to watch the way she always used to, for surely it was time for this sadness that plagued the girl to burn away as cleanly as the weeds on her great pyre.

Alice

I've always loved a bonfire. They remind me of when I was very small and my father used to light one out on the back lawn on Guy Fawkes night. I was only allowed to look at it through my bedroom window, kept at a distance by my mother who was afraid of the flames and anxious to protect her only child. I'd stay there from beginning to end if I could, watching it burn brightly and then die down to embers that glowed like precious things.

But, if anything, Babetta was more excited about this fire than me. She'd heaped up the waste I'd pulled from the garden and was planning some sort of party. She'd even produced a dusty bottle of brandy from her cellar that she wanted us to toast with.

'It's probably moonshine and we'll go blind if we drink it,' Leila warned as she peered at the messy pile of branches and weeds. 'Do you think this lot will even catch fire?'

To me, Leila still seemed like warmed-over food, all the flavour and zest gone from her. Mostly I left her alone to write because I wasn't sure what to say. The old Leila had always been half-laughing at life; this one only wanted to hide away from it.

'I guess we could always use the brandy as an accelerant,' I joked.

Leila didn't even smile. 'I keep thinking you're going to leave me, Alice,' she said in a low, intense voice. 'I wake every morning expecting to find you packing up your bags.'

'I said I'd stay, didn't I?'

'For the whole summer?'

'Yes … if you need me to I will.'

Leila gave me an odd sort of smile, then started moving round the pyre, first at a walk then a skip. Suddenly, she seemed to have too much energy rather than none at all. 'Let's fill the whole house,' she called out as she circled the unlit bonfire. 'Invite friends from England, have parties and make noise. Make Tonino come. Get Charlie to come with his daughters. And Guyon too, if you like.'

'Are you sure?' I was thrown by this sudden change of tempo. 'What about your writing – don't you need peace and quiet for that?'

'No, right now what I need is clamour.' She raised her voice. 'I need people … noise … life.'

'Leila?'

'Don't look at me like that. I don't want to be this sad person who wears black and grieves silently. I've had enough of it. So let's have a party when we light the fire tonight, just like Babetta wants us to. Let's wear red lipstick and too much perfume. We'll drink and sing and shout. What a shame we don't have any fireworks … I wonder if Babetta knows how we could get some …'

Leila spent a few moments thinking, then grinned and lit off over the grass, the old dog struggling to stay at her heels. A short time later I saw her with Babetta, heading up the hill on the Vespa. The limp, sad Leila had been worrying me. But this manic person she'd swung into being was a little scary.

About an hour later the pair of them returned with a large box, whispering to each other conspiratorially as they carried it into the kitchen. For a while I stayed well clear, busying myself by pulling out the odd straggler of weed and wondering if I'd gone too far hacking into the bougainvillea. There was a naked look to the garden now that really hadn't been my intention when I'd started out.

But I'd found it quite addictive clearing plants that had gone too far, chopping out pushy little colonials that had turned up where they weren't wanted. Now I had it all under control I felt much better.

By the time I went inside Babetta had started cooking the meal we were going to share. It was to be some sort of feast of shellfish in a soupy tomato base, but neither of them would let me help them prepare it.

'Out of the kitchen, go on get out,' Leila told me.

'But—'

'No, we're getting everything ready for the party. You've done all the hard work in the garden so now it's your turn to relax.'

Leila still had that look of forced gaiety about her so I didn't bother to argue. Instead I went and lay on my bed for a while and thought about Tonino who I wasn't missing as much as I thought I should. Just about the last thing I wanted was to invite him to Villa Rosa to be part of some big house party with my three old friends. And I began to wonder, had I really settled for him because he was the easiest option, just like Charlie had told Leila? The thought of them discussing me still infuriated me and I paced out onto the wisteria-covered terrace and back into the room, not knowing quite what to do with myself.

As the sun began to set I heard Babetta calling. 'A-leese, A-leese!'

'I'm coming,' I shouted back, relieved something was about to happen at last.

The three of us gathered round the bonfire, holding beakers full of red wine, and waiting for Raffaella to arrive and darkness to fall.

'This is how I want to say goodbye to my mother,' Leila said. 'With a big glorious burning.'

I nodded. 'OK, this is how we'll say goodbye to her then.'

Just as the sun was setting, Raffaella appeared. Soft light

and long shadows suited her. She seemed more beautiful than ever.

The four of us were solemn as Babetta held a torch to the pyre. For a moment I thought the flames wouldn't catch but Leila had taken me seriously and poured the brandy over it, adding kerosene too just to be sure, while Babetta had thrown in dry firewood that had been seasoned for who knew how long in the neat stack beside the most sheltered wall of her house.

None of us spoke. We stood around watching the flames lick at the debris I'd ripped from the garden. As the fire caught and began to roar, we took a few steps back, our faces burning, our eyes filled with wood smoke. Leila laughed and filled her glass with more wine. 'This is so beautiful,' she shouted. 'I love it.'

I glanced at Raffaella, wondering if she'd noticed anything off-key about my friend, but she was staring into the fire.

'If you look closely you see shapes,' Leila whispered to me. 'Galloping horses, phantoms ... can you see them?'

Babetta was feeding the fire with wood, a grin soldered onto her face. She seemed almost jubilant. Was I the only one who hadn't been infected by the sight of the flames? Who didn't find them exciting?

More wine was poured into our glasses by Leila who had wrapped a red woollen shawl round her shoulders and was dancing around the fire humming to herself. I walked back a few steps and tried to look at the scene as a stranger might. The bent shape of the old woman, the young one shrouded, the other still and staring.

Once it was properly dark and they had locked the dog safely inside, Babetta and Leila began to let off their fireworks. To begin with there were sparklers we twirled around our heads, then they lit a few Roman candles and Catherine wheels.

They saved the rockets till last. There were lots of them and they were spectacular, shattering the stillness as they blossomed against the inky blackness of the sky and then faded to a shower of sparks. As I watched I realised Leila had been right, this was the best way for us to say goodbye to her mother.

It was as though we were telling the sky she had gone.

Babetta

Babetta's cheeks still felt warm and taut from the fire. She busied herself in the kitchen, grating fresh Parmesan and hacking a loaf of hard crusty bread into chunks. The clams and baby octopus she'd bought would only need a few moments cooking in the soup they'd made earlier and then it would be time to eat.

Everyone had drunk a lot of wine, especially Leila, and the atmosphere in the kitchen of Villa Rosa was festive. Babetta listened to the three women talking and didn't mind that she couldn't understand a word they said. It was enough to hear the hum of them, to feel at the centre of something.

She had been watchful tonight, just as she'd planned. At first there hadn't been much to see but then she'd noticed the little English girl seemed wary of Raffaella. It wasn't obvious, most likely Raffaella herself hadn't seen it, but to Babetta the girl was like a timid animal drawing closer and then pulling away, head-shy at the last minute. Even now, here in the kitchen, she had circled the table before taking the chair furthest away from her.

Babetta ladled the soup into bowls and carried them over. She saw how Leila was topping up her glass again, how her cheeks were burning red against the paleness of her face and her fingers were in her hair, worrying at it constantly.

As she tasted the broth from the ladle, she turned her attention to Raffaella and was surprised by what she saw in her friend's face. For although she was smiling, raising her glass for a toast, proclaiming the fireworks a great success, her mood seemed laboured. And Babetta wondered what shadows might have fallen over Raffaella's life that happiness had become such hard work for her.

Alice

I kept trying to apologise to Raffaella but every time I came close I thought better of it. Tonino's secrecy had hurt us both and I didn't see how words could fix that. So instead I sort of tiptoed around her, hoping to avoid a confrontation.

Our dinner after the bonfire was difficult. I struggled to find conversations that didn't lead back to my life in London, keeping Tonino's name out of everything I said.

It was a relief when the night was declared over and Raffaella had stood up to go. Leila and I stacked the dirty dishes in the sink and Babetta headed for home with the uneaten slices of bread wrapped up in her napkin. I knew she would use them for something – breadcrumbs for meatballs or toasted for breakfast next morning, for in Babetta's kitchen nothing was wasted.

The last thing I'd intended was to be left alone with Raffaella but it took a while for her to gather her things: car keys, phone, dishes that had held little bits of food she'd brought, a jar of artichoke hearts Babetta had pickled for her. By the time she was ready Leila had said her goodnights and there was no one to act as a buffer between us.

For a moment we looked at each other expectantly. And then Raffaella took the lead, her voice harsh and her words uncompromising.

'So, Alice, were you too ashamed to tell me?'

'No, it's not like that,' I tried to tell her.

'It seems we all misjudged you, didn't we?' Raffaella

was so furious she was struggling to keep her voice steady. 'What kind of a woman stays with a man who won't even own her? And then to come here and think you can continue to hide your relationship with my son. I thought we were friends ... that my husband and I had been good to you and you appreciated that.'

I tried to defend myself. 'It wasn't me who insisted on all the secrecy. Tonino could have told you about us but he chose not to. Shouldn't you be angry with him rather than me?'

'Oh, don't worry, I'm angry with him too. Angry with both my sons for different reasons. I'm full of anger.'

'And what about Ciro?'

Raffaella shook her head. 'He's resigned to having the sons we have. And he tries not to look too hard at the bad that's in both of them.'

So Lucio must have upset her too. I wondered where he had gone wrong.

'I understand why you're offended,' I tried to assuage her. 'But Tonino thought there would be pressure on us to marry and have children. He wanted to avoid that.'

'Pressure?' Raffaella was dismissive. 'I've waited all night for you to bring the subject up. What were you so afraid of? What did you think I'd do?'

'I don't know ... it was awkward.'

'You love my son. What's awkward about that?'

'The thing is ... I don't think I do love him ... not really.' I stopped, appalled I'd spoken the thought out loud.

Raffaella made an exasperated hissing sound and, turning away from me, walked out quickly, slamming the kitchen door hard behind her.

I stood for a moment listening to the sound of her starting her car and driving it fast up the narrow road. Then I heard Leila's voice. She must have been hovering in the hallway, listening to our fight.

'That didn't go very well did it?' she said, coming back into the kitchen.

'Oh, do you think?' I asked drily.

'Don't worry about it. Raffaella has a terrible temper. By morning she'll have settled down and you can talk to her more reasonably.'

'I've made a mess of things, haven't I?'

Leila took a dirty glass out of the sink and poured the dregs of a bottle of wine into it. 'Life is messy, Alice. That's what makes it so interesting to write about. So are you really not in love with Tonino?'

'I don't see how I can be.'

'And you're sure you're not looking for something that doesn't exist?'

'You mean the grand passion? The great romance? No, I suspect you and Charlie were right. I'm with Tonino because he's the easy option. The safe one. And he's with me because I'm prepared to go along with life the way he wants to live it.'

'You can be happy like that for a long time, I expect,' Leila said.

'I have been. Sort of happy.'

'And now?'

'I ought to leave but I'm scared to. I don't want to be on my own.'

'You're not on your own,' Leila said gently. 'You have me, remember?'

'Yes, but you know what I mean.'

'Look, spend the summer here. Take a break from Tonino and get your head straight. Then go back to London and sort out your life there.'

'What about Raffaella? Won't she tell Tonino what I said?'

'Not likely.'

'How can you be so sure?' I asked.

269

'Raffaella is very pissed off with both her sons now. Tonino tells her nothing. Lucio tells her too much.'

'What do you mean?'

'Well, apparently last year Lucio got some local girl pregnant and they decided she was going to have an abortion. For some reason he confided in Raffaella who, of course, wanted to keep the baby, offered to raise it herself or support the young girl in any way she could.'

'But they went ahead with the abortion.'

'Yes, and broke her heart. My mother told me all about it. Word got out and it was a big scandal.'

'But abortion is legal in Italy, isn't it?'

'Yeah, but still ... nice girls don't, or at least not round here. It's fair to say there are some people in town who haven't eaten much pizza recently.'

'Poor Lucio,' I said.

'Poor Raffaella,' countered Leila.

'It explains why she lost it with me so badly tonight, I suppose.'

'She's got a big heart, you know, as well as a huge temper. Go and see her tomorrow. Sort it out.'

'Maybe ... I'll think about it.'

I didn't tell Leila that the person I really wanted to see was Lucio. Or that I didn't think I could wait very much longer.

Babetta

Babetta slept for a long time and when she woke didn't have the energy to do more than sit in the new cane chair Raffaella had helped her choose. She didn't like wasting money on new things but Nunzio's chair had begun to rot and collapse and she enjoyed sitting out on the terrace, his old rug draped over her knee, remembering him and their life together.

From time to time she glanced over at Villa Rosa, wondering if she'd heard voices or if it was just the call of a bird confusing her.

She had enjoyed every moment of the night before. The fire, the food, but most especially the fireworks Lucio had found for them. They had come from the schoolhouse, a whole box of the things confiscated from pupils over the last year or two. She hadn't asked him how he knew about them but she had her suspicions. There was a pretty teacher there, young and fairly new in town. Just the kind of girl Lucio liked to be friendly to.

Babetta thought it was a shame he hadn't come to watch. The thrill of setting a match to the rockets and waiting for them to fly was still with her. Lucio would have loved it too. But he had been reluctant to accept her invitation even though she'd offered to wait until he had finished working at the pizzeria before setting them off.

Tilting her face up to the sun, Babetta dozed for a while, letting the memory of the night mingle with the mysteries in her mind. What was wrong with Raffaella? And with

271

Alice? What could be done about Leila? She hadn't expected her life to become so tangled up with those of other women. But it seemed she was the only one who could see there were problems that needed fixing.

Not right now, though. This warm spring day was for other things. Babetta planned to doze away the morning, knowing there was nothing that demanded to be done. Her kitchen cupboards were well stocked, her house tidy, the garden of Villa Rosa under control. She was going to take this empty time and waste it, watching the pine martens darting through the trees, stroking the old dog if he nuzzled into her knees, staring out at the sea the way Nunzio always used to.

There was a comfort in such stillness, in a slow sort of day. Tomorrow, Babetta might drag out the old Vespa and point it towards the port or up the hill to Triento. She would look into the lives of her friends and see what might be done for them. But not now. This day was for her alone.

Alice

The morning after the bonfire was an anticlimax. After her frenetic burst of energy, Leila seemed exhausted and there was no sign at all of Babetta stirring next door.

So I filled an hour or so walking down to the sea and along the track that ran a little way along the coast. There were a few more houses down here now but all were shuttered, waiting for their summer visitors. Someone had built a proper pathway, shaded by trees and covered in pine needles. They'd put up a rickety old fence made of crisscrossed saplings and carved out some rough steps down to a little bay caught between two steep cliffs. It looked as though you might be able to swim here on warmer, calmer days, although the beach was shingle and the stones looked sharp. There was a smell of rotting seaweed, an upturned wooden boat pulled above the high-tide line and a coil of fishing twine left behind on the rocks.

Standing on the beach, staring out at the sea and the sky, the idea of spending the whole summer there became more appealing. After all, I was in no hurry to put my key in the door of Tonino's country home and slip into being the person who lived in it. The only thing I really missed was my garden, but land like that had a certain tyranny to it and I wasn't sorry to have left behind my lists of things that needed to be done. Let Tonino worry about it for a change. There would be someone in the village he could pay to keep things tidy. And meanwhile I had Leila's steep plot and the puzzle of how to plant it.

Perhaps a small garden of herbs and salad leaves right by the kitchen door, I mused, as I walked back up towards the house. The fruit trees would stay, of course, but on the upper levels of the garden I could put in a few palms to give structure, or something for shade. There was no point in beginning until I had a proper plan so I frowned at the bare earth for a while and then headed to the kitchen in search of something to cook.

There was hardly any food in the house. I found a couple of half-empty boxes of Arborio rice so infested with weevils they had to be thrown away, a jar of olives with a skin of mould growing over them and a hardened piece of Parmesan. Most of the meals we'd been eating had come from Babetta's kitchen: trays of lasagne she'd brought over and baked in our oven, clean-tasting broths of pasta and spring vegetables, steamed stalks of Swiss chard wrapped in bacon and fried in foaming butter, fresh young broad beans gently flavoured with sage.

While it had been a relief to sink into the lazy comfort of someone else's cooking, now I was longing to taste my own again. I wanted to chop an onion, my knife beating against the board, then swirl it through heated olive oil and smell it as it sizzled; to watch other people's faces as they took their first bite of a dense creamy risotto I had stirred for twenty minutes; to match a piece of veal with the flavours of the lemons that grew outside the kitchen door; to cook a squid in its own rich inky liquid.

First, I had to get up to Triento to shop for food. Already it was mid-morning and I knew the market closed at mid-day and there was a risk I'd arrive and find only the things other women had prodded and passed over. Aurora's old Jeep was parked by the side of the house and I considered taking it but it had stiff gears and soft brakes, and I wasn't sure I could handle it around the bends of the coast or up the steep road to the town.

Grabbing a jacket and cap, I went to see if I could find Babetta. She was on her terrace, her pickled walnut of a face browning in the sun. At first I thought she was sleeping but, as I drew nearer, her eyes opened.

'*Buongiorno*,' I said cheerily and she gave me a lazy nod in reply.

I tried to explain I needed a lift to the market, but watching me mime my request seemed to exhaust her. Before I'd even finished, she jabbed a thumb towards the lean-to where she kept her Vespa and closed her eyes again.

I was glad in a way Babetta hadn't wanted to come. It felt good to be driving the little moped, hooting on the horn as I negotiated the sharp bends and tunnels of the coast road. I'd forgotten how much fun this was.

I found a place to park in one of the narrow backstreets, pushing the old Vespa into the doorway of an abandoned building. Then I unstrapped the panniers and went in search of food.

I shopped carefully, the way Babetta had shown me, not allowing myself to be seduced by the great wheels of Parmesan, the teetering piles of spring vegetables or the strings of fat, spicy sausages. There would be time to buy all these things in the coming weeks but right now I could only carry what I needed for the night's meal.

Only once the panniers had grown heavy and I was considering turning back to retrieve the scooter did I hear the voice I'd been hoping for.

'Alice, is that you?' Lucio was standing beside the stall that sold fresh buffalo mozzarella. 'Is that really you?'

Time had touched him lightly. It had left fine lines around his eyes and begun to silver his hair. But the character of his face was unchanged; the high cheekbones, full lips and crooked nose. His smile was the same. And looking at him had exactly the same effect on me it always had.

He came and kissed me on both cheeks, took a step back

to survey my face then kissed me again, one hand on my waist, lingering there the entire time.

'You look wonderful,' Lucio told me.

'You too,' I replied.

'Leila told me you were here. I was going to come down and see you when I had a moment. But you know how it is working in a kitchen. Things have been quiet over winter but we're just starting to get busy again.'

His hand was still there, resting gently in the curve of my body like it belonged.

'I was thinking about coming to see you too,' I said lightly. 'But I've bought all this food and now I should go home and cook it.'

Lucio laughed. 'Still the same Alice ... still obsessed with food.'

I wondered if he knew about me and Tonino. Surely he must? But I didn't want to bring up the subject in case for some reason his mother hadn't told him yet.

'There's time for a quick coffee, isn't there?' I said instead. 'Or do you have to work?'

'Yes, of course there's time, but come and let me make one for you,' he offered. 'Then you can talk to me while I start getting things ready. Just like the old days, eh?'

I nodded an agreement and, sliding his hand into the small of my back, he guided me across the piazza and down the alleyway towards his pizzeria.

Inside, the oven was unlit and the place felt chilly. A fresh coat of whitewash had been put on the walls and there was still the faintest smell of paint. The long benches were scrubbed and polished and a planter box full of red geraniums was outside the door.

The menu hadn't changed at all. When he noticed me running my eyes over it, Lucio smiled ruefully. 'Still the primavera and the marinara,' he said. 'All the same favourites.'

'You don't do any specials?' I asked.

'Oh yes, when the tourists come in summer I make a pizza with chips on it for the children.'

'Chips? You bake them onto the pizza?'

He nodded and laughed. 'Yes, yes. I won't offer to make you one though, Alice. I can see from your face you don't approve.'

'What happened to food made with love?' I asked him. 'Surely you don't waste your love on a chip pizza?'

Lucio laughed again. As we talked he seemed to be looking for reasons to touch me; his fingers brushing mine as he passed me the coffee cup, his hands on my shoulders to steer me towards a stool he'd put beside the counter.

'So tell me what brings you back to Italy at long last,' he asked as he swept last night's embers out of the oven.

'Leila needed me. She's alone now that her mother has died.'

'Yes, very sad to have no mother. Poor Leila, life has been hard on her, I think. To me she has never seemed very happy. Not like you, Alice. You look like your life suits you.'

'Leila's a big success,' I defended her. 'She's worked hard and made a name for herself. I haven't done anything with my life really. Not in comparison with her.'

Lucio stacked the oven with dry wood and kindling, then fired it up. He would keep it burning all afternoon until the thick stone walls had absorbed the heat and the oven was the perfect temperature to cook a thin-based pizza.

'A successful life is surely one that fits you well,' he said as he watched the fire catch. 'Look at me, for example. I stay here making chip pizza for the tourists because it suits me. Would my life be more successful if I were in London offering tiny plates of fiddly food to rich people? I don't think so. I would be exactly like your friend Leila.'

There was a mean-spirited part of me that enjoyed

listening to him talk like this. That got a little thrill from it. All the old jealousies, his and mine, seemed to be bubbling up like wet pizza dough. Again I wondered how much Lucio knew about my life in England.

'I ought to go,' I told him. 'I've borrowed Babetta's scooter and she'll be wondering where I've got to.'

Brushing the loose shards of firewood from his hands, Lucio showed me to the door as though I were a guest, not the girl who had once helped out in his kitchen. As I went to leave he stopped me with a hand and I turned my face to his, stupidly wondering if perhaps he was going to kiss me.

Instead, Lucio shook his head. 'I can't believe you belong to my brother, Alice,' he said in a low voice, and then he closed the door on me and, through the window, I saw him turning back towards his pizza oven.

Babetta

Feeling rested after another long night's sleep, Babetta woke early and with a sense of determination. She had her usual breakfast of strong coffee and hard bread sweetened with a sticky plum preserve and, chewing on it, thought about where to begin.

It was Raffaella who had been on her mind most as she'd rested in her cane chair the day before. To Babetta, her friend's life had always seemed a sunlit one. She had a hard-working husband, fine sons, a successful business; and what else could a woman ask for? But now some dark cloud seemed to be shadowing her.

Babetta set off early, wrapped warmly against the breeze that rushed at her as she rode her Vespa round the coast. Soon it would be summer and she wouldn't need her layers of black wool but today she was glad of them.

She found her friend sitting in the morning sun at one of the outdoor tables, deep in conversation with her husband. They stopped talking when they saw her and Raffaella called out a greeting.

'Babetta, we missed you yesterday. I was going to come over later to make sure everything was all right.'

'No need, I'm fine. But that was a chilly ride. It would be good to have something to warm me up.'

Ciro stood. 'Of course, let me make you a coffee,' he offered. 'And maybe some of the *biscotti* I baked last night. If you enjoy them you should take some home, Babetta.'

Once he had gone, Babetta smiled at her friend. 'You

both look after me so well,' she said. 'Where would I be without you?'

'You have your family,' Raffaella pointed out. 'Sofia and the twins. They take care of you too.'

Babetta nodded. 'Yes, yes, but family is different. Look at my Sofia, always telling me what to do, how to live my life. You'd never do that.'

'That's true. Family can be the most wonderful thing ... and also the most difficult,' agreed Raffaella.

Babetta had heard the gossip about Lucio and the pregnant girl. Everyone had. For a whole week it was all people could talk about as they sat on Silvana's old bench outside the bakery.

'He's a good boy really, you know,' she told Raffaella. 'Just a little weak when it comes to women, like so many men can be.'

'But which one of my sons are you talking about?' There was a sharp note in Raffaella's voice.

'Well Lucio, of course. I'm very fond of him, you know,' Babetta added hurriedly. 'Almost everyone is.'

'Lucio is yesterday's problem.' Raffaella stared out towards the harbour. 'I have other things to worry about now.'

'Tonino?'

Raffaella nodded. 'Tell me this, why would a son refuse to tell his mother about the important things in his life?' she asked, her voice a bumpy staccato. 'About the things that might make her happy? Every morning when I wake up it's the first thing I think about. And it nags at me all day long.'

Out of the corner of her eye Babetta saw Ciro returning with a tray of coffee and biscuits. 'But I don't understand ...' she began.

'Never mind.' Raffaella shrugged her shoulders. 'It doesn't matter now. But let me say that Ciro and I are happy to look after you, Babetta. I hope that if ever I'm your age there might be someone who would do the same for me.'

Alice

I hadn't taken Leila all that seriously when she'd told me she wanted to invite more people to stay at Villa Rosa, but she brought up the idea again as we were eating an al fresco lunch, taking advantage of the first warmth in the sun.

'It's going to be a beautiful summer,' she said. 'Lots of swimming, delicious food, plenty of wine. What did Charlie say when you suggested he bring the girls over? And Guyon?'

'I haven't asked them,' I admitted. 'I wasn't sure you meant it.'

'Of course I did. I wouldn't have said it otherwise.'

'But what about your own friends? Don't you want to invite them?'

Leila looked thoughtful. 'My friends expect me to present myself a certain way and I don't feel like that right now.'

'What do you mean?'

'They invite me to their dinner parties to be fascinating, the famous author they can impress their other friends with. And straight away you're in a complicated place. Some resent you, others are determined not to like you. It takes a lot of energy to live in that world. A mental strength.'

'That you don't have?'

'Not now.'

'But Guyon and Charlie never really ...'

'Never liked me much?'

'Well, they were my friends really, weren't they?'

'I know, so I don't feel I have to make a huge effort.

They can just be here, filling the place with noise, making a party around me. There's no need for me to charm them, win them over. They'll be here for you, not me,' said Leila.

I laughed. 'I'm not entirely sure I understand but I'll invite them if you want me to. It'd be fun to have Charlie's girls here. They're so sweet.'

Leila looked wistful. 'My mother would have liked to see the house full of kids. She was sad I never had any.'

'So why didn't you?' I asked, curious now.

'I nearly did,' Leila admitted. 'I got pregnant by accident and it ended in a messy miscarriage. When they let me out of hospital I caught a cab straight to Battersea Dog's Home and adopted a couple of mutts. They're my best friends, aside from you. Sad, hey?'

'Where are they now?'

'At my place in Woldingham with my housekeeper. I'm missing them. What about you, Alice? Why did you and Tonino never have a baby?'

I chewed on my lip. 'Because he didn't want to, I suppose.'

'And you don't mind?'

'Yes, I mind,' I admitted. 'Although it's taken me a long while to realise it.'

'Do you ever wonder how things might have turned out for you if you hadn't been raped?' Leila asked suddenly.

I was taken aback. 'I really don't think about all that any more.'

'But it changed the whole direction of your life.'

'It's not the reason I don't have children though,' I argued.

'In a way it is. Ever since then you've chosen the safest course and stuck with it. Even now you say you're not certain you love Tonino, but I think at the end of the summer you'll go back to him. Anything else would be too much of a risk, wouldn't it?'

'Leila, I don't want you poking around in my life like this,' I said, standing up and throwing the dirty lunch plates into a stack. 'Why do you always insist on doing it?'

'Because I'm your friend,' she said. 'And because I care about you.'

Noisily and angrily, I washed up the plates, not caring if I chipped them. As I flung things into the kitchen cupboards I remembered how I'd been so determined to live life to the full. If Leila was right then I'd done the complete opposite.

Once I'd calmed down I called Charlie and Guyon, leaving messages imploring them to come. The more crowded the place was the less Leila would be able to trap me into meaningful conversations.

The less I'd have to deal with her.

Babetta

It was the children's voices Babetta heard first. Two little girls laughing and calling out to each other. Curious, she left her terrace and walked slowly to the gates of Villa Rosa. She saw they were pretty things with long fair hair wound into loose plaits. Someone had rigged up a swing for them, hanging it from the strong trellis covered in bougainvillea.

Watching them from beyond the pomegranate tree was a pale man sitting in a deckchair. He wore a hat to shield him from the sun and held a newspaper. Babetta stood by the gates for a while, wondering who these new people might be. And then another man came out of the kitchen. This one had a florid complexion and a brightly coloured shirt. He was carrying a teapot in both hands.

On other, more ordinary days, Babetta might have crossed the courtyard and knocked on the kitchen door. But the presence of these strangers made her shy. Even standing there, watching the children play seemed like an intrusion. So, reluctantly, she turned and went back to her own house.

As the day wore on cars came and went. Babetta listened the sounds of people eating outside, forks clinking with knives, the rise and fall of talk and laughter. Leila was the loudest but Alice could be heard too, rowdier than usual as she played with the children. For a moment Babetta considered going over to sweep the paths but it seemed much better manners to stay away.

And then the old dog Sky stood up from his basket and

gave himself a shake, his tongue lolling out of the side of his mouth. Stiffly, he walked down the steps and nosed about in a patch of long grass. His ears pricked up and he raised his grey muzzle in the air, barking hoarsely.

'Sky, Sky, here boy,' Babetta heard Leila calling out. The dog had heard her too. Wagging his tail, he set off at a determined trot towards the gates of Villa Rosa.

'No, you idiot dog,' Babetta hissed at him but he ignored her. She tutted to herself, certain the old animal shouldn't be trusted around children, their fingers were so tiny, his teeth so brown. What if they touched him roughly and he took fright? As quickly as was possible at her age, she headed after him.

She found Leila kneeling on the ground, showing the girls how to stroke the dog gently. Sky had surrendered to them, sinking down and rolling over, begging for his hairy stomach to be rubbed.

'It's OK, Babetta,' said Leila in her bad Italian. 'He likes the children, see. But you should come and meet our guests. They'll be staying for a few weeks over summer, so don't be shy of them.'

There were awkward introductions then, with Leila repeating the names until Babetta had managed to pronounce them properly. 'Charlie, Guyon ... Charlie, Guyon.' Neither man spoke a word of her language and Babetta wondered what their arrival might mean for her.

'*Momento*,' she said and, returning to her own house, searched through the kitchen cupboards. She lined a basket with a blue checked cloth and filled it with the most delicious things she could find: some biscuits she'd baked the day before, a jar of peach jam from last summer, a small *panettone* Sofia had bought and given to her. Then she returned to Villa Rosa where she found everyone gathered round the table, shelling fresh peas.

Nodding at the man in the bright shirt, Babetta held out

her small offering to him. He seemed pleased, smiling his thanks and straight away the tin of biscuits was opened. Then Leila went to make more tea and Alice moved over so there was a space for Babetta at the table.

She took the seat offered and, reaching into the plastic carrier bag in the centre of the table, pulled out a handful of pods and began popping them open, spilling the peas into a colander as the others were. Next to her Alice and Guyon chatted with each other as they worked. Now and then a pea escaped, rolling beneath the table where the dog was snuffling around, ready to eat them. Then Leila brought out the tea and her biscuits were quickly finished.

The sun on her shoulders, Babetta worked on shelling peas with the others as the foreign chatter round the table filled her ears.

Alice

This was turning into an idyllic summer. There was a part of me that felt guilty to be letting the days run away but it was easy to do little more than spend a morning at the beach and doze away the afternoon in a deckchair as Charlie's girls played on the terrace. We'd found all sorts of ancient toys locked away in the garage behind the house. Charlie had pulled out an old table tennis set and challenged Guyon to a tournament, and the girls had discovered buckets and spades. Some long-gone family who had lived at Villa Rosa must have abandoned it all but now we were making good use of the stuff they hadn't wanted.

For a while I'd been a little worried Leila might regret opening up her house to my friends. But she was joining in, playing ping-pong or taking the girls on rambling adventures round the grounds. She seemed to be enjoying herself. Even Babetta had slotted into our summer, appearing every day with treats she'd baked and insisting on taking turns with me in the kitchen.

'I feel bad letting the old girl cook when the two of us are chefs,' Guyon admitted. 'Shouldn't she sit down while we make meals for her?'

I looked at Babetta who was busy showing the children how to roll out a long snake of dough for gnocchi. 'Do you think you can stop her?' I laughed. 'She's in her element. I don't think I've ever seen her so happy.'

'It must be lonely for her here in winter,' he observed.

'Lonely and wild,' I agreed. 'Did you see Aurora's storm

paintings? Some of them are still propped up against a wall in the living room.'

'Ah yes, I did take a look at them. Talented women, both Aurora and her daughter. Amazing, really.'

I nodded. 'It must be nice to have one big talent. Must make it so much easier to see where you should take your life.'

'But you have a talent. You're a great cook,' said Guyon.

'It's nice of you to say that but it's not really true. I'm OK at it but not especially talented.'

'So are you sorry you ever got into it now?'

'Not sorry, exactly, but I do feel as though I've just woken up and realised I'm leading someone else's life. I keep wondering how I got here, how it happened.'

'Everyone feels like that from time to time, I think.'

'Other people I know don't seem to. You and Charlie, for instance. You never seem to be questioning whether you're on the right path. '

'We've got our problems though. And anyway it's not too late for you. You can still change. Do something you love.' Guyon paused and looked at me. 'Be with somebody that you love.'

'How, though? How do I make a change like that?' I needed someone to give me a clue. 'I don't know where to start.'

Guyon sighed. 'I've had a lot of therapy, Alice, as you can imagine. I'm not sure it's really taught me how to live life better. But I do know that sometimes you just have to do things and trust they'll work out. '

If Leila had tried to have this conversation with me I'd have run away but somehow from Guyon it seemed more palatable. For the next few days I thought about what he'd said. As I was playing with the girls on the sandy beach we drove to most mornings, or cooking them a simple lunch of macaroni and tomato sauce, I was thinking about it.

Sometimes I even took myself down to the rocks beneath Villa Rosa and sat there, looking out to sea. That was always the place where I could think most clearly.

For a long time, though, I could only think about all the things I didn't want. I'd realised being a chef wasn't my life. Neither was being an accessory for Tonino. It was easy enough to understand where I had gone wrong in the past. But I couldn't see my way forward.

And then, one morning, I was working in the little kitchen garden I'd put in for Leila and wondering why everyone didn't grow their own vegetables. Even if it were only a few salad greens and herbs they'd still get that sense of satisfaction, the special joy of picking and eating your own produce. For some reason so few people bothered these days, even those with decent gardens. And that's when I saw it. The thing I wanted to become.

I only dared to speak the dream aloud a few days later when Charlie and I were walking beneath the pines along the little path that led to the rocky cove.

'I've come up with an idea,' I began hesitantly.

'Oh yes,' he said encouragingly.

'I want to start my own gardening business.'

'But you're not a landscaper,' he pointed out. 'You only do edible gardens really, don't you?'

'I know, and that's just it. I thought I could start helping other people grow their own organic vegetables.' I was warming to my theme now. 'Maybe supply them with raised-bed kits and get them started if they needed it.'

'But food is your passion, isn't it? What about your career as a chef?' Charlie seemed surprised.

'It's been over for a long time,' I told him. 'Yes, I love food now, but I realised ages ago that I don't love restaurant kitchens. That sort of cooking is addictive. It's a great way to fill up your life and make sure you have no time to think about anything else. But it's not about food really. It's not cooking with love.'

'Isn't it? Why not?' He sounded interested now. 'I always thought you were obsessed by food.'

'Yes, I like growing food and dreaming up ways to make it into something delicious,' I agreed. 'To me it's a sort of alchemy. But being a line cook is all about turning out the same thing over and over again. That doesn't have the same magic.'

I explained what I'd read on the Internet about raised garden beds. How they could be built from wood to any height you wanted so you could garden without ever having to kneel or bend.

'You don't even have to dig,' I told him. 'Not everyone can have a kitchen garden like the one at Villa Rosa. They're so much work. But that doesn't mean people can't eat fresh things straight from the earth instead of out of a plastic bag from the supermarket. That's what food is all about to me.'

I'd expected Charlie to come up with a bunch of reasons why the idea wouldn't work but instead he seemed interested. 'You could sell them over the Internet,' he said. 'Do different sizes so even people with courtyard gardens could fit one. Untreated wood, of course, but still they'd last for years.'

'So you think it would work?'

'Why not? No reason why it shouldn't if you did your homework right.'

'Really?'

'Yep, really.' Charlie smiled at me. 'I think it sounds like a great idea. How on earth did you come up with it?'

Excitedly, I spilled out my explanation. 'I was trying to work out what I'm passionate about,' I told him. 'And I realised growing food has always brought me so much pleasure. Babetta helped me learn the basics and now I'd like to pass on her knowledge. I could sell starter kits of seeds, even supply recipes. I've got loads of ideas. I may have to do a bit of temping in a kitchen while I'm getting things up and running but that's OK. At least I'll be working towards the thing I really want to do.'

Later that afternoon we sat at the kitchen table and he helped me come up with an action plan. There seemed a daunting number of things to consider but Charlie worked through them methodically, head bent, chewing on the end of his pencil.

'I'll go in with you if you like,' he offered. 'Provide a bit of capital. Be a silent partner. Well, if you want me to, that is.'

'God, yes. I'd love you to,' I told him.

'Business partners then.' He looked up at me. 'Not quite how I thought things would turn out between us but better than nothing, I suppose.'

I didn't pick up on the hint, not at the time. Perhaps I was too busy plotting and planning for my new business to think about Charlie and the feelings that had once existed between us. It was later, as I lay in bed, trying and failing to sleep, that I remembered his words and wondered what they meant. All these years later, did Charlie still love me a little? And if he did, how did I feel about him?

Around six a.m., sick of thrashing around in bed and convinced sleep was never going to come with so many things buzzing in my brain, I decided to get up. The house felt surprised to see me; the shutters were closed, the early morning sounds of snoring and coughing were coming from behind closed doors. As I headed towards the bathroom I didn't expect to hear Leila's bedroom door open and close behind me.

'Can't you sleep either …?' I began, but then turned to see it wasn't Leila standing outside her room in the morning half-light. It was Lucio, his hair rumpled, wearing yesterday's clothes and carrying his shoes in one hand. He smiled at me and held a finger to his lips.

'Shh, she's still sleeping,' Lucio whispered.

I didn't say a thing to him. And to my surprise I didn't feel very much of anything either.

Babetta

With life behind the gates of Villa Rosa so irresistible, Babetta forgot about other things. She didn't bother driving up to Triento, to shop and gossip, or down to the port to see her friend Raffaella. Her days fell into a pleasant rhythm. In the mornings she slept for as long as she needed, then woke to bake biscuits or a loaf of bread. Before lunchtime she took her little offering to Villa Rosa where she swept the paths, interfered in the kitchen and then sat at the outdoor table to share whatever they had made for lunch. Usually the children were sticky with sand and salt water from a morning at the beach. They wore little hooded towelling ponchos in pastel colours and wandered round the garden clutching crusts of bread smeared with Nutella as the adults opened another bottle of chilled wine, moved from the shaded table out into the sun, nibbled on cheese and fruit or hard-baked rings of *tarallini*.

When she grew drowsy in the heat of the afternoon, Babetta returned home to doze in her cane chair. Often the others would head off on some sort of outing; to walk round the base of the statue of Christ on the mountain or drive along the coast, then have coffee and cakes in a café somewhere. The little girls always waved out of the rear window as their car climbed the hill and Sky barked an old dog's hoarse goodbye in return.

That afternoon they'd set off as usual and Babetta was left half dozing contentedly in her chair when she heard a car returning to the house. Surprised, she opened her eyes, and then felt a little stab of guilt as she recognised Raffaella's old Fiat.

'I'm so sorry, my friend, I've been neglecting you,' she called out as Raffaella climbed the steps to the terrace. 'I've been thinking I should come to see you soon.'

'I was a little worried. I thought perhaps you were ill. But then I saw Leila and she told me you'd been busy.' Sinking down on to the top step, Raffaella sighed. 'Ah, that's better. Those stairs are so steep, I don't know how you manage them. Maybe your daughter is right and you ought to leave this house before it becomes too much for you.'

Babetta's old face closed into a scowl. 'I'm not moving ... and I'm not ill.'

Her tone was sullen but Raffaella seemed to ignore it. 'So, tell me what you've been doing. Leila mentioned she's been seeing a lot of you.'

'Yes, yes, I've been helping the English people prepare meals and looking after the children,' Babetta told her, pride in her voice now.

'Ah, the two pretty little girls. I saw them running round after the seagulls down at the port.'

'Pretty but exhausting,' Babetta sighed. 'It's lucky I'm here to help or poor Alice wouldn't have a moment's peace.'

'And so how is Alice?' Raffaella asked curiously.

Babetta thought about it and realised how much the girl had changed since her friends had come. She smiled more often, filled the space she occupied more fully. She seemed less like a shadow of herself.

'Fine,' was all she said to Raffaella. 'They all seem fine.'

After they had talked for a while, Babetta made a pot of coffee to drink out on the terrace.

'I suppose they'll be gone soon, the Englishmen and the children?' she remarked flatly.

'I think so,' Raffaella agreed. 'They're only here for a

holiday. But Leila tells me she and Alice will stay for the whole summer. They want to do lots more work in the garden.'

Babetta looked down at the rows of tomatoes she'd managed to plant out in her own plot, already choked by a forest of weeds. 'Gardens do need a lot of work,' she said sagely.

Following the line of her gaze, Raffaella smiled. 'You know, I have a couple of hours free. Tell me where you keep the wheelbarrow and trowel and I'll see if I can rescue your tomato bed.'

The pair of them worked together, Babetta feeling guilty that her progress was so much slower than her friend's. 'If I bottle the tomatoes I'll be sure to give you some,' she promised. 'And lots of the sweet red onions if they're good this year.'

'You know, I could send my husband over to help out in the garden if you'd like,' Raffaella offered. 'At home we only have enough space for a few pots of herbs and I'm sure he'd appreciate the chance to plant things and watch them grow. No matter what you say, this place is too much for you on your own, Babetta.'

'It's a long time since I've had a man to help me,' the old lady conceded. 'I've missed that.'

'Well it's agreed then. We'll help in the garden some afternoons and whatever we grow that you don't need we can use in the trattoria. The perfect arrangement. I don't know why I didn't think of it sooner.'

For a while longer they worked on, freeing the tomato plants from the weeds until they heard the cars return-ing to Villa Rosa. Then there was a slamming of doors and Babetta looked up to see Leila and the children had climbed out and were walking the rest of the way, picking wildflowers from the roadside.

Watching their progress, her eyes narrowed. 'You

know,' she said almost to herself. 'I think that girl may be pregnant.'

'What? Raffaella sounded shocked.

'That Leila, look at her body. Her waist has thickened and there's a curve to her belly. But it's not just that. I've noticed she's barely been sipping the wine with lunch and yesterday she refused coffee. That's just how I was with Sofia. Couldn't touch either of them.'

'Pregnant?' Raffaella repeated stupidly.

'Yes, yes, I think so.'

Raffaella's eyes were on Leila now, watching as the two little girls presented her with clumsy bunches of flowers and she pointed to more they might pick.

'I think you're right. I see it too now. Oh my God.'

Babetta searched her friend's face. 'What's wrong?'

Raffaella hesitated, her handsome features looking strained. 'Please don't say anything to Ciro, not yet,' she pleaded. 'But I think I know who the father may be.'

There was no need for either of them to speak Lucio's name out loud. No need at all. And later, as Babetta wedged the gardening tools into the lean-to beside her old Vespa, she thought about the look on Raffaella's face and hoped that this time her youngest son would do the proper thing.

Alice

I'd expected Leila to be contrite, when eventually I told her I'd caught Lucio sneaking out of her room, but if anything she was defiant. Lighting a cigarette from the hob and pouring herself a glass of orange juice, she took the seat opposite me at the kitchen table and gave me one of her careless one-shouldered shrugs.

'So I suppose you're going to leave now,' she said.

Shocked, I asked her, 'Is that why you did it? Was it a test to see if it would make me leave?'

'Don't be ridiculous.'

'Well, why then?'

'I always have. Every summer when I came to see my mother I fell into sleeping with him. Why not? You'd disappeared from my life so it didn't matter what you thought.'

'And you couldn't be on your own. You always need to have a lover?'

'It makes life more interesting. People like Lucio and me, we understand that. But you weren't meant to find out,' Leila hastened to add. 'We've only been together a few times. I thought we'd get away with it.'

I watched while she stubbed out the last of her cigarette and went to light another.

'And anyway,' she continued out of the corner of her mouth as she sucked in her first taste of it. 'You're with Tonino now so I rather thought that meant you'd let your hopes of Lucio go. You can't have both brothers, can you?'

'I don't want either of them,' I snapped.

'Oh, for God's sake, don't be so sulky and childish. You might as well leave if you're going to behave like this.'

Before her operatic mood could move again, Leila swung her hips around and took off to her bedroom. She'd been spending more time in there lately, sleeping for longer than usual, perhaps finally finding the rest that her mother's death had stolen from her. For now it seemed best to leave her there until her blood had cooled and she was more easily reasoned with.

Outside, it was raining softly and, although the sky was bleached of its blue, everything in the garden seemed lush as a consolation. Escaping the house was my plan and I tried to think of some place the rainy weather wouldn't be a problem. The only thing that sprang to mind was the strange chapel in the cave that Babetta had taken me to years ago. On a day like this, with the gloomy light and dripping stalactites, it would be wonderfully atmospheric. I went to find Charlie and the girls to see what they thought of the idea.

Getting them out of the house caused the usual fuss, the tracking down of shoes, the finding of coats and cardigans. The bedlam of it drove Charlie crazy but to me it was still a novelty.

'Yes, Mia, you can bring your dolly if she wants to come. No, Grace, we're not going to get ice cream this time,' I called as Charlie hid behind an old issue of *Vanity Fair* and pretended none of it was happening.

We drove round the coast singing songs they'd learnt at nursery school and I laughed at Charlie for knowing all the words.

'You used to be so cool with your copies of the *NME* and your vinyl collection,' I goaded him. 'Now look at you.'

'Children change everything, as you'll discover yourself some day.'

I shook my head, quickly. 'Not me, I'm too old. I've left it far too late.'

'There are lots of women having babies later these days,' he pointed out.

'Yes, but they've got partners.'

Charlie took his eyes off the road for a moment to glance at me. 'And you don't?' he asked. 'Are you not with Tonino any more?'

'No. Although I must admit I haven't actually broken the news to him yet.'

'So you're going to finish it at last. Will he be upset?' Charlie didn't sound like he cared much. 'Or has he been expecting it?'

'I don't know, he's so self-contained. I expect he'll be peeved that I've messed up his life when he had it all perfectly arranged. His pride will be hurt. But I think that's all, to be honest.'

'So why not just ring and tell him now? What are you waiting for?'

'He's been good to me, given me a lot of freedom. I can't just dump him over the phone.'

For a moment or so Charlie said nothing. Then he muttered loud enough for all of us to hear, 'Controlling, conceited ass.'

'What's an ass, Daddy?' piped up Grace from the back seat.

'Like a donkey.'

'Are we going to ride on one?'

'Um, no, we're going to see the cave Aunty Alice wants to show us. We're steering well clear of asses.'

I'd forgotten how steep a climb it was to reach the entrance of the chapel. Halfway up there was a lot of whining from small girls with short legs so Charlie hefted Mia onto his shoulders and I piggybacked Grace. To strangers we'd have looked like a family. Even to me it was beginning to feel like we were almost one.

Once inside the wide limestone cavern filled with altars

and marble statues, the girls were entranced. They ran off to explore, calling to each other in loud stage whispers.

'Weird place,' remarked Charlie. 'I've never seen anything like this.'

'I think this is where Babetta and her husband married.'

'What a cool setting for a wedding.' Charlie gazed around at the limestone grotto. 'Can you imagine it? I think it would be incredible.'

'I guess so, but I don't suppose either of us will have to worry about settings for weddings at this rate will we?' I said.

'It doesn't seem like it.' Charlie sounded wry. 'What's the story with you and Tonino anyway? Why suddenly decide to change things?'

'It's not sudden. I should have done it ages ago. But I've only just realised I've been letting the years click by and getting a lot of things wrong.'

'So, new job, new man then?' Charlie asked jauntily.

'I don't know about that but a new apartment definitely. I can't go on living in his house.'

'You're being very brave, Alice.' He watched as his daughters tried to peer through the dusty windows of a locked side chapel. 'But then you always have been.'

'Brave? I don't think so. I go where life pushes me. Or at least I have till now.'

'So long as you know I'm here to help if you need me ... practically, emotionally, whatever you want really.' Charlie had forgotten about the girls and was looking straight at me now. 'Just say the word.'

'Thank you. I don't know where I'd be without friends like you and Guyon. I'm not sure I deserve you.'

'Oh no? Guyon says you're the reason he still has a job. And as for me ... well you and me, we'll always deserve each other.'

The girls came screaming back then, begging me to

change my mind about the ice cream. And since we could see through a big gap in the cave wall that it had stopped raining and we knew there was a stony beach nearby, we gave in to their demands.

Charlie had pistachio, I chose lemon sorbet and the girls both wanted strawberry, of course. As we were sitting on the nearly empty beach, watching the waves and other families doing the same, I thought how easily they could have been my kids. Just a couple of turns, decisions made or not made, and life might have turned out differently.

'Do you still have that emerald?' I don't know what made me ask it. 'The one you proposed to me with?'

Charlie seemed unfazed. 'Yes, Alice, as a matter of fact I do still have it.' Then he bit off the bottom from his cone and his little girls laughed as the ice cream came dribbling out of it.

Babetta

Babetta had given up trying to help people look for happiness. Things changed too quickly, the ground shifted then shifted again. She was too old to keep up or understand. She could do other things though. Pull a salad of herbs and peppery leaves from her garden, bake a loaf and dust its golden crust with flour, show a little girl how the dough she squeezed between her fingers became a plate of pasta. She could share her food, her company, her knowledge. But there was nothing she could do about the tremors that shook other people's lives.

She was certain now the artist's daughter was pregnant and just as sure she didn't know it yet. Yesterday, when Babetta had gone over to Villa Rosa to make a spaghetti sauce, Leila had complained about the smell of frying garlic so early in the day. The colour had fled from her face and she'd left the kitchen quickly. Later that afternoon Babetta had given her some dry biscuits she'd flavoured with ginger and the girl had nibbled on them gratefully.

'Just exactly what I felt like,' she told Babetta. 'I must have a bit of a stomach bug or something. I'm not feeling myself at all.'

Babetta had said nothing. By then she was distracted by the other one, little Alice, who'd always had such a core of sadness and now seemed lit with joy. Her colour was warmer, her beauty less of a fleeting thing. Babetta saw how the men watched her, Guyon in one way and Charlie in quite another. She wondered about that. Often she drew the girls away, pushed them on the swing or took them over to her garden and kept them for as long as she could, smelling flowers and picking herbs. If it helped much, she wasn't certain, but Alice and Charlie were always together when they returned.

Still, she wasn't always able to run around after other people's children. At least every other day she made a point of waking early enough to drink a morning coffee with Raffaella and help her set up the trattoria tables for lunch. She polished the cutlery carefully, shined up the glasses and made sure every place had a neatly folded serviette. Usually there was something in the kitchen they wanted her to taste to see if it needed another pinch of salt, a drizzle of balsamic vinegar. Or she would join in as they decided what to make with the seafood Ciro had bought that morning. Once or twice she even stayed to take orders and tell the customers what she thought they might enjoy eating that day.

Babetta had decided to give up worrying about other people's problems. She simply didn't have time for them.

Alice

There were only a few days to go before Charlie and Guyon had to drive back to Rome with the girls. The plan had always been for them to spend some time walking round the famous places: the Coliseum, the Trevi Fountain, the Spanish Steps. Hotels were booked and paid for, decisions made, but now neither of them seemed keen to leave.

'Honestly, I don't know when I've been more relaxed than this,' Guyon told me. 'Rome with its crowds and in this heat is going to be a nightmare.'

I'd been worried when Guyon first arrived, feeling almost like I was responsible for him not drinking so long as he was staying with me. But if at any point he'd felt like lapsing he hadn't shown it, sipping on mineral water or juice whenever we were guzzling wine.

'I wish you could stay a bit longer,' I told him. 'To be honest, the thought of being alone with Leila is slightly terrifying.'

Guyon frowned. 'There's something not right with her, isn't there? I mean, besides her grief for her mother and her customary level of madness. She seems even more off-key than usual.'

'I don't know what's going to happen once this summer is over. I don't think she should be left alone.'

'Well, you've got weeks yet. Maybe she'll sort herself out.' Guyon sounded doubtful.

'She doesn't seem able to decide on anything: whether to sell this house, where she'd prefer to live. She's sort of stuck.'

'All you can do is be here, Alice.'

'I know that.'

'Charlie and me, we thought the same about you for years,' Guyon admitted.

'That I was stuck?'

He nodded. 'And you're freeing yourself now, aren't you? But you had to want to. No one could help you.' Then he laughed. 'Listen to me sounding like someone who's had too much therapy. I have to stop doing that.'

I had much the same conversation with Charlie as I was helping the girls decide which of their clothes they were going to wear in Rome, setting aside the special outfits to put on the very top of all the other frilly pink things stuffed into their suitcases.

'Not those.' Mia pointed to her jeans. 'Princesses don't wear trousers. Only pretty dresses.'

Charlie gave me his world-weary father look. 'Please come to Rome with us. I don't think I can cope alone.'

'You know what, I'd love to come. But I don't think right now is a great time to abandon Leila.'

'Yeah, she's edgy, isn't she?' Charlie agreed. 'She seemed to be having such a good time when we first got here but then something changed.'

'Well, she's been feeling really nauseous which can't have helped. Have you noticed she's been sitting on one glass of wine all night long? Now that's not like Leila.'

'She's barely been touching her morning espresso either.' Charlie's eyes widened like he'd suddenly been woken up. 'Bloody hell, you know what – she must be pregnant!'

Now I felt nauseous too. 'Surely not? I mean she's over forty and she's had a miscarriage.'

'So what? It all adds up, doesn't it? She sleeps more. She lives on those ginger biscuits Babetta keeps plying us with. Don't know why it's taken me so long to notice, actually. Mary was pretty much the same with both the girls.'

'Oh my God, maybe she is pregnant.' I realised it had to be true. 'But she hasn't said anything.'

'Perhaps she hasn't realised it herself. Mary was four months gone with Mia before she worked out what was happening. She'd assumed she was just off-colour and stressed. Leila might be thinking the same. She's just lost her mother, after all.' Then he paused and thought for a moment. 'I wonder who the father is.'

An image of Lucio creeping out of Leila's room in the half-light of an early morning flashed up in my mind. 'I think I might know,' I admitted.

'So who?'

'You haven't met him. It isn't important.'

'By the look on your face it is,' Charlie countered. 'Not an ex-boyfriend of yours, is he?'

'No, just someone I used to think was going to be special,' I said reluctantly. 'But it hasn't turned out that way.'

'Oh well, perhaps he'll be special to Leila now,' he said lightly. 'She could do with slowing the pace a bit, couldn't she? It's one thing sharing yourself around like that when you're in your twenties but at her age it's getting a bit sad.'

'Charlie!' I poked him. 'Don't be so sexist.'

'I'd say the same if she was a bloke,' he argued.

'Not everyone has to settle down and behave themselves. Maybe she won't even want to keep the baby. Some other girlfriend of Lucio's fell pregnant and she got rid of hers.'

'Lucio.' Charlie said the name thoughtfully. 'So he's the one who was meant to be special, eh?'

'But he isn't,' I told him. 'Not special at all.'

Babetta

Babetta was certain nobody knew. On Silvana's old bench outside the bakery the talk was of other things, a wife caught cheating on her husband, a scandal involving the mayor and money. It had been a while since she'd heard Lucio's name mentioned. And the English folk down the hill had long since stopped inciting comment. If people had known anything they would be talking about it, especially to Babetta who might be able to fuel the gossip with more facts. But no one had said a thing.

All the same, the next time she went to Triento she took a detour from her normal route around the market stalls and wandered along the alleyway to Lucio's pizzeria. He was inside, with the oven lit, working in the stifling warmth of a summer's day.

'Ouf,' Babetta complained as she walked in. 'What heat you have in here.'

Looking up, Lucio smiled a greeting. 'Ah, Babetta. Are you searching for more fireworks? Or do you want to taste the best pizza you've ever eaten?'

Without waiting for a reply, he picked up a ball of dough and began stretching it between his fingers. 'I'm guessing your liking would be for something simple, sliced tomatoes, torn basil, chunks of buffalo mozzarella. Nothing too fussy for you, eh, Babetta?'

'If you say so.' She climbed onto the stool he kept behind the counter. 'But I didn't come here to eat.'

'Oh no? What then?'

She stared at him for a moment. Lucio, who had always been so handsome, still had the look of a boy, hair flopping into his eyes as he bent his head over her pizza. Babetta could see how easily he might charm a woman and for a moment was grateful she had married Nunzio so young and never had time to be tempted by a man like this.

'I came to talk to you but I'll taste that pizza first, I think,' she told him.

She ate it all, even the hard, smoky crust, relishing the melted mozzarella against her tongue and the sharp tang of the tomatoes.

'You have an appetite,' Lucio remarked admiringly.

'And so do you, apparently.' She pushed the empty plate away and wiped her mouth with a serviette.

'I'm not sure I know what you mean.'

'Oh, I think you do.'

Lucio looked at her quizzically. 'You'll have to explain, old lady.'

Babetta glared at him. 'In my day when a man got a girl pregnant he was made to marry her. There was no going to a hospital and getting rid of it. No leaving a girl disgraced.'

'This again.' Lucio sighed. 'I'd have stood by her if she wanted but her family wouldn't hear of it. They wanted something better for her than a pizza-maker. They've sent her to London now, well away from me.'

'I'm not talking about that young girl,' Babetta told him.

'Who then? To the best of my knowledge I haven't made anyone else pregnant.' He stopped and looked at the expression on Babetta's face. 'Who? What do you know?'

'Just how many girls are there?'

Lucio took her empty plate and set it in the sink. 'That's none of your business really, is it?'

The tartness of his tone affronted her. 'In the old days if a man refused to marry a girl he'd disgraced then the police would be sent to make him,' she reminded him.

'I know that. But we aren't living in those days, are we?'

Babetta climbed off her stool. 'Then you must choose to do the right thing yourself, mustn't you, Lucio?' She turned to go. 'This time it's up to you.'

'Wait.' He called after her. 'Aren't you going to tell me who it is?'

Babetta considered the idea for a moment, then gave a sharp shake of her head. 'You'll find out soon enough, I expect. But thank you for the pizza. It was just as good as you promised it would be.'

Alice

It was early morning and I heard the sound of Leila's empty retching. I found her bent over the toilet bowl, tears filling her eyes, holding her hair back from her face.

'Can I get you anything?' I asked. 'Water? A towel?'

She sat back on her haunches. 'No, but God, I feel terrible. Maybe later I should go to find a doctor. This stomach bug is hanging round way too long.'

'Have you never felt like this before?'

'Hell, no.'

I sat on the edge of the bath. 'Not even once, maybe?'

'What are you on about? Can't you just leave me here to die?' She bent over the toilet bowl again and I winced as there was another bout of dry retching.

'I'm just saying that perhaps it's not a stomach bug,' I explained once she had finished. 'Being sick in the mornings, going off alcohol, coffee. Apparently they're all signs of something else entirely ...'

Leila looked at me for a moment and I saw the change on her face as it dawned on her. 'Shit ... you think I'm pregnant?'

'Might you be?'

'I didn't feel like this last time. I wasn't sick at all.'

'But still you might be, yes?'

Leila buried her face in her hands. 'Oh God, isn't this the last thing I need, to be pregnant.' She seemed to be laughing and crying at the same time. 'Wouldn't it just be my luck?'

'We should buy a test from the chemist. One of those stick things you pee on.'

'Yes, we should,' she agreed. 'Oh, how could I have been so stupid?'

'If you're pregnant ... will you tell Lucio?'

'No.' She seemed certain.

'What will you do then?'

'I don't know. How could I have a baby alone? I can't even look after myself properly at the moment.'

'Well maybe Lucio—'

'No! That's not how things are between us. I wouldn't want to be linked to Lucio for ever by a child.'

'But you couldn't get rid of it?'

'No,' she said more softly this time. 'No, I don't think I could do that either.'

'Well, you wouldn't have to cope all alone,' I reminded her. 'You've got me. I'd be the baby's auntie. I'd like that actually. To share a baby with you.'

There were tears washing her face now. 'Really?'

I reached out and stroked her tangle of grey-shot hair. 'If you're pregnant life's going to change, Leila, but that's not necessarily a bad thing.'

'I'm the one who's always telling you that, aren't I?'

'Well now it's my turn, maybe.'

Leila rested her hands on her stomach in that pregnant woman's classic pose. 'A baby,' she said wonderingly. 'All this time I've been trying to decide what to do and now it seems to have been decided for me.'

Funnily enough, once we were certain Leila was pregnant it seemed more obvious. Her shape had changed, the trunk of her body thickening, her belly rounding out. We began to wonder if Babetta had guessed long before we did. That constant supply of ginger biscuits seemed telling and, although we hadn't said a thing, she had started making other dishes especially for Leila: bland broths, tiny portions of delicate ravioli, food most unlike her usual hearty cooking.

I fell into looking after Leila, making sure she had the peace to rest and the time to come to terms with what was happening. We took long slow walks, the old dog Sky at our heels and often, during the hours I spent working in the garden, Leila would pull a deckchair close and we'd talk about the future.

'If it's a girl I'll call her after my mother, of course,' she would say. 'But a boy, I don't know. There aren't any special boy's names in my life. Something Italian maybe.'

Both of us were aware that just beyond the gates of Villa Rosa, Raffaella and her husband were working in Babetta's garden. They'd started coming three or four afternoons a week, disciplining the rows of vegetables, keeping the ground clean and finely hoed. Leila stayed away from them, avoiding any questions. This baby would never be part of their family, she remained definite about that, this baby was ours alone. For a while I tried to argue, reminding her that she and Raffaella had always been friends, that it seemed unfair to punish her. But Leila had set her face against the family. She refused to relent.

'Lucio and I were only ever playing,' she told me repeatedly. 'It was never meant to be a serious thing. And a baby definitely makes things serious.'

'But he'll want to at least see the child, won't he?' I pushed her.

'You still don't really get Lucio, do you?' Leila sounded almost amused. 'He's a small town boy, trading on his looks. He doesn't want anything to change. He's got life set up the way he likes it.'

'You make him sound awful.'

'Oh he's not awful, just selfish.'

'I suppose Tonino is like that too.' It had only just struck me. 'The pair of them have always seemed so different but in fact they're the same. Everything is fine so long as life is the way they want it.'

'I suppose Italian Mammas must spoil their sons and that's what they end up with.' Leila looked thoughtful. 'That's not why I don't want Raffaella involved with my child though.'

'Why then? If you'd just tell me I might stop nagging you about it.'

'I was raised by my mother alone and I'm fine,' she said softly. 'And this will be the only child I ever have.'

'So you want things to be how they were for you and Aurora?'

'I want things to be perfect.'

I tried to talk her round many times but always Leila shook off my arguments. She didn't need another family involved in her child's life, telling her what it should wear or eat, where it should go to school. 'It's my baby, not theirs,' she repeated stubbornly.

As the summer wore on, both of us began to feel stronger, ready for the way things were about to change. Ready to say goodbye to Villa Rosa, knowing soon it might be sold and we would never return. Ready, at last, to go back to London and get on with different lives.

Babetta

The days had grown cooler and Babetta sensed an ending. At Villa Rosa sheets and towels were being washed and folded into linen cupboards. Gardening tools had been cleaned of their dirt, oiled and put away. Kitchen cupboards emptied of food that might perish.

A week ago, Leila had insisted on having a phone installed in Babetta's house. It was in a corner of the kitchen on its own table, a shiny plastic thing with buttons that she had dusted twice but not yet used. She'd promised to answer it when it rang, had thanked Leila several times but secretly she thought the girl had wasted her money. All these years Babetta had managed without a phone and she saw no need for change.

'We can call you once we're back in London,' Leila explained. 'You'll keep an eye on the house for us as always, won't you? And sweep the paths, of course, although there'll be a gardener coming in to look after the work Alice has done.'

She was rubbing at her belly, a habit she'd fallen into. Dressed in clothes that were looser than they needed to be, her pregnancy remained an unspoken thing, a secret shared yet somehow not acknowledged.

Even Raffaella still hadn't found a way to talk to the girl. The gates of Villa Rosa remained closed and Raffaella reluctant to push herself through. Her son Lucio had tried and been turned away at the door. He hadn't bothered to come again. Only Babetta was allowed in, bearing gifts of soothing foods and ready with domestic kindnesses. The gates opened for her. No one else seemed welcome.

And now this packing up and stowing away of things, these signs that summer was coming to an end. Soon it would be time to pick the pomegranates from the trees. To pull the spent tomato vines from the garden, dig in manure and sow a winter crop of lupins. To pickle and preserve, to fill the storecupboards and stack more wood along the long sheltered wall of the house. Soon the sun would fade, the sky's mood darken and the coast would be swept by storms.

As Babetta braced for winter she wondered if they'd ever come back, these English girls? Or would Villa Rosa lie empty and shuttered for another stretch of years until the smartly dressed signora returned with her leather folder to ready it for sale?

On the final day she helped load their suitcases into Aurora's old Jeep, let them put their arms around her and kiss her cheeks, the pregnant one's fuller belly poking into hers. She watched as they waved goodbye from open windows and then disappeared up the hill in a smoky belch of exhaust fumes.

Babetta felt almost certain this was the last the place would see of them.

Alice

The thing I'd been most dreading was telling Tonino. I should have realised he'd never made things difficult and wasn't going to start now. He helped me pack my things into cartons he'd supplied and carried them to the van that Guyon had driven over. And then he sat with me on a bench overlooking the gardens I'd spent a decade of my life shaping, and we had our final conversation.

'You'll be all right? You have enough money?' he asked.

'I'll be fine. I'm going to stay at Leila's place for a bit.'

'This is the right decision for you. I see that.' His tone was low, his voice controlled, just as it had always been in the days at Teatro when he'd been showing someone how to make a dish or pointing out how they'd gone wrong.

'And what about you?' I asked him.

'I'll miss you, of course, Alice.'

'But you'll find someone else?' His hair had greyed, his skin had tempered but Tonino was still an attractive man.

'Yes, and so will you.'

Getting up from the bench, I went to tug out a couple of weeds that his new gardener must have missed. 'I'm not really looking,' I told him. 'That's not why I'm leaving. I need to spend some time alone. Find out who I am and who I want to be.'

'I've never stopped you doing anything, least of all being yourself.' Tonino sounded hurt.

'I know.' I sat back down beside him. 'You made it easier for me to avoid myself though.'

'Don't you find all this impossible to leave?' He nodded towards the garden. 'You worked so hard here and now you're going to walk away.'

'There'll be other gardens, I hope. Lots of them.'

He took my hand, so roughened by soil and kitchen work that it almost rasped in his. 'I'm sorry if I didn't give you what you needed, if I was too caught up with my own life. It's the peril of being with a chef, I expect. And, to be honest, I wouldn't do things any differently, even if I had the chance.'

Then he leaned over and brushed his lips against mine, barely even touching them, just as he had that first time he'd kissed me on his balcony above the Thames.

'I'd better go,' I told him. 'Guyon is waiting for me.'

'Goodbye then, Alice.' He squeezed my hand one last time. 'Be who you want.'

When I slipped into the passenger seat of the rental van I was on the crest of tears. Guyon, however, seemed jubilant. He took off quickly, chanting, 'Don't look back, Alice, don't look back,' as he sped down Tonino's gravel driveway.

We turned onto the road, Guyon whistling in triumph. 'If I was a drinking man I'd be taking you somewhere for a bottle of champagne,' he told me.

'I don't feel much like celebrating.'

'But you're free. This has been hanging over you all summer and now you've done it.'

'Yes, and now the hard part starts,' I pointed out. 'Getting Leila through the birth of this baby, getting my business off the ground. There's so much to do.'

'Nothing you can't manage though. Just take it bit by bit.'

I scrunched up my face. 'One day at a time, you mean?'

Guyon laughed. 'I didn't say that, did I? Not even I'm that much of a cliché.'

We drove straight to the flat in Maida Vale and piled up my cartons in the spare bedroom. It was strange to be back there after all these years. Leila was staying in the country for the time being, in her big old house south of the city with an acre of garden surrounded by tall yew hedges, so I had the flat to myself. I remembered how I'd arrived there the first time, fresh off the train and full of fear and determination. All these years later and I still felt much the same.

Life had come in such a full circle that I even picked up a couple of shifts at the brasserie. The place had new owners, a new coat of paint and different furniture but it was still a bustling neighbourhood café, and on weekends I ran the kitchen, slipping back into my chef's whites almost effortlessly.

During the week I put long hours into planning my business. Often in the evenings Charlie would come over and we'd share a bottle of wine and talk about what I'd achieved so far. He seemed excited to be part of it but wary of me too. I noticed how he always kept himself at arm's length, avoiding any situation where we might need to come closer. If I cooked dinner, he washed up. If I curled up on the sofa to watch TV, he stayed in the armchair. And when he left, there was no kiss on the cheek, just a wave and a promise to send me a text in the morning.

For a while at Villa Rosa it had seemed as though an easier intimacy was growing between us. Now Charlie had backed away from that, and on the evenings we didn't spend together I wondered if there might be someone else. I imagined him taking some other woman to movies, sharing meals with her.

And I minded about it much more than I thought I should.

Babetta

Babetta pulled the rugs and shawls from her cupboards and kept the fire banked up with logs. Her life slowed down for winter, just as it always had. Wool-lined and warm, she kept to her house. People came to see her there, Sofia with her daughters to share a bowl of lunchtime soup, or Raffaella as a late afternoon softened into darkness. But mostly she was left alone.

The first time the shrill call of the telephone broke the silence she was too surprised to answer it. And when she did manage to pick it up and heard Leila's voice, the conversation was stilted. The girl's poor command of Italian, the secret that lay between them, the uncomfortable pressing of hard plastic to her ear, all made for an awkward exchange.

Babetta had so little to say anyway. Her days repeated themselves; there was nothing new. When Raffaella came she was always prepared with a titbit of gossip she knew would be appreciated. She filled the silence with words while Babetta listened gratefully.

Some days, if Raffaella was early and the day a fine one, she let herself be coaxed outdoors and they walked quickly into the grounds of Villa Rosa, through the garden, starved and wintry bare, and down to watch the sea crash against the rocks.

'The summer I lived here I spent a lot of time sitting on these rocks,' Raffaella recalled as she let the sea spray wet her face. 'It was always the place to come to when you needed to think. But that was a long time ago, before I was married and had children. When more of my life lay before me than behind.'

'You're not that old yet,' Babetta reminded her. 'There's still plenty of life ahead of you.'

'But some days I feel there is nothing left to hope for.' Raffaella's voice was bleak.

'In England you have a grandchild coming. You must have some hopes for that.'

'How can I? Leila has made it clear she doesn't want my son to have any part in it. I suppose he could insist, force the issue ... but he won't, of course. Not Lucio.'

'I tried to talk to him, you know.'

'Yes, he told me.' Raffaella smiled at the memory. 'He was shocked, actually. Then he realised it was Leila he'd made pregnant and I think he was relieved. She's a woman with money, a career. She can afford to raise a child without him.'

Babetta grunted and looked out at the sea, waiting for her friend to continue.

'Why both my sons should be this way, I don't know. Have Ciro and I not provided them with a good enough example? Did we do something wrong when they were growing up?'

'You can't blame yourself,' Babetta murmured.

'I think it comes from my side of the family, the way they are. I had a brother, Sergio, who was very much the same. I'd never have had sons if I'd known they were going to take after him.'

'You don't mean that. You love your boys, Raffaella.'

'Of course, I do. But the more I love them, the more they hurt me. Sometimes it's easier to be angry with them.'

'They aren't bad boys ... not really. Tonino is a hard worker. Lucio is charming and loving.'

Raffaella said nothing, her face folded into a frown.

'They aren't bad boys,' Babetta repeated not sure how else to help her.

'Not bad but flawed,' Raffaella said at last. 'All of us are, I realise that. But Lucio's flaw means my grandchild will grow up in England and never know me. Can you imagine how that makes me feel?'

'What does Ciro say?'

'That I should wait. Things will sort themselves out. But I don't believe that. I don't have hope like he does.'

Taking her friend's arm, Babetta turned back towards the steps that led up to Villa Rosa. 'Remember when Nunzio died I was so lonely,' she began as they walked together. 'You helped me then. I thought the good part of my life was over, all my hopes finished and gone. Thanks to you, I got on that old Vespa.'

'I remember, of course I do.'

'And now it's you who's lonely. I want to be able to help you.'

'But there's nothing you can do.'

'Remember the night of the fire, the four of us so close?'

'Yes, yes.' Raffaella sounded impatient.

'You were good friends then, you and Leila.'

'I suppose so.'

'What do you think would happen if you went to her now?'

'To London?'

Babetta nodded.

'Leila would tell me to leave, shut the door in my face. That's if I could find her. I don't even know where the girl lives.'

'But I have addresses and phone numbers,' Babetta said quickly. 'They insisted on giving them to me. You'll find her easily enough. But are you prepared to take the risk?'

Raffaella stared at the pink walls of the empty house. 'They might never come back here,' she said. 'They'll spend the summers somewhere else like all the other families who've owned Villa Rosa over the years. It's fated to be abandoned, isn't it? It's an unlucky, lonely place.'

'Perhaps it is,' Babetta agreed. 'But if you wanted to, you could change that.'

'I don't believe I could.' Raffaella sounded certain. 'That child is lost to me. There's no point in hoping.'

Alice

At long last Leila's stomach had settled and so, it seemed, had her mood swings. She came up to London so I could help her shop for baby things and looked to be enjoying the whole business of preparing, taking pleasure in spending money, filling drawers with tiny clothes and cupboards with all sorts of equipment.

I did worry about the reality of a child that cried for half the night in the pretty crib she'd bought or vomited down the Baby Dior. As I wandered through clean white places that smelled of lotions and talc, I looked at her belly, full to bursting with Lucio's child, and wondered how things were going to be once it was born.

It was Charlie who made me see how unprepared Leila was. 'I've talked to her and she's got no idea,' he kept telling me. 'Late-night feeds, nappy changes, colicky crying … And no support apart from you, apparently.'

'She'll manage though, won't she?'

'Has she ever been the type who manages?'

'I don't suppose she's had to before now.'

'I can't see this going well,' Charlie warned me.

'But what can I do?'

'There's some family over in Italy, at least. Can't you talk Leila into letting them be involved?'

'Lucio was just some guy she slept with,' I said doubtfully. 'She doesn't want to be tied to him.'

'What about his parents? How do they feel? Or is Leila

doing her usual self-involved thing and not worrying about them?'

'I don't know.' I felt guiltier than ever about Raffaella. 'I can try to talk to Leila, I guess, but I don't hold out much hope.'

The dull glow faded from Leila's face as soon as I brought up the subject. She reminded me there was no reason why her baby needed a father when both she and I had managed without one.

Each week she grew bigger but no less stubborn. Christmas came and we spent it together at the house in the country, Guyon, Charlie and the girls joining us for a few days over New Year, all of us tiptoeing around Leila, keeping things nice for her.

I spent most of my time in the kitchen, cooking rib-sticking stews to warm us from the inside, simmered for hours until the beef yielded and the gravy thickened. I roasted free-range chickens and made velvety soups from browned stocks I'd bubbled all day long, bowls full of robust, comforting goodness. Outside there was a frost on Leila's lawn and the muddy track to her house was hard and rutted. We stayed indoors, close to the old Aga, baking coarse grainy bread we spread thickly with salty butter, or indulging in cakes sticky with toffee and treacle.

Leila had discovered her hunger. She ate with a quiet determination, spreading snowdrifts of grated Parmesan over her soups and dollops of thickly whipped cream onto anything sweet. The stuff she'd worried about before, fat content and calorific value, seemed forgotten as she lost herself in eating. Guyon produced a smoky spiced dhal and I found her, hours later, spooning up the cold leftovers and savouring the flavours. Charlie barbecued a fillet of beef and she devoured whole slices of it coated in horseradish. Each mealtime, we gathered round the solid, country table, the fire flickering in its grate and candles lit at night, and she made her way through generous plates of whatever we had made for her.

'Ah, another feast,' Guyon said as we sat down for dinner on the final night. 'I've already loosened my belt a couple of notches. This has been my most delicious New Year ever.'

He and Leila raised their glasses filled with sparkling water, Charlie and I joining them, toasting with our vast balloons of pinot noir. 'To the future,' I said. 'To all our futures.'

It was Guyon who touched on the subject we'd all been avoiding. 'What a pity Babetta isn't here to share a meal with us like in Italy,' he remarked as we piled our plates from bowls and platters. 'I wonder what the old dear does for Christmas and New Year. Will she have been all alone, do you think?'

'No, she has family,' Leila told him crisply. 'I expect she's spent it with them.'

'And so will you go back there this summer?' he continued conversationally. 'To the lovely Villa Rosa?'

Leila looked uncomfortable. 'Most probably I'll sell the place. There's no real reason for me to go back there now my mother has gone.'

Seemingly oblivious, Guyon ploughed on. 'But the father, the guy from the pizzeria, right? Won't he want to see his child? And the grandparents too? Surely you'll have to go back?'

'Actually, I don't have to do anything.'

Guyon heard the metal in her tone. 'Oh, I see. This is a bit of a thing with you, is it?'

'What do you mean, a thing? It's nothing to do with you, Guyon. None of your business.'

He shrugged. 'You're right, it isn't, but I'd hate to see you making a mistake.'

'Fine, let's talk about it then, if you insist.' Leila sounded

326

furious now. 'The father – Lucio – tried to come and see me just once when he realised I was pregnant. His mother didn't bother at all. I don't think they're interested in my baby and that's fine by me.'

'We both know that's not true,' I said quietly. 'There's no way Raffaella would want to miss out on this child. It's all she's wanted for years and years.'

'And what about Babetta?' Guyon sounded shocked.

'She'll be fine ... she's always been fine. She has family, remember.'

'Yes, and so does your baby.' I dared to say it even though I knew how the words would curdle her.

That ended our New Year celebrations on a low note. Leila retreated to her room to sulk while Charlie and I drank too much wine and Guyon satisfied himself with ranting.

'She'll expect you to run round after her, you know, Alice. And if you do then you're as much of a fool as she is.'

Charlie and I were on the sofa together, sitting side by side on the plump cushions. 'No, no, Alice won't do that,' he told Guyon, 'I won't let her.'

'Oh, just you watch. She won't be able to stop herself. That's how the relationship between those two works. Leila is the queen bee, Alice is the handmaiden.'

'I am actually here, you know,' I interrupted them. 'And it's not a one-way thing. Leila's helped me when I've needed her.'

Guyon snorted, then bitched on about Leila a lot more until he grew tired of himself and went up to bed. We stayed there together, me and Charlie, enjoying the last of the warmth being thrown from the fire, our hips almost touching as the cushions from the sofa sagged together.

'It's funny,' I remarked sleepily. 'I've always thought you were my real family, you, Guyon and Leila.'

'I suppose we are,' Charlie agreed. 'Actually, Leila feels very much like a sister. She annoys the crap out of me but I care about her all the same.'

'And Guyon's the bossy big brother.'

'What about you and me?' Charlie's leg was almost touching mine.

'Hey?' I was a thrown for a moment.

'What relationship do we have? Because you don't feel like a sister to me, Alice. You never have.'

'No,' I agreed. 'We've been friends such a long time though, haven't we? You really are my family.'

Charlie relaxed his leg and it lolled into mine, resting there warm and heavy.

'The way Leila is being. I suppose I was a bit like that with you,' I tried to continue. 'Shutting you out ... blaming you for everything that went badly. I'm sorry, you know. I do regret the way I've treated you.'

He put his arm round my shoulders and squeezed.

'Charlie?' I leaned into him and forced out the words I'd been thinking for weeks. 'Is there someone else in your life? A woman?'

'Nah,' he told me. 'I've given up on women. I couldn't have the one I wanted.'

'What if you could though? What if she'd realised at long last what she wants from life?'

He stared at me, his eyes wary and shifted his arm from my shoulders.

'Charlie.' I made myself say it. 'Do you think after everything that's happened you might possibly consider marrying me?'

He gave a dry, nervous sort of laugh. 'Marry you, Alice? So you really do want that emerald after all.'

'No, Charlie,' I told him, feeling very certain, 'what I want is you.'

Babetta

Spring came and Babetta waited for the signora with the leather folder. She was sure that she would come, bustling about the place making lists of things that needed to be done. And then a sign would be nailed to the gates of Villa Rosa, proclaiming the place was for sale again, even though there was barely anyone there but Babetta to see it or care.

She said nothing, but some afternoons she watched through her kitchen window as Raffaella and Ciro planted out the garden just as they'd promised to, and she worried they were wasting their time. Would they be there to enjoy the first of summer's tomatoes or see the wispy parsley seedlings growing lush and green? Not if the signora came as she was certain she was going to.

Babetta felt as though a season had changed within her. She tried to remember how long ago her walk had turned into a shuffle. When had she started taking the terrace steps so carefully and dozing away the afternoons? This past winter had hurt her bones, made them ache, and now spring's newness seemed too bright for her. She stayed inside, watching and waiting.

Even the phone had stopped ringing. Babetta didn't miss the struggle of her conversations with Leila but still she thought about her often, trying to imagine her life in England. Perhaps by now there was a baby, Lucio's child in a newly decorated nursery. Alice would be there too, taking care of things Leila hadn't realised needed doing. Babetta could imagine them both, fussing and doting, letting the hours drift by just feeling the warmth and weight of the small child in their arms.

She remembered how that felt, the very beginning. Children grew up and away from you soon enough but those first few months they were more completely yours than anything had ever been. Babetta imagined Leila discovering that. And then she stared out of the window at her friend Raffaella planting beans in the slowly warming ground while her husband hoed the earth just like Nunzio used to, and thought how great a hurt those two must be feeling.

She felt it too. At times, over that last summer, Babetta had painted herself into the picture, imagined rocking a pram with one hand as she sat beneath the shade of the pomegranate tree, or taking care of the child while Leila wrote and Alice cooked. She had seduced herself with dreams of the summers ahead.

But then she'd come to realise there was to be none of it. Leila had taken the best part of the future and kept it for herself. Lucio had let her do it.

Babetta looked at the empty cane chair out on her terrace. It sat in a fall of sunlight, a rug draped over it, tempting her to come. She sighed, pulling the threadbare curtains over the kitchen window, and thought perhaps Raffaella was right after all.

There was nothing much left to hope for.

Alice

For a second time I found myself keeping a relationship a secret. Charlie's emerald stayed in its box and only we knew how things had changed between us. There was a deliciousness in how hidden it was, a stolen pleasure in rediscovering the comfort of each other's bodies. I didn't want that ruined by what other people said or thought.

In time, those judgements would come. Charlie's family would disapprove, so would Leila. His ex would have an opinion and his daughters too. Even Guyon would offer something. But not yet. Not until we told them.

I wanted to wait till after Leila's baby had arrived. Since Christmas she'd seemed shaky, as though the truth of what was happening was only just becoming plain to her. We needed to get her through the birth and the first few weeks before I explained I had plans that didn't involve her.

In the final weeks of Leila's pregnancy I sweetened her with treats. Softly whipped mousses of chocolate and ricotta, fingers of lavender shortbread, moist little honey cakes covered in butter icing. I filled tins that I left at her house and when I went back they were empty. So I baked more goodies, carroty cupcakes iced in pastel colours, little squares of lemon tart, seedy syrupy slices.

And as I drugged her with sugar I realised I didn't envy Leila, so full of Lucio's baby, so occupied by it. When she made me lay my hand against her belly to feel it kicking, I didn't wish myself in her place. I was happy to have Charlie and his two ready-made girls, a new life waiting for me.

So I felt kinder towards Leila. My days were spent in the nitty gritty of setting up a business, my nights in the softness of Charlie's bed. The time left over I gave to her. She needed it.

Just before the due date she moved back to Maida Vale and we lived together for a short while, just like we had when we were girls.

'I don't want a moony spoony home birth,' she kept telling me. 'I want doctors and beeping machines and someone else cleaning up all the mess. And I want you there, Alice. You promised me. You haven't forgotten that?'

Her son was born with a sheen of dark hair and skin more olive than his father's. I watched his squashed little face open, heard him scream his first shock and confusion and I held tight to Leila's hand until I was certain I could let it go.

'I feel ready,' she told me. 'I didn't expect to be. But I am.'

'Do you feel different? Changed?' Almost certain I was never going to have this experience, I wanted to hear exactly how it was.

'I feel needed.' Leila touched his fingers, his cheeks. She breathed in the smell of him. 'I'm glad it's a boy.'

Neither of us mentioned Lucio. I didn't ask if she might put his name on the birth certificate or let him know the child was safely come. The last thing I wanted was to sour this time with unwelcome questions.

Very quickly Leila discovered she was good at being a mother. She moved the crib from the nursery she'd set up so carefully and put it right next to her bed so she could hear her son breathe all night long. She read about things on the Internet; breastfeeding regimes, sleeping patterns, and she parroted the information back at me. To my surprise she even started cooking.

'I'm going to have to make meals for him eventually,' she pointed out. 'So I might as well learn now.'

The baby still didn't have a name. For weeks all of us amused ourselves by texting mad suggestions to her, Guyon and Charlie vying to see who could come up with the most ridiculous: 'Tristan', 'Crispin', 'Gaylord'. She took it in good humour, but the baby remained unnamed.

'It will be the first definite thing about him, the first big decision of his life. I want to get it right,' she explained.

Spring had turned to early summer before either of us was brave enough to share our secrets with each other.

'I've decided on a name,' Leila told me, as we sat between the towering yew hedges in her grassy acre of garden. 'Actually, I knew from the moment he was born, I just couldn't quite manage to admit it. I'm going to call him Ricci.'

She'd spoken the word with an English accent but still it was clear. 'You're giving him his family name?' It was the last thing I'd expected. 'Why?'

'He deserves to have some heritage,' Leila said simply.

'So are you changing your mind then? Do you feel differently about Lucio's family now you're a mother?'

'Everything feels different, Alice,' she admitted. 'But I don't know yet what I'm going to do, just what I want him to be called.'

Then it was time to tell my news, to speak Charlie's name in a different way and watch Leila's face to see which expression crossed it.

She laughed out loud. 'After all these years and everything that's happened you're marrying Charlie.'

'Yes.' I smiled too. 'It's what I want, where I belong.'

'Oh God, and all those years I spent insisting he wasn't right for you,' Leila said ruefully. 'And it turns out I was wrong after all.'

'Maybe you weren't,' I admitted. 'I don't think Charlie

was right for me, not then. But he's changed since he's had kids ... and I've changed too. We're right for each other now.'

'You and Charlie.' Leila laughed again. 'You'll have to get married here, of course. A summer wedding in the garden with a big marquee. I'll help you organise it.'

I paused for a moment. 'That's lovely, thank you. But it's not what we want.'

'No? What then?'

'Charlie and I have discussed it ...'

'Yes?'

'And we've decided to get married as soon as we can in the place things first started to change for us.'

'Oh God, no, please don't,' Leila guessed with a grimace. 'You're going to say Italy, aren't you.'

'Yes, that's right,' I agreed. 'A place in Italy. A very special place.'

Babetta

It had been many years since Babetta had been to a wedding. There were brand new shoes on her feet and her stout little body was wrapped in a soft blue dress, that Sofia had made her buy, and a matching shawl to keep her shoulders warm. Outside there was a high summer sun, but here in front of the altar it was chilled and damp.

'What sort of place is this to get married?' Sofia hissed at her.

Babetta glanced round at the rough walls of the cave and the white marble statues half-nibbled away by the constant drip of water from the roof. 'This is where I married your father,' she hissed back. 'We started our lives together here. Why shouldn't Charlie and Alice?'

She didn't see any need to mention that there was another new beginning unfolding before their eyes. Leila and Raffaella sharing a pew, the new baby in its buggy between them, both sitting a little stiffly and speaking in short, formal sentences. Babetta had sensed a softening, a blurring of Leila's hard edges. When the girl had been faced with the only other woman in the world who loved her child as much as she did, how could she not have yielded?

She watched them now; Raffaella so very careful, holding back, letting Leila come to her; Leila unable to resist. It would take some time, perhaps, but this was definitely a beginning.

Surrounding them in the other pews were strangers. Charlie's family and Alice's mother, friends gathered over the years and held loosely ever since, people whose only link was blood. Babetta wiggled her toes in the uncomfortable but stylish shoes she never meant to wear again and smiled a welcome at the foreigners.

And then there was Guyon, his shirt a medley of stripes and flowers, his face pink with pleasure. He had taken Babetta's arm and helped her up the steep incline then settled them in a spot close to a hole in the cave wall where there was a tiny warm shaft of sunlight. She saw how he kept turning his head, straining to see if Alice had arrived.

Babetta turned too, in time to hear the music begin and see a flurry of white lace and tulle. She hoped this wouldn't be a long service, that the priest wouldn't preach till his mouth grew dry. She wanted to hear Charlie and Alice, see what happened on their faces when they looked at each other. And then she wanted to return to Villa Rosa where she knew there was a feast waiting for them.

Babetta had offered to cook the meal herself and had been relieved when they turned her down. Instead she had given the best from her garden: crisp fennel and blood oranges for a salad, sheaves of herbs and leafy greens all picked fresh in the cool of the morning. She hoped they weren't being ruined by the clash of chefs in the kitchen; that the bitterness lying between the two men didn't somehow flavour the food they were making.

Even Raffaella had been surprised when first Lucio and then Tonino had decided on cooking the wedding feast. Neither had wanted to be in the church to witness the ceremony, nor had they thought to share a kitchen. But both had insisted and both refused to back down.

Babetta imagined the clanging of pots and ladles as the two Ricci boys cooked together, determined to outdo each other. There would be course after course, a whole afternoon and evening of eating. Tonino had filled a mountain of delicate ravioli with crabmeat and slivers of preserved lemon. Lucio had made a hearty timballo of macaroni and meats. They'd hired plates and glasses, set long tables beneath the pomegranate trees and hung lanterns from branches that would be lit once the light had faded. Only when it was dark and still would Babetta light the bonfire that Guyon had built for her and then set off the fireworks Lucio had again procured.

She was looking forward to seeing Villa Rosa filled with light and colour. The party would go on late, with drinking and dancing, and endless toasting of one another's happiness. Even once her energy faltered Babetta would be part of things, sitting in her cane chair on the terrace, enjoying the noisy hum of people and the warm glow in the night sky.

Babetta craned her neck to watch as Alice walked up the aisle. The girl had cast off her sadness like a winter coat on the first day of spring. She hoped it would be a long, long time before the season changed for her again.

Alice

I was so worn out I posted myself between the sheets and lay without moving. Charlie was already there – I could hear the rhythm of his breathing and feel the heat coming from his body. There was no need to touch him. No need to kiss. It was more than enough just to stay there breathing beside him.

The day had been a perfect one, despite the fears that had crowded in on me: my mother and Charlie's family cold-shouldering each other in the pews, Leila meeting up with Raffaella again, her warring sons taking over the kitchen. It had nearly soured things but then Charlie had reminded me of the worst that could happen. An emotional scene, too much salt in a dish. Neither would ruin his happiness.

He insisted I dress like a bride even though I was sure I'd look too old and feel ridiculous. And he was right that there was something seductive about the rustle of silk and lace as I walked up the aisle. The white gown had a grace to it against the rough caste walls of the cave and the music of the dripping stalactites.

My satin shoes had been ruined by water-stains from pools of damp. And now the dress lay discarded on the floor of our bedroom at Villa Rosa, crumpled and creased. It didn't really matter because I'd finished with those things. There would be no looking back for me, only forward: to coffee-breathed kisses in the morning, to a honeymoon with our friends in Villa Rosa and then a new home and another life.

I couldn't wait to put my hands in the earth again and make things grow. It was intoxicating, the thought of showing other people the things Babetta had taught to me. To share with them my recipe for life.

'I'm forty-four and I feel as though I'm just beginning.' Charlie was half asleep and most likely didn't register the words. But that was fine.

It was saying them that really mattered.

Babetta

Babetta was so soundly asleep it seemed a shame to move her. Raffaella draped more rugs around her shoulders and over her knees in case a chill blew off the sea but the night was warm enough. Soon it would be dawn and Raffaella had made plans to return this way in the morning. The old woman would come to no harm sleeping outside for a few short hours.

Raffaella stood for a moment listening to the soft sound of Babetta's snoring. Her head had fallen onto her chest and her eyes were closed tight. At her feet the old dog Sky was sleeping just as soundly. He didn't stir, even as Raffaella found a spare rug and tucked it round him.

She rested a hand on his warm hairy head for a moment and then looked back at Babetta. Her body was gnarled, her limbs grown heavy like an ancient pomegranate tree. No one knew how old she was or how long she might stay rooted to the earth. Perhaps she would be here for years to come, or maybe only one more winter.

Leaning down, Raffaella kissed her cheek, warm and polished as old leather. 'Goodnight, my friend,' she whispered. And then she left Babetta to rest through what was left of the night until the view of a layer of sea beneath the paler blue of the sky greeted her the next morning.

ACKNOWLEDGEMENTS

A few years ago I went for a job interview to ghostwrite the autobiography of famous baby photographer Anne Geddes. I didn't really want the job but needed the money. Fortunately, I was rejected pretty much straight off by her husband Kel, who included in his e-mail the quote with which I opened this story. Actually, he sent me a longer version which goes like this:

> 'Your time is limited, so don't waste it living someone else's life. Don't be trapped by dogma – which is living with the results of other people's thinking. Don't let the noise of others' opinions drown out your own inner voice. And most important, have the courage to follow your heart and intuition. They somehow already know what you truly want to become. Everything else is secondary.'

For a while I had this stuck up on my fridge because I realised that's what I'd been doing – leading someone else's life. And it got me wondering about how we end up where we are, and how easy it is to fill up life with busyness and never think too hard about it. That's when Alice and Babetta's stories began forming in my mind, so I owe a big thank you to Kel Geddes – never has a job rejection been so helpful.

Since Alice was a chef it gave me all the excuse I needed to indulge my love of reading about food. There were three excellent books I found especially inspiring: *Heat* by Bill

Buford, *Kitchen Confidential* by Anthony Bourdain and *Made In Italy* by Giorgio Locatelli, and all are highly recommended.

This is the second book I have set in the town of Triento. It is, of course, a thinly disguised, fictionalised version of Maratea in Basilicata where they really do have a huge white statue of Christ on the mountain and where I have been fortunate to stay in a beautiful house owned by my father's cousin Clara DeSio and her husband Antonio. So another big thank you to them, and also to Anna Bidwill for the use of Northcote in Martinborough where a chunk of this book was written.

Also thanks to everyone at Orion and at Hachette NZ and Australia for their support of my work, thanks to my agent Caroline Sheldon, to the friends and family who listen to me carp, moan and whinge when things aren't progressing so well, and to my husband Carne Bidwill who, whenever I claim I can't do something, has a tendency to say 'Well don't then', which is a lot more helpful than it sounds.

1	21	41	61	81	101	121	141	161	181
2	22	42	62	82	102	122	142	162	182
3	23	43	63	83	103	123	143	163	183
4	24	44	64	84	104	124	144	164	184
5	25	45	65	85	105	125	145	165	185
6	26	46	66	86	106	126	146	166	186
7	27	47	67	87	107	127	147	167	187
8	28	48	68	88	108	128	148	168	188
9	(29)	49	69	89	109	129	149	169	188
10	30	50	70	90	110	130	150	170	190
11	31	51	71	91	111	131	151	171	191
12	32	52	72	92	112	132	152	172	192
13	33	53	73	93	113	133	153	173	193
14	34	54	74	94	114	134	154	174	194
15	35	55	75	95	115	135	155	175	195
16	36	56	76	96	116	136	156	176	196
17	37	57	77	97	117	137	157	177	197
18	38	58	78	98	118	138	158	178	198
19	39	59	79	99	119	139	159	179	199
20	40	60	80	100	120	140	160	180	200

201	216	231	246	261	276	291	306	321	336
202	217	232	247	262	277	292	307	322	337
203	218	233	248	263	278	293	308	323	338
204	219	234	249	264	279	294	309	324	339
205	220	235	250	265	280	295	310	325	340
206	221	236	251	266	281	296	311	326	341
207	222	237	252	267	282	297	312	327	342
208	223	238	253	268	283	298	313	328	343
209	224	239	254	269	284	299	314	329	344
210	225	240	255	270	285	300	315	330	345
211	226	241	256	271	286	301	316	331	346
212	227	242	257	272	287	302	317	332	347
213	228	243	258	273	288	303	318	333	348
214	229	244	259	274	289	304	319	334	349
215	230	245	260	275	290	305	320	335	350